DEATH ROAD TO LODGEPOLE CREEK

THE MAN WITH THE LEMAT

BOOK ONE

ZACHARY LANE

LEMAT BOOKS

To my wife who has always been my Encourager in Chief.
Zachary Lane

PROLOGUE

Present Day

I never met my great-grandfather. He died in 1920, years before I was born. My dad liked to say, "Your great-grandfather died before you were even a twinkle in your mother's eyes," whatever that means.

I grew up in Nebraska on family stories about my great-grandfather. These stories made him larger than life. As I grew to manhood, my skepticism increased. To me, the reality of my great-grandfather's life took on the reality of a John Wayne movie: *"When legend becomes fact; print the legend."*

Permit me to share two examples of the legend surrounding my great-grandpa Jones. One I have proven; one I have debunked. First, there was the legend that at Shepherdstown, Virginia my great-grandfather took possession of a rare LeMat pistol belonging to a Confederate Colonel. The story is "he carried it with him all the way to

Appomattox Courthouse" and then to the remote outpost of Fort Sidney, Nebraska. This legend is true.

A second family legend is that he was once mistaken for Wyatt Earp. I debunked this legend when I discovered an old photograph of my great-grandfather taken about 1870. All I can say is that whoever started this legend was drunk or blind. Probably both. There is no resemblance.

To further research great-grandfather's life I turned to the Nebraska Historical Society archives. One day I spent six hours combing through microfiche files. I remember the strain on my eyes, but I found the following obituary.

Jesse Jones

Longtime Cheyenne County resident Jesse Jones died on Thursday May 20, 1920 at his home west of Sidney, Nebraska. Mr. Jones came to Nebraska in 1867 with a contingent of U.S. soldiers guarding the Union Pacific Railroad and then stayed to make Cheyenne County his home.

Jessie Stephen Jones was born to Henry and Elizabeth Jones on June 1, 1840, in Detroit, Michigan, the first of eight children born into this union. Mr. Jones served in the 4th Michigan Regiment at the Battle of Shepherdstown. Members of the 4th Michigan mustered out in June 1864 with veterans and recruits assigned to the 1st Michigan Regiment in October. Jones was proud to have been present at Appomattox Courthouse for the formal surrender of Confederate troops under General Robert E. Lee. Jones remained in the military after the war and came to Cheyenne County with Federal troops to establish Sidney Barracks (later Fort Sidney). Jones rode with Buffalo Bill Cody and Ned Buntline.

He was married to Sarah (nee Fitzpatrick) on June 1,

1871 and he built their home along Lodgepole Creek. Mrs. Jones was murdered in the fall of 1871, leaving behind no children.

Jones spent several months tracking down his wife's killers. He later served as Cheyenne County Sheriff. He married his second wife Martha (nee Belt) on October 23, 1874. Into this union, God gave three children: Jesse, Annabelle, and Elizabeth.

Survivors include his wife Martha of the home, Jesse (Amanda) Jones, North Platte; Annabelle (Mrs. Frank Chambers, Omaha); and Elizabeth (Mrs. Bart Hickman, Lodgepole).

Funeral Services for Jesse Jones are Saturday May 22, 1920 at 10:30 a.m. at the Christian Church with the Rev. Stanford Turner, presiding. Burial in the Boot Hill Cemetery. Remaining members of E.V. Sumner Post G.A.R. to provide military honors.

With this discovery, I now had my first real clues to the identity of Jesse Jones, and not the Jesse Jones of family lore. On a white-lined notepad I bullet pointed my finds:

- Born in Detroit, Michigan
- Came to Sidney, Nebraska
- House on Lodgepole Creek
- Murder of his first wife, Sarah
- Burial in Boot Hill Cemetery with G.A.R. Honors
- LeMat Pistol (family legend)

What I did not find was a reference to great-grandpa Jones as a Wyatt Earp look-alike in his obituary.

Questions formed:

- What is a "LeMat Pistol"?
- Who murdered my great-grandfather's first wife?
- What was his relationship with Bill Cody
- Where do I continue my search: Detroit, Michigan or Sidney, Nebraska?

That last question led to a simple answer. When I compared the cost of flying to Detroit to the five-hour drive to Sidney, the choice was a "no brainer." Sidney is where my great-grandfather is buried. I'd start there.

Before I traveled to Sidney, I gathered information on the Internet. In the search bar, I typed: What is a LeMat?

I found the first entry interesting, but not helpful. I passed several other entries, and found what I was looking for.

LeMat Revolver

The distinguishing characteristic of the LeMat Revolver is that its 9-shot cylinder revolves around a separate central barrel of a larger caliber than the chambers in the cylinder proper. The central cylinder is smooth-bored and is a short-barreled shotgun (hence the name 'Grapeshot Revolver').

Nine cylinders? Plus a shotgun? Are you kidding me? The entry went on to say that this was a Confederate officer's handgun used by Generals Beauregard, Bragg, and J.E.B. Stuart among others. So my great-grandfather picked up a Confederate revolver during the Civil War and wore it the rest of his life? Jeepers. Nine bullets in the chamber and a central cylinder shotgun. Nine 42 caliber shells with a 20-gauge shotgun; a short, stubby 20-gauge. Deadly to be sure, but I'll bet it bucked like a wild bronco when fired. I would not want to be on the business end of that! Can you imagine a gunfighter counting shots and charging after six shots only to walk into three .42 slugs and a 20-gauge?

I drove seventy-five miles per hour in the right lane of I-80 to Sidney. Semis, pickups, SUVs, and one hippie van from California passed me like I had a slow-moving vehicle sign on the back bumper. Other than that, the drive was uneventful. Scenery changed past Grand Island: acres of ripening corn and soybeans replaced by undulating hills good only for grazing livestock. Sometimes, a bluff appeared out of nowhere like a monolithic sentinel. To the north, a two-mile long train weaved its way to the coal fields of Wyoming for another load.

The sexton at Boot Hill Cemetery in Sidney offered me directions to my great-grandfather's grave.

"Too hot to take ya there m'self," he said through slipping dentures.

I found the headstone just where he said I would. I looked it over. Nothing unusual about the marker. Government issue white marble. A cast aluminum five-pointed star punched into the stone confirmed his membership in the Grand Army of the Republic, the GAR.

I was curious how many walked by his grave, saw the letters: GAR 1861-1865 and wondered what it all meant. If they had asked, I would have told them it's part of our nation's history and history tells us where we've been so we can avoid doing stupid stuff in the future. If I'm remembering correctly there's an appropriate saying: "Those who don't know history are doomed to repeat it."

Next to my great-grandfather's grave, I found two others. One belonged to my great-grandmother Martha, who died in 1929. They chiseled her name into a red granite obelisk. The second marker was a plain wooden one, like you might see in any other Boot Hill cemetery in the west. Thin wooden lathes nailed across the front and back held it together. A small inscription placed in front of this old marker read:

Sarah Jones: Murdered
Fall 1871

There was nothing easy about finding my great-grandfather's "home place." No one remembered where the Jones homestead was located. I traveled west into the last rays of a dazzling sunset on the only road I could find near Lodgepole Creek. A nearby sign read MINIMUM MAINTENANCE ROAD. My Nissan pickup found it hard to keep its footing on the path even while driving twenty miles per hour. Squinting helped somewhat, but I was afraid the ditch and I would tangle.

What was I looking for, anyway? I did not know. A clearing, maybe? A peter-tumbledown shack?When the last rays of the day disappeared, darkness fell. The kind of darkness you get when the lights go out.

Headlights. Thank God for headlights.

The road-grader hadn't passed this way in a while. There was loose gravel all over. And there were potholes. I tried to avoid hitting them, but it was like an attempt to avoid a prize-fighter's nasty right hand only to get hit by his left.

I hit a pothole. The impact almost jerked the wheel out of my hands. All the while I kept thinking I've done a lot of crazy stuff, but this topped it all.

Except for my headlights and the moon overhead darkness surrounded me. Alone. In the middle of no-where. What sense did that make?

With headlights on low-beam I saw a dead tree out of the corner of my eye. But it was too late. I didn't swerve in time.

CRASH!

The engine was still running. That was a good sign. Could I back up? Now that was another question. I slammed the transmission into reverse and gunned it.

No movement except spinning tires and flying gravel. I was stuck and my best guess was it was a good eight miles back to town: A long walk for a late night.

I could call someone. But who would I call? How would they find me? Besides I didn't know anyone in Sidney outside of the Boot Hill sexton, and we hadn't exchanged phone numbers.

Ah, shoot. My wife was right; I should have signed up with Triple A.

If she was here, I'd have gotten a scolding. Well deserved, too.

Upon inspection, the only damage was a broken right headlight. Shattered glass, like hundreds of tiny prisms, reflected the moonlight. The right front tire was fine, but wedged between two long-dead, barkless branches. I kicked the glass away from the tire and thanked God for the full moon.

If I could break the smaller of the two branches, I should be able to back up and get free.

I balanced myself against the truck, and stepped on the branch wedged under it. Several times, I bounced on the branch like a trampoline. It winded me before it gave way with a pleasing crack.

I threw the truck in 4-wheel drive and felt it lunge free.

How about that? No Triple A needed. Now where's the road? There was no road. It occurred to me if Shel Silverstein found *Where the Sidewalk Ends*, I'd found where the Lodgepole Creek road ends. My sense of humor delighted me.

There was a clearing in front of me. It was overgrown, of course, but still a clearing.

Was this the place great-grandfather Jones called home? The moonlight and my flashlight brought a seedy shack into view. The same tree that had once held my truck secure had collapsed like an accordion when it fell. No wonder no one knew where my great-grandfather had lived. A person could fly a drone over the spot a dozen times and never see the shack buried under a tree and a hundred year's worth of undergrowth.

I thought I should leave, but I couldn't remove my eyes from the shack. Something drew me closer. Call it curiosity, if you like. I was in the middle of nowhere. Yet something was telling me I *am* somewhere. Somewhere close to completing a journey I started years ago. Was my great-grandfather calling me from beyond the grave? No, I don't believe in all of that stuff. Yet, something was drawing me.

What was that? Is that a tarp?

A piece of dark fabric showed beneath a broken window.

I grabbed it while thinking all I needed now was to reach out and shake hands with a rattlesnake.

I yanked. Nothing. A struggle followed. Whatever held the tarp in place was not about to give in. Not with my one-handed grip, anyway. I grabbed with both hands and tugged. Still nothing. I gained a better grip and pulled.

R-i-i-i-p. The tearing fabric sent me flying backward.

Gathering myself and standing upright, I found the aged lathes once forming a wall in the shack had splintered, exposing a metal box measuring approximately two feet by three feet.

What's this? A strongbox?

My pulse raced. My bare hands clawed to free the stubborn box. In an instant, I cradled my trophy. It was a strongbox alright. My one lone headlight illuminated the scene. I put the strongbox in its light, spun it around and looked for a keyhole, and found it. But no key.

What I needed was a key. What I found was a jack handle in the spare tire compartment.

This would have to do.

I was a man possessed. What was inside did not want to be revealed.

"C'mon! Open up!" This was one tough strongbox. So, this was how my investigation ends? Years from now, someone will clear away the brush and discover my body. Dead from a heart-attack while prying on this stupid strongbox, bearing silent witness to a man who came so close.

Those who know me know I have a temper. The strongbox took that temper and laughed. A dent or two from the jack handle later, the box held firm.

I could hear my wife's voice at my funeral. "I told him his anger would kill him, but did he listen to me? No. And for what? His great-grandfather? Great. This is just great, just great!"

My thoughts moved from the jack handle to dynamite. Dumb idea.

Explosives would blow things to smithereens. Besides, there was none available. I also nixed driving my pickup over it.

Something prodded me to reach through the broken windowpane again. Carefully running my fingers around the broken glass, lathe and plaster, I felt metal.

Was this a key? Yes, it was a key alright. But was it the right key?

All my frustration melted like a snow cone on a hot day at the fair when the key fit the lock perfectly. A match.

But would it turn without a quick squirt of WD-40?

My luck, the key would break off in the lock and I would be back at square one.

It didn't.

The tarp, the plaster, lathe and the shack itself had preserved the lock. Some rust, but not much. The key turned. The lock snapped open.

Was I sure I wanted to do this? After all I had been through, I now arm-wrestled my reluctance. What if my discovery should remain hidden? Had I considered the implications of my curiousity?

My impulse was to close the lid. I didn't follow that impulse. I let my one good headlight and the fall moon reveal the contents as I lifted the lid. There, neatly placed on top, was a piece of yellowed paper. I opened it and read it half out loud.

To Whom It May Concern,

I, Jesse Jones, on this 4th day of August 1900, placed these items in this box. Each item has meaning for me. First, the only photograph taken of my first wife Sarah and me on our wedding day. Her love for me carried me through some bad times. Second, the only thing left me after my first wife's murder. Her Bible. She circled a verse in her own blood before she died. Third, a blanket given me by Chief Dull Knife when I rode with Bill Cody. Then there's my gun. Got this LeMat off a dead rebel at Shepherdstown. Wore it from then on even when I came west. Saved my life more than once. Lastly, my diary. Started writing in it on the trail to Sidney. It's got names, dates and personal stuff. Didn't want it falling into the wrong hands and hurtin' someone, so I stashed it. Almighty God has changed me. Not the same

*man anymore. Parson Abel told me once that I was forgiven
in Christ. God be praised.*

Jesse Jones

MY GREAT-GRANDFATHER'S first wife was beautiful. In the faded photo, her hair hangs about her shoulders. There she was, standing next to a handsome man a head taller. Was I looking into my great-grandfather's face? Someone had written a simple note on the back.

Jesse and Sarah Jones on their wedding day,
June 1, 1871

A wedding photo? A typical wedding photo for its day.
Why so stoic?
Then I remembered other wedding photos from that era. Yeah, stoic brides and grooms were commonplace.
I lifted a tattered Bible from the strongbox. Inside the front cover, a different handwriting greeted me. One word only: *Sarah*; the name of my great-grandfather's first wife.
But who wrote her name there?
The blanket was in worse shape. Just age, I guessed. Great-grandfather Jones did something special for a chief to be given a blanket like this. I wondered if he wrote this story in his diary. I lifted the blanket from the strongbox and did a double-take.
A pistol! Great-grandfather's pistol!
It was a heavy pistol, but felt good in my hand. I'd seen nothing like it; only read about it on the internet. Nine

chambers with a cylinder in the center to hold a .20 shotgun shell. Great-grandfather's LeMat.

The gun's action was stiff, but not bad, considering its age. Great-grandfather picked up this gun on the bloody field of the Civil War. And family legend had it that he wore it throughout his life. That is until he placed it behind plaster and lathe. The gun couldn't talk of the hardships he suffered, but my mind went there. I remembered reading the Battle of Shepherdstown happened two days after the Battle of Antietam where the 4th Michigan, my great-grandfather's unit, was held in reserve.

If this LeMat could talk, the stories it would tell. My research told me that unlike the storyline of the 1950s *Johnny Ringo* television western or movies like the *League of Extraordinary Gentlemen*, this gun's story was real. It's my great-grandfather's story.

At the bottom of the strongbox, I found the diary. I tried to read it on my knees, but the moon and the headlight bleached the letters. While I wanted to read it right away, I would have to wait. I packed everything but the diary into the strongbox but I wasn't about to use the padlock again until I oiled it.

The diary rode shotgun, the strongbox sat on the floor. It was 11 o'clock when potholes gave way to pavement of a Sidney street.

My stomach grumbled. *When was the last time I had eaten? My best guess? I couldn't remember.*

Neon 'No Vacancy' signs greeted me as I drove into town. Forget the diet. I was thinking cheeseburger, fries, and a cold root beer. *Comfort food*, I reasoned.

I set my sights on food, sleep and deciphering the hand-written diary of one Jesse Jones, my great-grandfather.

I relied on my great-grandfather's diary and some pages

torn from the account of Buffalo Bill Cody written by Ned Buntline, both of whom, it turns out, my great-grandfather knew on a first name basis, to write an adventure set in western Nebraska. My great-grandfather wrote extensive notes in his diary. Writing this book allowed me to get to know my great-grandfather and those influencing his life. He worried over the harm his diary may cause because of his specificity in naming names and places. I do not share his reluctance, but I attempted to treat each individual with respect. I moderated the language and softened the edges of the account of my great-grandfather's life, spanning the diary entries from August 12, 1869 until September 23, 1871 and titled this adventure *Death Comes to Lodgepole Creek*.

CHAPTER ONE

Sarah Fitzpatrick shuffled along the timbered sidewalk, putting behind her the admonitions of Madame Rogers to never walk the streets of Sidney alone. She ignored the warning like so many times before.

I don't need to be school-girled. Just because I work for her doesn't mean I have to follow her every instruction, Sarah told herself.

Madame Rogers had stopped her in the parlor of her bordello again this morning. "Now, where do you think you're going?" she'd asked.

"For a stroll," Sarah responded.

"Don't you remember I want my girls traveling in pairs for their own safety?" Madame Rogers admonished.

"I'll take that chance," Sarah fired back, freeing herself and escaping out the door. What she had in mind was buying the new dress she'd seen hanging in the window of Swede's Mercantile and checking her mail. Swede's served as the town's lone post office. The mail, of course, was always weeks old, but that didn't matter to Sarah. Her brother in Georgia was the only one who wrote to her. And that was seldom. She wrote to him that she was a singer and waitress in a saloon, never once mentioning that she was a 'working girl of ill repute;' the name respectable women called women in Sarah's line of work.

A humidity haze hung over everything after an early morning rain that attempted to wash the air clean, but then the August sun drove the rain away leaving behind the haze. With the high humidity, clothing clung to every nook and cranny. Sarah's parasol blocked the sun but did nothing to prevent her clothes from sticking to her. She walked down a step, crossed the dirt street, and then up a step to the timbered sidewalks. City fathers had elevated the sidewalks to prevent rain water from entering the front doors of retail businesses.

Sarah kept her head down when she walked. At five foot seven, she stood a head taller than many women and at twenty-four years of age, she possessed a beauty women envied and men paid good money for. She was not proud of the hand life dealt her. She often thought how disappointed and hurt her parents would be and she thanked God they were not alive to see her, one of six prostitutes working for Madame Lorraine Rogers, and ignoring the snide comments of Sidney, Nebraska's leading women who passed her on the sidewalk. Hearing their comments, she wanted to raise her head and say, *Why do you talk to me that way? Your husband was with me last night.* But she resisted. *Let them think what they want*, she said to herself.

Children scampered by and nearly ran Sarah over in their haste to return to school. They would be in class until harvest when their parents needed them again. The younger children giggled as they passed. Sarah recognized the voice of Charlie Smith. At twenty-three he was the oldest member of the fifth grade. His father had died in the dusty street in front of Swede's while his mother looked on. A man named Custus killed him. The same Custus who frequented Madame Roger's and spent many nights in Sarah's room. He disgusted her, but nothing she did drove him away. She hated him for it.

"Well, looky here. I've gone lookin' for a dove of the evening and she flies right into my arms."

Someone grabbed Sarah around the waist and lifted her into the air. She recognized the boots and the voice of the man who wore them. Both belonged to Custus Leverette, a behemoth of a man; unkempt and uncivil. "I'm not working right now, Custus. Put me down!" she said.

"'Not working right now'. Do ya believe that, boys? She's 'not working right now.' Come on; give 'ole Custus a kiss. How 'bout it?" Custus belched out the words with a laugh.

Sarah aimed a well-placed kick at Custus' groin. Her pointed-toed shoes found their mark.

"Awf!" he shouted in pain, dropping her in a heap to the ground. Sarah struggled to regain her footing, but each time her boots tangled in her red gingham dress and prevented her from doing so.

Custus tried to stand erect but his pain would not let him. "Grab her, boys. Grab that little tramp!" he yelled.

She recognized his men. Iggy was the skinny one with a pock-marked face. Stinson the fat one. Both delighted in Sarah's predicament. The two of them forced Sarah against the front door of Higgins' Lumber, trapping her.

It was a few minutes before Custus stood to his full 6 foot 3 inch height and even then not without pain. "Iggy and Stinson here, say ya ain't going nowhere," Custus said. "So, ya won't give 'ole Custus a kiss, huh?" He pushed his men out of his way. "Well, we'll just see about that. I'll teach ya to kick me." Custus struck her face with his open hand.

"Help me!" she cried out in agony. Tears streamed down her face and she lifted her hand to touch the welt rising on her cheek.

A crowd gathered in the street. Custus stared them down. "Get outta here!" he barked. "Unless you want the same thing to happen to you, you'd better scram. DO YOU HEAR ME! I SAID, 'SCRAM!'"

No one dared raise a hand in Sarah's defense. They knew better. Custus had killed men for less. Sarah's screams went unanswered over the sinister laughter of Custus' men.

Two soldiers rode up and she made eye contact with one of them and thought she detected a hint of sympathy in his eyes. But he never stopped. He just looked at her, sized up the situation, and rode on.

"Help me!"

Iggy put his filthy hand over Sarah's mouth. "Shut up! You know how Custus hates it when someone screams, don't ya?"

"Yeah," Stinson joined in. "If ya don't quit screaming, Custus here is gonna cut ya." Stinson was right in her face, so close she smelled his whisky-soured breath.

"What's going on here?" Sarah heard a man ask. She looked up to see the crowd part and the soldier she'd made eye contact with standing directly behind Custus and his men. "I think this has gone far enough," he said.

The crowd moved away leaving the soldier all alone. "Did you three hear what I said? I think this has gone far enough!"

Custus' face turned red with anger. He turned from Sarah to face the intruder. "Me and the boys are just having a little fun with the town pump. Ain't we, boys?" Iggy and

Stinson nodded in agreement. "Now, you mind yer own business, soldier boy, while I mind mine."

He turned back to Sarah.

"I'm making her business my business. Leave the lady alone," the soldier answered.

"She ain't no lady. She's a prostitute. That's what I'm tellin' ya. Now, we're gonna beat ya to a pulp fer interruptin' us, soldier boy."

Custus motioned Stinson into action and took his place holding Sarah against the door.

Stinson neared the soldier, who backed into the street. The crowd separated further. "Take him, Stinson!" Custus shouted. Stinson took a huge swing. The soldier ducked beneath it and drove his right fist into Stinson's belly, doubling him over in pain and making himself an easy target for the soldier's uppercut.

Whap!! Stinson dropped in the dirt.

Custus pulled Sarah away from Iggy and stood behind her. Iggy drew his gun, but the soldier was faster and on top of him in a heartbeat. The butt of the soldier's revolver hammered Iggy's face. Blood splattered everywhere. "My dose!" Iggy screamed while both hands covered his bleeding nose.

The soldier brought the revolver down on Iggy's head with a hollow thud.

No more screams. Only silence. The lights went out in Iggy's eyes and he took two staggering steps before collapsing on top of Stinson.

The soldier holstered his pistol.

Custus' eyes filled with hate and with all his might he shoved Sarah aside and stalked toward the soldier. "How did you learn to fight like that?" he said.

"The War," the soldier replied. "I'm used to dealing with scum like you, all bull and no go."

"His knife!" old man Higgins yelled from the doorway. "Watch out for his knife."

In a heartbeat, Custus drew cold steel from his belt; an extra long Bowie knife. "This says I cut ya. Ya can bet I'm gonna cut ya."

He lunged and missed as the soldier side-stepped. With one blow to the face, the soldier spun Custus around. The soldier's boot found Custus' backside, pushing him head-long into the horse trough.

The soldier stood over him. "Next time treat a woman with respect—prostitute or not."

It took a while before Custus drew himself from the trough and stood in the dusty street glaring at the man who'd bested him. His pride hurt and his cheek throbbed. The townspeople melted away. The soldier had given them a lot to talk about.

Custus shouted orders and he and his men mounted up and rode away. Custus stared back at the soldier, trailing angry words behind him like the dust their horses kicked up.

The soldier turned toward Sarah, who stood in the doorway with old man Higgins. "Ma'am," he said.

"Dang, Jesse," the second soldier said. "What the heck was that?"

"You hold your tongue, sir, there's a lady present," Parson Abel pushed the soldiers aside.

"Pardon me, Parson. Didn't see you standing there," the second soldier replied.

"It doesn't matter whether or not you did," he said. "That's no way to talk." Parson Abel's gentle face and calm demeanor heightened the impact of his words as he took Sarah's hands in his. "You alright Miss Fitzpatrick?"

"I am, Parson, thanks to--" her voice trailed off. "I'm so sorry, gentlemen, but in the scuffle, I don't believe I caught your names."

"Jesse Jones, Ma'am. And this here is Adam Potter."

"Ma'am," Potter added.

A gentle smile accompanied the Parson's words. "Come, Miss Fitzpatrick. I'll walk you home."

"Wouldn't you be ashamed to be in my company, Parson?" Sarah said.

"I already know who you are and what you do, my dear. All of us are sinners. You are no different. God loves you and sent a Savior. Kinda' like Mr. Jones here. Only on a much bigger scale. You'll learn all about this Savior in my sermon on Sunday. I'm inviting you to come."

After a few steps with Parson Abel, Sarah turned back to Jones and Potter. "Thank you, gentlemen. Thank you for your kindness."

ABOUT A HALF HOUR'S ride east of town, Custus found a clearing and drew his rag-tag bunch to a halt and dismounted, tying his horse to a scrub tree.

The sight of his own blood made Iggy squeamish, so he had torn a piece of fabric from his filthy shirt, wadded it and stuffed it into his left nostril. To stem the bleeding, he'd ridden one-handed with the other hand clamped over his nose. Blood covered the front of his shirt. "My nose," he said, but with the rag in his nose, the word came out 'doze.' "He broke my doze," he moaned, looking every bit like he could upchuck at any moment.

Stinson kept rubbing his head where the soldier clubbed him. "Got double-vision. I see two of ya, Custus. I got a busted toof out of the deal," Stinson said. He nursed a bruised jaw and stuck a grimy finger in his mouth and poked around. All the swelling let him know where the bigger of the two soldiers clobbered him. "Bet I gotta busted toof in here."

Custus' face hurt as well, but he wasn't about to give his men the satisfaction of thinking he was hurt. He paced the grounds in anger. "There ain't nothin' gonna take my mind off of what's just happened. Wet clothes and all. Quit 'yer dad-gum belly-achin'! We got whooped today. I won't let that go. No, sir! Ain't no one ever done that to me before. Ain't no one gonna do that to me again, neither."

Stinson took his finger from his mouth. "What 'er we gonna do?" he asked.

"I gotta cut that soldier boy. Don't know when or where, but I gotta cut him." Custus stopped pacing just long enough to draw his Bowie knife from its sheath. "I gotta cut him." An evil grin crossed his face. "Ya, that's what I gotta do. I gotta cut him."

"WHAT KIND of life is this for you to live?" Parson Abel asked while he and Sarah walked side-by-side.

"We've been through this, Parson," Sarah said.

"I know, but I can't help but ask again. Being a prostitute is a dangerous business, especially with a man like Custus around."

"That thought has occurred to me."

"It should. Those men could have killed somebody; if not you, then one of those two soldiers who helped you. Give that some thought." They walked a while without talking, and then Parson Abel left her in front of Madame Roger's.

Sarah wasn't getting any younger. The dreams of a man to sweep her off her feet returned. She'd suppressed that dream long ago when warring men set fire to her family plantation outside of Atlanta. The hatred of those Yankees had scared her. She wanted no part of men like that. *Jones is different.* She entered her depressing room and shut the door behind her.

"REVENGE IS A CRUEL TASKMASTER," old man Higgins said to the two soldiers. "There will be more trouble now that you put Custus in his place. Custus will never forget what you did to him. His reputation is at stake."

"Where did Custus come from?" Jones asked.

"No one knows fer sure," Higgins continued. "He and his men showed up a while back. It was obvious even then that Custus was used to getting his way through intimidation. And if that didn't work--murder."

"That's why you warned me to 'watch out for the knife.'"

"Yep. Several haven't and bear the scars. You remember a prostitute named One-Eyed Mary, don't you?"

"Wasn't she found dead in an alley?" Potter asked.

"That's her alright," Higgins continued. "She found out the hard way what happens when you cross him. She failed to give Custus sex on credit and she paid with her life. Her screams for help went unanswered. Those who heard Mary's cries closed their windows on a hot summer night to suppress the sound. Next morning, One-Eyed Mary lay in a pool of blood behind the pool hall, hacked to death.

Everyone knew who the murderer was, but no one stepped forward to testify. Custus had free rein. No one stood up to him then like you did today."

Jones thought about old man Higgins' words as he and Potter rode south to Sidney Barracks. Custus had asked Jones where he learned to fight like that. Jones had told him 'during the War,' but now Potter wanted specifics.

"The War taught me many things," Jones said. "I learned to read the eyes of the men I've faced. I came to recognize either fear or hatred in their eyes. Hatred clouds your judgment so you can't think straight. You miss minor advantages you would otherwise notice if your judgment wasn't clouded. The War taught me that eyes tell you everything."

"Hatred *was* in Custus' eyes." Potter said. "I saw it in the way he tossed that girl around."

"The girl's name is Sarah," Jones said. "Hatred clouds the thought processes. Control those two things in yerself— fear and hatred—and you have the advantage."

"Fear and hatred," Potter repeated the words like a mantra.

"And there's one more thing."

"What?"

"Sometimes it just comes down to stupid luck," Jones said with a laugh. "I also learned something else during the War and that's that people talk and when a story like this one gets told over and over again, someone embellishes it and the story grows bigger and bigger. It's kinda like Robert E. Lee's legend scaring the bejeezus outta everyone except General Grant who faced him head-on and won. When a story is told over and over it gets bigger and bigger to become a legend. Imagine the hatred the retelling of this story will stir up in Custus when he hears that you and I bested him and his gang—they'll say stuff like we took down twelve men instead of three and had it not been for you and me, ol' man Higgins and a prostitute named Sarah would be dead. That's the stuff of legends."

CUSTUS HATED what happened to him in town. He stewed over it. He lost sleep. "No one does this to me! No one! Not some wimpy soldier and his friend. Not nobody! It may not be today, it may not be tomorrow, but someday it will happen. What happened to that little one-eyed prostitute will pale in comparison to what I'm gonna do. Ain't nobody gonna stop me neither. Do you hear me, soldier boy? Nobody!" he yelled to the surrounding prairie.

CHAPTER TWO

Sarah approached Parson Abel's home, invitation in hand. She'd finagled her way around Madame Rogers *rule* of never walking alone by taking Brandy Dawson with her, another of Madam Rogers' girls. Brandy stayed in the room across the hall from Sarah and long ago the two had struck up a friendship.

Brandy was seeing a young man on-the-side, so when Sarah found the invitation from Adeline Abel, Parson Abel's wife, stuck in her mailbox, the two of them hatched up a plan for an outing.

Brandy and Sarah left the brothel together, but once out of sight of Madame Roger's watchful eyes, they separated. Brandy met her young man in front of Swede's Mercantile and Sarah walked four blocks to the Abel's home. The two agreed to meet in front of Swede's an hour and a half later.

Sarah fell in love with the Abel's home the moment she rounded the corner at Fifth Street and Main. There, three blocks ahead of her, standing on a slight rise, was a beautiful white, Victorian home complete with wrap-around porch. The stateliness was reminiscent of the plantation where she'd grown up. Childhood memories popped into her head, memories of times spent with cousins and friends playing on the bowling green, of servants bustling about the place, and how her papa treated each servant with respect.

Papa.

His memory flooded in while she navigated the front steps and found herself on the wrap-around porch complete with porch swing.

It sure is pretty. She imagined what the home looked like inside. *This would sure be a fine place to come home to. All I've got is a sleazy bedroom in a brothel—a bed, a busted chair, a cigarette-stained dresser with a washstand and cracked mirror. Madame Rogers says 'a working girl don't need nothin' else,' but I do so miss my home—and you Papa.*

Sarah knocked. No answer. She waited and tried again. Nothing. She was about to turn away, when she heard footsteps near the door. Adeline Abel peered through the stained glass of the front door and her hurried fingers fumbled with the lock and opened the door.

"Come in, child, come in," she said. Sarah guessed Adeline's age was somewhat younger than her husband, making her fifty-five or so. Sarah noticed Adeline's rounded face, hazel eyes and pleasant smile.

"You have a lovely home, Mrs. Abel," Sarah said, looking about and assessing the interior even more beautiful than she imagined.

"Thank you. God has blessed us since coming to Sidney five years ago. Our little congregation takes wonderful care of us. Come sit in the drawing room," she said, leading the way. "Here we are. Do sit down. In my invitation I promised you some tea. It was presumptuous on my part, I know, to assume you drink tea, so let me ask you, would you care for some tea?"

"Yes, please. I learned to drink tea when I was growing up. It was my Papa's favorite."

"Is your Papa still alive?"

"Papa died during the War and Mama a couple years before that."

Adeline took Sarah's hands in hers. "Oh, my sweet child, I am so sorry."

"It seems so long ago."

Adeline reflected on Sarah's comment and patted her hands. "Now, if you'll excuse me, I'll get us both some tea. And Sarah, my husband has already told me what you do for a living. Make yourself comfortable. I won't be a moment."

In Adeline's absence, Sarah wandered about the room and noted what she saw: A settee, a couple of overstuffed chairs, a family portrait on the wall, and Parson Abel's theological diploma. The room felt comfortable. Homey. Feelings she hadn't felt since the War of Northern Aggression, as her Papa had called it.

"Here you are my dear," Mrs. Abel announced. "Are you in the least bit curious about why I invited you here today?" Adeline did not wait for Sarah to answer and continued. "Most likely, you thought I invited you here to condemn your choice of vocations. Not the case at all. I want to get to know you. Everyone has a reason for coming west. For me, it was the opportunity to join my husband in ministering to new people and talking to them about Jesus Christ." Adeline seated herself on the settee. She set the tea service on the small table in front of it and poured two cups. "Sugar?" she asked.

Sarah nodded.

"One spoonful or two?"

"One, please."

Adeline spooned sugar into Sarah's tea, stirred it, and handed the cup and saucer to her. "Tell me a little about you."

Sarah sat on the overstuffed chair to the right of Adeline. "I was just thinkin' about that on my way here," she began. "I was eighteen when the Yankees came. I saw their hatred first-hand. They came south burning, looting, raping on their way to Atlanta. Ya'll can't imagine what it was like in the summer of '64."

"Oh, my dear child," Adeline said, "You poor, poor thing. I am so sorry this has happened to you."

"When the soldiers left, there was nothin'. Cotton fields gone, trampled underfoot. Plantation house ablaze," Sarah spoke through her tears. "A Yankee straggler tried to straddle me in the barn. Papa stabbed him with a pitchfork but another Yankee blew Papa's head off, splattering me with his blood." Sarah lowered her head to her hands and cried.

"It's alright, you are safe here," Adeline said.

"I got up and ran," Sarah said. "I haven't looked back since. It's like I got all these feelin's inside and I can't outrun 'em."

"So you ran to the ends of the earth or what seemed like it and you wound up in Sidney, Nebraska." Adeline smiled.

"No matter how far I run, no matter how hard I try, I cannot outrun the things that happened in the past," Sarah added.

"Oh, my dear."

Sarah felt secure and vulnerable and this new relationship that was beginning brought about a confession. "In every relationship with a man, all I experience is hatred. I want to change, but that's how it is. Forcing myself to have sex to suppress my feeling does not work either. My hatred compounds with feelings of remorse and shame. My parents raised me to be a good girl. I know better than that. Tears flowed down Sarah's cheeks. I was a 'good girl' I don't know why I'm telling you all this."

Adeline wrapped her arms around Sarah. "My poor, poor, dear," she said.

Sarah had not received a hug like this since her mother died. She felt protected. When Adeline returned to the settee, Sarah sipped her tea in silence.

"Tell me about last Thursday," Adeline said.

"Custus and his men attacked me that morning. It's not the first time. If the two soldiers hadn't stepped in we would not be talking," Sarah said.

"Have you considered leaving Madame Rogers? Then, at least, you would get out of that environment."

"I would, 'cept Madame Rogers doesn't pay me that much. If I quit, I've got nothin' to live on."

"My dear, a girl should never feel like she's out of options." Adeline stood. "If you'll excuse me, I want to get something for you."

Sarah sat alone with her thoughts and her tea. Adeline returned with a book. "Let me give you something. Consider it a little token of our friendship and time together today." Adeline handed Sarah a Bible.

"I can't take this," Sarah said, handing it back.

"Oh, but I insist, my dear. You'll discover yourself in this book. In this Bible, you will see that you are a woman of value. A woman forgiven. You've been on my mind and I've prayed for you, by name since Parson Abel told me about you. I slid a piece of paper between some pages. Start by reading these stories first. Do that for yourself. I think you will find yourself on these pages. Now, Parson Abel and I have already discussed it and we won't take 'no' for an answer. Consider it our gift to you."

"I'll borrow it and bring it back."

"How about this? Read what I have marked first and then decide if you want to bring it back or not. Can we agree on that?" Adeline said.

Sarah paused for a long moment then nodded.

Smiling gently, Adeline asked, "More tea?"

THAT EVENING, before the paying customers arrived, Sarah sat alone on her bed. She opened the Bible. 'You'll discover yourself in this book,' Adeline had told her. Sarah wondered what she meant by that. She found the first slip of paper and read *John 4* on it. She found the words Adeline had circled with a pencil and read the account of a woman who had five husbands and was living with another man. Sarah read that Jesus, who knew everything about the woman, never condemned her. On the second slip she found the words *John 8*. Again, she read what Adeline circled. Some men brought a woman caught in adultery to Jesus. They wanted to stone her. Jesus said, "I do not condemn you."

"I do. I do see me," Sarah cried. "I've got to tell Adeline."

Sarah raced down the stairs and headed to the door. But before her hand reached the doorknob, Madame Rogers grabbed her arm and spun her around.

"And where do you think you're goin'? You got work to do. The men will be here any minute."

Sarah was emboldened. "That's none of yer business."

Madame Rogers slapped her. "This is my business. You are my business. Now get back upstairs. And what's this?"

Madam Rogers tore the Bible from Sarah's hand. "A Bible! So, you think you're too good for us, huh?"

"Give it back!" Sarah shouted. "Adeline Abel loaned it to me."

"Oh, she did, did she? I'll put a stop to this right now. Get along back upstairs. The men will be here soon. If'n you ain't a layin' than I ain't a payin'!"

The door swung open. In stepped Custus. Iggy and Stinson followed. He walked over to Sarah. "Now, that's what I call perfect timing. You're here and I'm here. You're available. And so am I," Custus announced.

"She's the reason I got dis here busted doze," Iggy said to Madame Rogers through the gauze that overflowed his nose.

"And looky here at this knot on my jaw," interjected Stinson. "Whatta ya know, she ain't got her soldier boy to protect her now."

They all laughed.

"She ain't got a soul in the world," Custus said. "C'mon, honey, 'ole Custus'll take care of ya."

Custus dragged her toward the stairs. "Room seven, ain't it?" He aimed this question at Madam Rogers, who nodded.

"Well, fellas, for tonight anyway, it looks like seven is my lucky number."

Sarah struggled to free herself, but Custus' grip was sure. She had denied him sex last Thursday, but not tonight.

"Ride 'em, cowboy. Yee haw!" Iggy said.

"Careful, Custus, don't get bucked off," Stinson added.

Like immature schoolboys, Iggy and Stinson fired off snide remarks while Custus pulled Sarah up the stairs. She struggled but could not free herself. Custus kicked opened the door to room seven and flung Sarah into the room. His breath reeked of cheap whiskey. He fumbled for his belt buckle.

Sarah screamed.

"Don't scream," he said. "I don't like it when a gal screams. Somethin' inside me snaps. Ya heard of One-eyed Mary, ain't 'cha? She screamed." He sighed. "So I cut her. I cut her real bad. If'n I cut you, ain't nobody gonna care."

His left hand covered Sarah's mouth, his right continued fumbling with his belt. "Never was very good at undoin' my belt one-handed, but I'll keep practicin'." He laughed.

Custus' weight on her made it hard to breathe. She drifted in and out of consciousness. In her mind she saw the Yankee who tried to rape her, but this time, her Papa never came to her rescue. There was no pitchfork, no emotionless face of a dead Yankee.

"You're nothing," Custus chided. "Nothin'. Yer southern scum, and that's all you'll ever be."

Sarah wanted to strike back but thought better of it. She breathed in the smell of Custus' sweat, the rancid smell of someone who hadn't bathed in a while.

At last Custus was done. "Catch," Custus tossed a ten dollar gold piece in her direction on his way out the door. "Yep. Seven is my lucky number."

Sarah lay curled on her bed in her sleazy brothel bedroom—the room with the busted chair, the cigarette-stained dresser with a washstand and cracked mirror and no hope. She cried herself to sleep.

THREE A.M. CAME, the time when cowboys and rowdies sleep off their drunken stupors. Sarah had seen this hour many times before. With soft footsteps, she crept out of her room, down the stairs and down the hall toward the front door. She caught sight of the Bible Adeline Abel had given her, discarded near the fireplace. She snapped it up. Somehow, she found a new resolve. *I'm much too young to feel this old.*

Sarah unlocked the door of Madame Rogers' brothel and stepped outside. A humid late August night greeted her— hot and still. Sweat clung to her like Custus had hours before. His putrid breath lingered in her mind. She gagged. When her feet hit the sidewalk, she quickened her pace.

Near the Painted Lady Saloon she spied a drunken man face down on the sidewalk. She noticed the gauze in his nostrils. *Iggy.* She resisted the temptation to kick him and reopen his wounded nose.

Sarah turned the corner and walked north. Parson Abel's house came into view and she steered her aching body in that direction. The reality of the day struck her harder than Custus had. It was men like him who paid money to sleep with her. Men like him who pawed her body without love. Men like him that stirred up memories. Bad memories. She wanted to puke. *I can't go back. But I'm in too deep,* she whispered to the dark.

The first few knocks on Pastor Abel's door brought only silence. Sarah upped the ante and knocked harder. The flicker of a candle in a second story room gave her hope. She knocked again. The window sash rose, and a head appeared, the candle light cast an aura contorting the face.

"Who's there?" Parson Abel asked with a welcoming tone.

"It's Sarah."

She heard feet scurry and an indistinguishable female voice. Then Adeline appeared at the window. "My dear child," Adeline said, "what are you doing here at this time of night? Are you alright?"

Not waiting for Sarah's reply she sent her husband to the front door. "Don't move we'll be right there."

Sarah's ears followed hurried feet on wooden steps and down the hallway. She heard someone undo the latch, and the heavy front door opened. Adeline invited her in. "Are you alright?" Adeline asked.

Not knowing where to start, Sarah held out the Bible. "I've been reading yer book. Can we talk about it?"

Adeline sent her husband to the kitchen to boil water for tea. "Of course, we can talk. Where would you like to start?"

Tears flowed down Sarah's cheeks. "You were right. I discovered myself in this book," Sarah said. "Can we start with that?"

CHAPTER THREE

Jesse Jones found himself six miles south of Sidney Barracks at the shooting range; a spartan place dotted with an occasional sage brush. Soldiers had carved out a shooting range in the side of a sand dune to safely hone their shooting skills.

The dunes provided parameters for their shooting, but sometimes the men took aim outside those parameters when jackrabbits happened too close. Such shooting was frowned upon by Sergeant-Major Kelly.

Once Jones had wounded a jackrabbit from a hundred and fifty yards and the wounded jackrabbit cried like a baby. Since Kelly was the father of five children all under ten years old, he wanted no more of that.

"Don't be a doin' that," Kelly ordered. "'Tis dangerous to fire outside the range. None of ya here can hit the broadside of a barn but Jones and Potter anyway."

Today Company A of the 37th Infantry Regiment, to which Jones and Potter belonged, a young company with fifteen new recruits, had come to this secluded spot to practice small arms fire. For this exercise Kelly used the heel of his boot to scratch a line of fire thirty-five yards away from the paper targets mounted waist high, each with ten evenly spaced concentric circles around a red bulls-eye.

"Gentlemen," Kelly began. "Points are tallied based on where 'yer bullet strikes the paper. One point for a strike furthest from the bulls-eye, up to ten points for a bulls-eye.With the exception of Jones, all of Company A will fire the standard issue Colt Single Action Army revolver. Fer all ya new recruits, single action means that afore the weapon is fired, the hammer is pulled back and cocked."

He demonstrated for the benefit of new recruits. "Only then can ya squeeze the trigger and discharge the weapon. Ya may have noticed that Jones carries a different revolver, a battlefield souvenir retrieved during the late War. Because of his years of service, Jones has permission to carry a LeMat revolver. Would you be so kind as to demonstrate, Mr. Jones, sir?"

"Yes, Sergeant-Major." Jesse cocked his weapon. Aimed. Squeezed the trigger.

BAM!

Down range his slug tore a hole in the paper target.

"Bullseye!" Potter shouted and then repeated himself eight more times as Jones found his mark with his LeMat's .42 caliber slugs. The men of Company A stood in awe.

"As ya can see, men, the LeMat is a special handgun, but there is one more feature to her, isn't there Mr. Jones?"

"There is, Sergeant-Major."

Jones slid the firing pin down, cocked his LeMat a tenth time and fired.

BOOM! It roared into action tearing out the bullseye.The entire company cheered.

"Can we have a gun like that?" asked a new recruit.

Sergeant-Major Kelly calmed his men. "In answer to yer question, No, ya can't have a gun like that. Ya got the best in yer government issue. I wanted you to see what marksmanship looks like from the best Sidney Barracks has ta offer in Jesse Jones.

A private asked about the gun.

"It's a LeMat." Jones held the empty revolver for all to see.

"It holds nine .42 caliber rounds with a 20-gauge shotgun under the main barrel," Potter chimed in. "He got it off some dead Rebel officer during the War."

"That's enough, Potter," Jones said. "That was a long time ago."

"Alright, now lads, I have one other surprise for ya 'afore you be a gitten yer practice in. I said that Jones is the best marksman our Barracks has ta offer. Now, I want ya to see me in action—the second best marksman—'ole Irish."

"With all due respect, Sergeant-Major," Jones whispered to his senior officer. "I've never let anyone fire my LeMat before."

Kelly, the most experienced Indian fighter among them, answered Jones in the best way he knew how. He pointed to the three yellow chevrons on his sleeve."I'm pullin' rank on ya," he whispered back.

"Yes, Sir," Jones replied. Jones reloaded by cracking open the breach and dropping in the 20-gauge shell first, then the nine .42 caliber cartridges. Irish watched in gleeful anticipation.

"I'll be havin' yer revolver," Irish said and he extended his right hand to receive Jones' gun.

"But, Sergeant-Major," Jones injected.

"I know how to handle her. Yer sidearm, if you please, Mr. Jones." Kelly looked downrange and spoke to no one in particular. "Someone be a settin' a target. Watch now, lads. 'Ol Irish'll show ya a thing or two."

A private scrambled to put a fresh target in place while Irish waited. The men of Company A looked on.

"But..." Jones said.

"For the love of God, man, will ya stop 'buttin' me?" A broad smile formed under Irish's handle-bar mustache. "Hold this." Kelly removed his hat with the pushed-up front, handing it to Jones in exchange for his LeMat. Everyone waited as Irish stared down at the weapon in his hand.

Kelley had heard of a LeMat before but never held or fired one. It was heavier than he had imagined. "I like the feel," he said. He looked downrange to the fresh target, pulled back the hammer and took a last look at Jones. "There will be no more buts, sir," he said.

He squared himself to the mark and held the LeMat at arm's length. He squeezed the trigger. Nothing.

"Begging your pardon, Sergeant-Major," Jones said, "but you forgot to cock it."

"So I did! Thank you, sir." He smiled a wry smile and cocked the LeMat, again before holding it out at arm's length and squeezing the trigger.

Boom! The 20-gauge exploded to life. The vicious recoil brought the weapon back toward Irish's face. He ducked, spun around and fell flat on his backside. Everyone laughed, except the disheveled Sergeant-Major, who sat with a bewildered look.

"But, I tried to tell ya, Sergeant-Major," Jones said while extending his hand to help Kelly up.

"I 'spoze, there's the reason for the 'buts,' Mr. Jones?"
"Yes, sir."
Irish struggled to regain his feet amid the chuckle of his

men. "It's a tad bit late now, but what was it ya wanted me to know?"

"Well, sir. I wanted to explain that in your hurry to shoot my gun, I didn't have a chance to switch the hammer to fire the 42s instead of the shotgun. The recoil is a bugger if you don't know it's coming."

"Ohhhh, is that so?" Kelly said. A smile broke out on Irish's face, followed by laughter all around. "Is that so?" he said again. He handed the LeMat back to Jones. "Alright men, 'tis time fer you to practice. This is the only break you'll have until lunch, so get crackin'."

Some time later, Kelly looked down at his pocket watch. "That's it, gentlemen. Time to report back to the barracks. Mr. Potter I'm puttin' ya in charge a addin' the scores and reportin' 'em to me."

It wasn't long, and twenty-five men had stowed their gear away and four pack mules began the process of trekking to Sidney Barracks and home.

Jones and Potter rode side by side behind the Sergeant-Major and kept up a continual dialogue about the day's events. "What are the chances that conversations the next week or so will retell the story of the gun range and the Sergeant-Major?" Potter asked.

"I'd give you ten to one odds that that will happen." Jones said.

"I have the perfect title for that retelling."

"You do?"

"Yep. They'll remember it as the day you shot ten for ten and the day your LeMat knocked the Sergeant-Major on his butt," said Jones.

"I like that. I really do," said the Sergeant-Major.

SOME THREE MILES from their encampment, Sergeant-Major Kelly halted to view the scene from the top of a hill. A steam engine puffed out smoke while it chugged across the open prairie. It made its prescribed stop in Sidney where passengers disembarked and others boarded. Near the tracks a crew of workers let down a pipe from the water tower to fill up the engine's tanks. The water entered the boiler and was converted to steam to turn the mighty wheels.

"Let this be a reminder to ya about why we're here, men," Kelly said. "We've an important job to do. Guard the railroad from Indian attacks. We're here to protect citizens from war parties of the Pawnee, Cheyenne and Sioux. We came to protect the track layers and stayed to defend a state, now only a little over three years old.That's why we do what we do out here."

"May I add something, Sergeant-Major? With your permission, of course," Jones said.

"Permission granted," said Kelly.

"Remember what Colonel Englewood told you," Jones began, "when you first reported for duty. Your mission is to protect the lives of those laying the track and the lives of those who choose to make their homes, lured by whatever reason—to make a place for themselves or to hide from their past, it doesn't matter, we guard them all willingly and with the understanding that we may give up our lives in their defense."

"Well said, sir," Kelly noted.

Jones continued, "When I arrived a year ago there were but a handful of sod houses near the railroad. Log houses sprang up shortly after my arrival. Construction on a village followed, and now a town needs our protection. More people have increased the responsibility of Sidney Barracks. That's why we're building a new fort soon. Take a good look men, this is your responsibility. This is your home."

The men remounted and rode on. In the distance Jones saw a mule train bearing wood. Sergeant-Major Kelly told them the wood came from the abandoned buildings of Fort Sedgwick, Colorado, to be repurposed into the buildings of the new Fort Sidney.

"Our protection extends to a pretty girl in town, too, doesn't it?" Potter said.

"It does," Jones said. "And by the way, her name is Sarah."

Jones, Potter, and the Sergeant-Major made their way to Colonel Robert Englewood's tent to issue their reports. Sergeant-Major Kelly being the first to answer Englewood's request for the small arms assessment. "Small arms fire 'tis much improved, sir," he said. "Tomorrow's mounted drill will be another matter entirely."

"Begging the Sergeant-Major's pardon, but don't you want to report on your morning at the shooting range, sir?" Jones asked.

Kelly's face flushed.

"Well, Sergeant-Major?" the colonel prompted.

"It's nothing, sir. Mr. Jones is only havin' a wee bit of a joke at my expense, sir." He gave Jones a look and Jesse and Potter did everything they could to keep from laughing.

"Would you three step into my tent, I have a couple of gentlemen I'd like you to meet," Englewood said.

Home-like comforts filled the tent. A large four-poster

bed, dresser, and washstand. Scattered on the Colonel's table and writing desk were trail maps, and locations of key western forts, reminding Jones that the colonel administered the barrack's affairs here.

"At ease, gentlemen. We have visitors with us. I want you to meet Buffalo Bill Cody and his friend," Englewood said. "Gentlemen, this is Sergeant-Major Kelly, we call him Irish, for short, along with Jones and Potter who assist him in our shooting regimen."

Cody rose from his chair. The other man never looked up but continued to write. "And gentlemen," Englewood said, "This is Cody's friend; Edward Zane Carroll Judson."

"You know him better as the dime novelist Ned Buntline. Ned is writing about my adventures," Cody announced. "He's very good at putting down facts along with a lot of B.S."

"B.S. sells," Buntline interjected with a laugh. "How many men have a reputation like yours, Cody? My readers know how you single-handedly supplied meat for the Kansas Pacific back in '67 by killing four thousand buffalo in eighteen months."

"See what I mean, gentlemen?" Cody replied. "Ned always has a line of bull."

Jones was close enough to Buntline to look over his shoulder and read his latest entry. *The beginnings of a mustache adorned Cody's upper lip; his chin remained clean-shaven. On each hip, he wore a Colt 1851 Navy revolver. With a firm grip, he took the Sergeant-Major's hand.*

Buntline looked up and Jones quickly looked away when Englewood got down to business. "Irish, Bill Cody's looking for marksmen."

In an instant, Irish recalled Jones' success at the range. "Ten fer ten," he said, thinking aloud.

"What does that mean, Irish?" Englewood injected.

"Jones was ten fer ten this morning at thirty-five feet. That's what I mean. If you will excuse me, sir, I saved his target in my saddlebag. Ain't never seen a ten fer ten b'fore."

Jones glanced down at Buntline's journal as he wrote how Irish bounded out of the tent and lifted the flap on his saddlebag and produced the paper target.

"Jones put nine rounds around the bullseye before blasting it out," Irish said. "And that makes him ten fer ten." He held up the target for everyone to see.

"Huh, only a LeMat's that accurate. How accurate are you at a gallop?" Cody asked.

Before Jones could answer, Englewood spoke. "We'll find out tomorrow. We have a mounted drill scheduled. I'll have Irish take you out."

Cody turned to Jessie with a grin. "And now, Mr. Jones, how about giving me a good look at your LeMat. I've heard about 'em, but never had my hands on one."

"Colonel, I want this demonstration done away from prying eyes," Cody announced. Colonel Englewood excused Company A from mounted target practice. Only Jones, Potter, Cody, Buntline, and Sergeant-Major Kelly rode to the range. An early morning sun baked the riders. Jones had convinced Cody and Buntline to take Potter along. He told them of Potter's accuracy with a rifle secured in previous visits to the range.

Jones and Potter each made four riding passes, two passes into the sun and two passes away using carbines loaded with seven rounds of .56 caliber metallic cartridges.

The sergeant-major placed paper targets in random

locations two hundred paces apart along an imaginary line the horses would travel. Speed and accuracy mattered, with points for shots nearest the bullseye as was the case the day before with handguns.

"Pin-point accuracy is required," Cody said.

In answer to Cody's command Jones put twenty-five of twenty-eight rounds into the targets and Potter twenty-three of twenty-eight.

Cody and Buntline found the accuracy they sought in the shooting prowess of Jones and Potter.

The men returned to Sidney Barracks, where Cody produced a special authorization from his tasseled shirt pocket and presented it to the colonel.

"Special orders from General Sheridan. I am authorized to transfer whomever I see fit into the services of the Fifth Cavalry," Cody said.

In his journal Buntline wrote *What General Sheridan had in mind for them, Cody could only guess. All information was on a need to know basis and for the moment, Cody did not need to know.*

CHAPTER FOUR

Sarah had her best night's sleep at the Abel's. Alone and without interruption. No young man waking her once or twice in an attempt to prove his manhood or an older man who falls asleep on her and snores. This was restful, rejuvenating sleep. Sarah and Adeline had stayed up to almost dawn enjoying each other's company and carrying on like a couple of schoolgirls. There was a bond, a commonality between the two of them.

It's as if we have known each other for a long time, Sarah thought. And because of this closeness Sarah entrusted Adeline with personal information without fear of betrayal.

Something inside Sarah whispered Adeline never would sell her out. They talked, as dear friends do, on subjects as diverse as the Bible, their histories, life in Sidney, and of course, men. And it was around a small table in the kitchen of the Abel's home where Sarah found peace, forgiveness and restoration.

One evening Sarah and Adeline stayed up past midnight

and Sarah woke the next morning in a panic among unfamiliar surroundings.

Where am I? She wasn't at Madame Rogers, that was obvious, but where was she? But once her head cleared of sleepiness she realized where she was.

I am in the Abel's guestroom. I'm safe and no one can touch me. One floor below she heard a mantel clock struck seven times.

Sarah pushed off the covers and made her way to the washstand where a mirror reflected her image. *It is true. I am beautiful, just as Adeline said. It's amazing, how different I feel living here than when I worked for Madame Rogers.* She splashed cool water from the basin onto her face, and she laughed. Her mirror image laughed back. *Isn't it something, how someone can come along and speak into your heart and change everything?"*

No longer stigmatized by shame, Sarah knew forgiveness. She had confessed her sins and Parson Abel had forgiven her, telling her she was now a new creation. She had not believed this last night either. Somehow, someway, she believed it this morning and the peacefulness of forgiven sins flooded over her like water from a basin.

BOOM! BOOM! BOOM!

A sharp hammering of fists and the yelling of a familiar voice interrupted Sarah's thoughts.

"Open the door! Do you hear me? Open this dad-blamed door!"

"Oh, God, that's Custus. He's found me," Sarah cried.

More pounding. This time only seconds apart.

"Open this door, or I'll bust it in!" Sarah could make out that Custus was attempting to open the door, but the solid wood remained secure.

"What do you want, son? How can I help you?"

"That's Parson Abel. He must be going to the door," she whispered.

"You know good and well what I want. No sense in denying it. I got witnesses that say she's been staying here."

"Son, quit banging on the door and give me a minute to unlatch it."

"I shouldn't be here," Sarah mumbled. "If Custus finds me, he'll kill me just like he did One-Eyed Mary. Parson Abel won't be able to stop him. He'll die trying standing between me and Custus."

Sarah stood stock still. Footsteps sounding from the back stairs. She couldn't move. She didn't dare.

From across the room she watched as the doorknob turned so slowly it was barely noticeable. She took a deep breath. She could either stand there and get killed, or do something. And maybe still get killed.

Grabbing the water pitcher from the washstand, she quickly moved behind the door and silently watched the doorknob turn and the door open slowly.

Adeline sprang through the narrow opening.

"Hurry, child," she said. "Get dressed! The Parson will keep the man at the front door busy long enough for you to slip out the back door. I was out riding this morning so my horse is saddled out back. Get dressed quickly, get mounted and ride."

Sarah dressed in seconds. "I've gotta get away from here, but where can I go where Custus can't get to me?" she asked.

"I'm not sure," Adeline said. "But I do know you can't stay here. It's not safe."

Adeline led the way down the staircase to the back door. "Can you ride, my dear?"

Sarah nodded.

"Then ride like you've never ridden before. Ride for your life."

Sarah recalled how her Papa taught her to ride as a young girl. She mounted in haste. From behind the alley fence, she saw Iggy running toward her. She pulled back the reins and Adeline's horse rose on hind legs and freed itself from Iggy's vicious grip.

Sarah's boot found Iggy's face then she dug her heels into the horse's sides. The bay sprang into action, racing down the alley and into the street. She turned in the saddle to see Iggy and Stinson scrambling toward the front of the house.

Sarah reined in the bay and scanned the crowded street before her and screamed, "Get out of the way!"

"Look out!" shouted the town drunk as Sarah raced by.

Where do I go? Sara wondered while she rode east down Sidney's Main Street. To her right she saw troopers, stripped to their waists building Fort Sidney. *I must find Jesse, but he's three miles south of town at Sidney Barracks.*

Sarah looked back. No one followed her, yet she did not allow her horse to slow.

She turned right, racing south on Sidney Barrack's road with the barrack's blockhouse looming ahead on a ridge now two miles away.

Another look back.

To her horror, Custus, Iggy, and Stinson rode in hot pursuit four blocks behind and gaining. She could hear Custus yelling, "Get out of the way!" at those daring to cross the street in front of him.

The race was on!

"Heeee-haaah!" Sarah shouted. The bay responded with more speed. "Good girl." Sarah leaned forward and whispered into the horse's ear, "Good girl."

Although Sarah's reaction time had been fast, Custus and his gang gained on her. Their horses were faster. Closer they came.

She felt them and wanted to sneak a look over her shoulder, but resisted. Troopers dotted the hill now only a quarter mile ahead, cheering her on as if they had money on the outcome of this impromptu race to the top of the hill.

Sarah thundered into camp with Custus, Iggy, and Stinson right behind. Troopers surrounded the four of them with one soldier holding each bridle. Adeline's bay panted to catch her breath. Sarah repeatedly patted the mare's damp neck. "Good girl."

"I told ya she would win," one of the soldiers said. "Now, pay up!"

Colonel Englewood emerged from his Headquarters tent and stood before Custus. "Gentlemen, what's the meaning of this? This is U.S. Government property and all of you are trespassing!"

"Give us the girl and we'll be gone," Custus responded.

"You'll be leaving without her, gentlemen. I'm placing this woman under my jurisdiction until I can determine what to do next. Do I make myself clear?"

No response.

At Sergeant-Major Kelly's command, troopers drew their weapons and pointed them at Custus and his men.

"That's the end of this conversation, gentlemen," Colonel Englewood said. "Either ride out upright or draped over your saddles. It's your choice, and frankly, I don't care which you choose."

Custus pulled his reins free, turned his horse around and led his men back the way they'd come and as before after the incident in front of Higgin's Lumber, Custus looked back in anger.

"This isn't over! Not by a long shot," he yelled at Sarah. "Yer nothin' but a cheap whore and that's all you'll ever be."

His words penetrated deep. She felt small, useless, and ashamed, not at all like she had an hour ago.

Colonel Englewood turned his attention to Sarah. "Lt. Colonel Englewood at your service, ma'am."

"Jones," she said. "I need to find trooper Jones?"

Troopers helped Sarah dismount.

"Take care of her mount," Kelly told the men who held horse fast.

"Trooper Jones isn't here right now, ma'am, but we expect him later this morning. Would you mind telling me what's going on?"

Sarah looked around and noticed all the men milling around, ogling her. Colonel Englewood noticed the same. "Dismissed, gentlemen," he said. "Follow me, ma'am. We can speak freely in my tent."

Once inside the tent's canvas walls, Englewood began anew. "Now, ma'am, would you mind telling me what this chase was all about?"

"It's hard to explain," she said. "A couple of days ago, Jones saved me from Custus. He's after me again. He wants to kill me."

Colonel Englewood took it all in. "You're safe here," he said.

"Beggin' your pardon, sir, Cody is back," a trooper interrupted from outside the tent.

"Stay here, ma'am." Englewood stepped outside.

Sarah peered through the tent flaps. Her eyes searched for Jones.

"Colonel Englewood, I've found the two men I need," Cody said. "Jones was the best of the lot, with Potter right behind him. I'm asking you now to transfer both men to me upon General Sheridan's orders."

"I hate losing these two men, but orders are orders. Congratulations, men." Englewood grasped their hands and gave each man a congratulatory handshake.

Sarah found Jones at last and ran to him.

"What is she doing here?" Jones asked Colonel Englewood.

"Some men on horseback chased her all the way from town," he replied.

"Custus chased me." Sarah pointed down the hill at the three riders just reaching the city limits. "I was so frightened. I didn't know what else to do. They came after me. They're trying to kill me."

Disjointed thoughts tumbled out of Sarah's mouth. "Parson Abel and his wife are in danger.They took me in. I don't want to go back to Madame Rogers. I'm tired of being alone and scared."

Sarah buried her head against Jones' chest and cried.

"I got you," he said, holding her close. "Ain't no one gonna hurt you or anyone else. Enough's enough."

Jones broke free of Sarah. "Permission to defend the lady's honor, sir," Jones asked.

"I'm afraid I can no longer give you that permission," Englewood replied.

"But, I can," Cody replied to interrupt the proceedings. "You're under my command now and quite frankly, I'm up for an adventure."

"Me, too," Buntline announced, noting the account in his journal.

"You're not leaving me behind," Potter said.

"Gentlemen, we've got a lady's honor to defend," Jones

said. Sarah responded by giving Jones a hug around his neck.

"Nothin' like that ever happens to me," Potter said to Buntline.

"Or me either, for that matter," Buntline replied.

Jones' powerful arms grabbed Sarah by her waist and lifted her back onto her horse. She took the reins from him and waited for the others to mount. For Sarah those peaceful feelings of earlier in the day returned to crowd out the worthless feelings Custus had created within her. The difference she felt around Jones was restoring her faith in men. She wanted more of that feeling.

"Gentlemen, let's mount up," Jones said.

Custus and his men reached Sidney and stopped to liquor up and lick their wounds at the Lodgepole Saloon. It was Custus' favorite place to be when not at Madame Rogers. Some found the décor in the place repulsive with its mounted buffalo heads, but Custus didn't mind being around dead things. They matched the bitterness inside him, especially after his ill-fated ride to Sidney Barracks.

"This is the last time someone steps between me and Sarah," he said before slugging down his whisky. "This whole idea of someone keeping me from her makes me want to cut someone." He retrieved his Bowie Knife from its sheath and laid it on the bar.

"Not here, boss," Iggy said.

"Yea, boss, you remember what happened the last time you did that. We all got chased out of here," Stinson added.

"We didn't get chased out. We walked out," Custus said. "And we walked out when we was good and ready."

"But we was asked to walk out," Iggy added.

Custus looked both of his men directly in the eye. "Alright, boys. Alright. But I want ya to know that I ain't no coward and nobody tells Custus Leverette what to do and when to do it. Got that?"

"Yes, boss," Iggy said. "We got that."

Custus returned his knife to its sheath and ordered the bartender to pour them another round.The bartender poured three shot glasses and moved to put the bottle away, but Custus grabbed his arm."Did I tell you you can put the bottle away?"

"No, sir," the frightened bartender said.

"If I didn't tell ya, then leave the bottle."

"Yes, sir."

Custus removed a small pouch from his pocket and ordered the bartender to look inside the pouch. "This says the bottle stays."

"Gold flakes have a way of changing my mind," the bartender said. His beefy hand grabbed the pouch and put it in the till.

"Where's Billie tonight anyway?" Custus asked him.

"Our piano player? Is that who ya mean?"

"Yeah, that guy," said Custus.

"Out sick."

"Always like to hear him play. Can't tell what he's play-ing, but he always makes me laugh."

After the men finished their second round of whiskey Custus announced, "Boys, I've decided on our next move. We're gonna make a visit to that interferin' Parson. He and his wife are keepin' Sarah from returning to work. I say that he's gotta pay for what he's done. Grab a quick shot for the road and let's get outta here. We got us just one last stop before leaving town."

CHAPTER FIVE

J esse Jones used the ride into Sidney to think matters
through. The hill on which Sidney Barracks was built
sloped downward in a northerly direction before flattening out when it neared the railroad tracks. Jones used
this flattening out space as a place to pull up the horses. The
Civil War had taught him not to act impulsively; no matter
the situation. "Some never learned this lesson," he often
said, "and because of it, many men died. Impulses get you
killed when coupled with hate."

"I'm thinking," Jones said to no one in particular, "that
we don't just ride into town, 'cuz Custus may be planning
an ambush."

"I agree with you," Potter said.

"Agreed," Buffalo Bill added.

Jones continued, "If our priority is protecting Sarah and
returning her safely to Parson Abel's, then I suggest we wait
until nightfall to do that. If our goal is to ride into town after
Custus, it could be a mistake. He could be holed up somewhere
just waitin' for us to ride by. I'm suggesting that we make our

way to Parson Abel's and be ready in case Custus comes after her again. It's better to be on the defensive than on the offensive in this case. Potter, I want you and Ned to take Sarah. Hide out until sunset and ride into town from the northwest. I'll take Buffalo Bill with me. At sunset we'll ride in from the southwest under cover of that line of trees over there." Jones pointed to a line of Lodgepole pine. "This gives us a two pronged approach in case Custus has planned a surprise. At all cost keep Sarah safe."

A small grove of trees provided sanctuary for Jones and Cody for the afternoon. An open meadow rendered sufficient grass for their horses to nibble. As evening fell, Jones borrowed Cody's spyglass to watch the Abel's home about a mile away.

"Doc Halsey is climbing aboard his surrey and driving away," Jones reported. "Let's wait a little longer and ride in."

At nightfall, the two men arrived at the front of the Abel home where a single candle illuminated the drawing-room. Jones drew his LeMat and crept up the wooden stairs leading to the wrap-around porch and peered into the dimly lit room. Through the window he saw Adeline Abel kneeling near the settee where someone lay with a face covered in bloody bandages.

Jones banged on the front door. He was soon greeted by Adeline Abel who burst into tears at seeing him.

"He's hurt bad. It was awful, just awful. If only you had been here." She collapsed in Jones' arms. The back door flew open and Potter barged down the hallway.

"We were completely undetected coming in except for somebody's gray cat that had the misfortune to occupy the spot where Buntline planted his size eleven boot. Boy, did it hiss and skedaddle," he said.

"Where's Sarah?" Jones asked them.

"We left her outside," Buntline answered.

"She can't stay outside," Jones said. "She isn't safe. Bring her in."

Ned retraced his steps to retrieve Sarah. Adeline led Jones into the drawing-room where Jones discovered the person he saw through the window. It was Parson Abel writhing in pain on the settee. The parson moaned and fought against the restraints that prevented his hands from contact with his bandaged face.

"Custus came at him like a wild beast," Adeline said through her tears. "He slashed at Edgar's face."

"Edgar?" Jones said.

"The parson," Adeline continued. "Custus came at him with a big knife. I've never seen such hatred in a man's eyes before. Evil. Just pure evil." Adeline buried her face against Jones' shoulder. "Doc sewed him up the best he could," she continued, "and I wiped up all the blood. Doc said that they laid open his cheek like it was done to Secretary Seward the night Lincoln died."

"Cody, take Ned and see if Custus is somewhere around town, then leave the rest to me," Jones said.

AT THE DINING ROOM TABLE, Sarah and Adeline talked. "This happened because of me," Sarah said.

"We've gone through all this before, child. Don't blame yourself. We want you to know the love of Christ. Parson Abel and I opened our home to you gladly. We were well aware of the risk we were taking." Adeline patted Sarah's hand. "This isn't our first rodeo."

Sarah found Adeline's *rodeo* expression funny but stifled

her laughter. "I have a question, if y'all don't mind my askin'. Don't you hate Custus for what he's done?"

"No, my dear, I don't," Adeline said. "I have been through a lot in my marriage. Thirty-three years come November eighth. God transformed my heart and his. Back then, Edgar was a professional gambler with no regard for God."

Sarah listened to Adeline's soft words.

"One time, he accused a man of cheating and took a terrible beating for it. They left him for dead. A pastor found Edgar in an alley. He remembered that the pastor knelt by his side and prayed saying 'Save this soul and keep him from seeking revenge.' God did."

"HOLD HIM." Doc commanded.

Jones tried, but Abel refused to cooperate, fighting both the pain and to free himself. "If you can hold him still, I'll pour the laudanum. It'll quiet him down and help him sleep."

Jones took hold of Parson Abel's forearms. It took all his strength to secure the thrashing man. Abel let go an inhuman cry. Doc poured. A gurgle. A swallow. And it was done.

"How much longer, Doc?" Jones asked. His arms ached, but he held the Parson down.

"His pain is insufferable. Saw this during the War. Men fight to stay alive."

Doc put the laudanum back in his satchel. "Should only be another minute before the laudanum takes hold. I stitched him the best I could, but this is a massive wound. There's a high risk of infection."

Adeline, Sarah, and Bill Cody stood in the doorway. Jones gave them a nod.

"My poor darling." Adeline cupped her hands over her mouth.

Doc rubbed his chin and rose to calm Adeline. "It's gonna be alright," he said. "A couple inches lower and we wouldn't be talkin'. We'd be arranging a funeral. I'll come back tomorrow. In the meantime, we've got to make sure he remains still. Otherwise, he'll start bleedin'."

Doc opened the door to leave and walked into Potter and Buntline lugging Iggy between them.

"Howdy, Doc," Potter said.

"Don't look like you boys need any help," Doc noted. "Seems like you've got the situation well in hand." He exited and closed the door behind him.

"Looky what we got here," Potter announced, dragging Iggy into the parlor. "Ned and I rode until we spotted a familiar horse tied up at the Lodgepole Saloon. Iggy's horse. So we went in."

"Don't know the song that piano player at the Lodgepole had in mind, but he played real bad," Buntline said, "but we saw saloon girls and gamblers all scrunched together at a few tables. Any space in the Lodgepole big enough to have a table had one."

Potter cut into Bunline's story telling. "Yeah, and I saw one of the saloon girls reach across the table to retrieve the dice, giving all the men an unrestricted view of her merchandise. She just laughed and tucked 'em away.' Talk about someone who drew men to her like bees to honey."

"Potter, Ned's dime novels are rubbin' off on you. Cut to the chase, will ya?" Cody said.

"We're gettin' there," Potter said. "At the bar stood Iggy

with his bandaged nose. Five empty shot glasses sat in front of him.”

“I went over and struck up a conversation while Potter snuck up behind him,” Bunline said.

“And here he is,” Potter said. He shoved Iggy into a chair.

“Well, if it ain’t our old friend from Higgins’ Lumber Yard,” Jones announced. He squatted so he could look Iggy in the eye.

“Ya dirty buzzard. Yer the one that broke my doze.”

“Gonna break a lot more if ya don’t tell us where your buddy is.” Jones grabbed Iggy by the collar and lifted him out of his chair.

“Custus’ll kill me, if I do,” Iggy fired back.

“And I’m going to kill ya, if you don’t,” Jones replied. “What do they call this, Bill? A Mexican standoff?”

Cody nodded his reply.

“More like darned if ya do and darned if ya don’t,” Potter interjected.

“Yep.” Jones brought the barrel of his LeMat alongside Iggy’s nose while Potter held him upright. Jones continued, “My pappy used to say ‘This will hurt me more than it will hurt you,’ but this won’t be the case for you.” He cocked the LeMat. “This is gonna be really loud and will probably wake Parson Abel over there, but as he’d say, “An eye for an eye and a cheek for a cheek.”

“Actually,” Potter interrupted, “It’s gonna be a nose for a cheek.”

Iggy squirmed to free himself “I’ll talk! I’ll talk!” he shouted.

“I’m not so sure we can trust him,” Cody interrupted.

“You can. You can.” Iggy said, pleading with his eyes.

“Alright, let’s hear it,” Jones said, still holding his gun against Iggy’s nose.

"Custus headed west to get some help. He's friends with a Cheyenne named Black Arrow. He's got some braves. They're going to raid Sidney and kill the troopers." Iggy stared at Jones. "And you and that tramp called Sarah."

"Why does he want to kill troopers?" Cody asked. "If he does that, the army'll just send more."

Silence.

"Answer the question." Jones nudged Iggy's nose with his LeMat causing Iggy to wince.

"Alright! Alright." Iggy pleaded. "Custus plans to let the Cheyenne under Black Arrow murder the troops and step back and watch. Black Arrow broke away from Chief Dull Knife's tribe. Black Arrow hates all white men and their squaws. Dull Knife speaks peace. And because of it, Black Arrow called Dull Knife a woman. Dull Knife drove him out of his camp, but Black Arrow took about two dozen braves with him. And when he left, Black Arrow grabbed Dull Knife's granddaughter Two Moons, giving him an enormous bargaining chip."

Buntline made notes while Iggy continued. "Custus bought rifles for Black Arrow's braves. He figures that more troopers will arrive to protect the settlers. Black Arrow will shift the blame to Chief Dull Knife. Two Moons is his bait. Custus figures that with Dull Knife out of the way, he can get rich on Black Hills gold. All he has to do is to control Black Arrow."

Bill Cody shrugged. "Now all we have to do is find Custus and stop him."

CHAPTER SIX

I ggy poured out all kinds of information that night and Buntline wrote everything down, but the truth of the matter was that only some of what Iggy told Jones was usable information. Some of that information, at Custus' urging, was misinformation told to Jones to throw him off Custus' trail. Custus had rehearsed every word Iggy spoke until Iggy could recite everything verbatim.

Custus planned to trap Jones, but as he told Stinson when the three men split up, he intentionally left Iggy behind in the Lodgepole Saloon where Potter could find him.

Among the misinformation Iggy doled out was Custus' location. Iggy told Jones Custus was camped west of Sidney when the reality he was east of town sitting next to a warm fire and sipping his coffee from a tin cup. The red rays of dawn flared over the eastern sandhills.

It was just after six o'clock and Custus had already stoked the fire and boiled the coffee. *Nothin' like a hot cup of coffee. Sometimes I think if I cut myself, I'd bleed coffee instead of blood.* He smiled. Custus appreciated his own humor. He raised his cup to take one last sip, found it empty and pitched the dregs. Using his dirty handkerchief for insulation, he poured another cup from the dingy coffee pot, and took in his surroundings.

To his left, about ten yards away, the sun highlighted where Stinson slept with his head resting on his saddle and his hat pulled down over his eyes. It irritated Custus that Stinson was still asleep, but what irritated him the most was Stinson's snoring. He snored all night, a phlegmy, raspy snore that woke Custus often, making his sleep anything but restful. Custus stood, reared back, and kicked Stinson's booted foot hard.

"C'mon, ya lazy bum, yer snoring again. Get up, it's time to ride."

"Okay, okay." Stinson stammered through the dense fog of a rude awakening. "What's yer gall darn hurry?" He sniffed the air, sat up and sniffed again. "That coffee sure smells good."

"Yeah, it does," Custus said. He took a long, deliberate sip. "And it tastes good, too. And if you'd gotten yer fat rump up earlier, you could have had some." With deliberate movements he lifted the coffeepot and poured the remaining coffee on the fire, extinguishing it. "Put all this stuff away. We got a day's ride ahead of us. I'm already saddled."

Custus removed a piece of paper from his chambray shirt and read out loud. "Follow Lodgepole Creek toward the sun. Black Arrow will find you." "Don't move," Custus whispered. "There's someone behind you, out about a hundred yards."

Custus walked to the shrub where their horses were tied. Something was spooking the horses. They whinnied and stomped their hooves. "Steady, Hombre. Steady, boy,"

Custus told his horse while stroking his muzzle. "Steady." Custus withdrew his Winchester from the right side of his horse, chambered a round and watched Stinson attempt to pull himself into a standing position. Because of his immense girth, Stinson had to press himself against a nearby tree to help him stand.

"What do you see?" Stinson asked. "I don't see nothin'."

Custus pointed to a distant grove of trees. "By that elm tree," he said. "Look close. There's a man standing behind it. You gotta look close or he'll blend in."

The man walked toward them with his rifle across his arms. His buckskin loincloth worn over trousars and long, dark braided hair told Custus that he was most likely a Cheyenne. The brave made a gesture of peace as he neared the camp.

"Custus. I seek man named Custus," he said.

"I'm Custus. Come ahead." Custus kept his rifle trained on the brave who walked toward his camp. The brave never flinched or wavered, but kept a steady, even pace.

"Can I ask ya somethin'?" Stinson asked.

Custus nodded.

"I just noticed that your rifle scabbard is southwest. I've only seen that from guys in the military. How long ya been doin' that?"

"That's a stupid question at a time like this," Custus said keeping his eyes on the brave as he came closer and closer.

"I am called Many Eagle Feathers," the brave said. "I bring word from Black Arrow. You follow me. I lead to Black Arrow's camp."

The brave turned his back on Custus and Stinson and headed back the way he'd come, leaving them to follow.

Traveling until sundown, Custus guessed that he was somewhere near Lodgepole Creek, about twenty-five miles east of Sidney. Trees along the creek sheltered Black Arrow's camp from anyone approaching from the west. Here the creek bent to the south, and then curved back east where more trees hid his camp from the south. Sandhills kept those traveling from the north and east from seeing the camp. Hidden from sight on all four sides were Lodgepole pine tent frames with buffalo hides stretched over them.

A few braves encircled Custus and his men and ordered them to dismount. Breaking free would be suicide. These braves were deadly accurate with bow and lance. Custus' only advantage was his Winchester, which remained in its scabbard since his Navy repeater was already confiscated. *Yes, sir, any escape would be futile. 'Sides, I'm quite fond of my hair; no matter how little of it there is,* Custus thought.

"What do we do now?" Stinson asked as the two men entered Black Arrow's camp.

"Let me do the talking," Custus answered.

"I'm scared," Stinson said after a brief pause.

"Shut up, will ya? I'm trying to think."

Black Arrow came out of a teepee and walked in front of six older men. He spoke in broken English. "Ah, my friend, Custus. Many moons have passed since you promised long guns. These guns I do not see."

Black Arrow was so close to Custus he could hear him breathe and feel the icy stare of Black Arrow's deep, brown eyes. "No wagons. No guns," he said.

Custus reached into his pants pocket. In a heart-beat a dozen arrows were trained on him. He withdrew his hand with a wadded up paper held by the tips of his fingers. Many Eagle Feathers grabbed the paper and unwadded it.

Custus spoke, "Great leader among the Cheyenne, I rode here to tell you that this paper speaks of long guns coming from the east. Long guns I will sell to you. Custus keeps his promise to his old friend, Black Arrow."

Black Arrow snatched the paper Many Eagle Feathers held. "What good is paper? Paper mean nothing," he said.

With a wave of his hand several braves grabbed Custus and Stinson and held them secure. "Your word no good, my brother. You speak of paper, not of guns." Black Arrow tossed the wadded paper toward the fire, missing it by inches.

"In my world, that paper keeps my word," Custus replied. "It speaks of what will be. It speaks of two crates of Winchesters from Omaha arriving in Sidney. Soon Black Arrow and his braves will have long guns to avenge themselves on their white enemies."

"Is this so, Many Eagle Feathers?" said Black Arrow.

Many Eagle Feathers retrieved the crumpled paper from near the fire and read the contents outloud. "Mr. Custus Leverette. We confirm your order for fifty Model 1866 Repeating Rifles. Arrival in Sidney, Nebraska within the week. Sincerely yours, Oliver Winchester, Winchester Repeating Arms Company."

"What mean 'con . . .firm?" Black Arrow asked.

"It means 'this is true,'" Many Eagle Feathers told him. "It means that our white friends tell the truth. Long guns coming."

"All is well, my brother," Custus said, shaking himself free. "Soon you can avenge yourself and hunt buffalo again."

"Until guns arrive, you speak only empty words," Black Arrow said.

Custus felt the sting of Black Arrow's rejection as the mighty chief and his entourage turned their backs on him and walked away.

CUSTUS TRAVELED WEST. The events of the day did not please him. He was not in control. Had it not been for Many Eagle Feathers knowing the meaning of the word 'confirm,' everything would have disappeared in a puff of smoke, including his and Stinson's lives.

"What are ya thinkin' about, boss?" Stinson asked at last.

"Thinkin' about whether Iggy did his job. You and I have work to do and I don't need no interference from Jones or anyone else until I'm good and ready. And those guns better be on that train in a couple of days or you and I will both lose our hair."

Stinson drew his hat further down over his head.

CUSTUS AND STINSON traveled to Sidney where they rented a wagon and prepared to meet the three o'clock train. Custus liked the odds that his shipment would arrive today, but there was always the chance that the shipment was delayed. To ease his uneasiness, Custus pulled the wagon into the alley behind Madame Roger's brothel and walked down the street to the Lodgepole Saloon where he and Stinson found Iggy at the bar where they had left him a week before.

"By the way," Iggy added after the pleasantries had ended, "Jones took the bait. Jones and that Potter fella headed west four days ago trying to track you down. Oh, yeah, Buffalo Bill, Ned Buntline and two Pawnee scouts followed along."

"Ah, that's a problem," Custus thought out loud. "Those

scouts won't take any time at all to figure out that we didn't head west."

"I thought they'd be back in town by now," Iggy said. "But I sure ain't seen hide nor hair of 'em; and I aint been exactly hiding from anybody.

THE WEST BOUND Union Pacific was late. That did not help Custus' disposition. By the time it steamed into Sidney at four p.m., Custus was in a bad humor and everyone within hearing distance knew it. They knew better than to complain because Custus was like a rattlesnake, coiled and ready to strike. The only difference being that Custus, unlike a rattler, never warned anyone before he struck.

While residents greeted trains bringing family members from back east, Custus wondered if the guns were on board, otherwise Black Arrow would have his scalp.

To his delight the manifest the conductor produced showed there were two heavy wooden boxes with his name on them. "Boys," Custus said, "our special packages are here."

"My hair thanks you," Stinson added.

"What does that even mean?" Iggy asked while scratching his head.

"It means we all get to keep our scalps a little while longer," Custus said. "Now go get the wagon so we can load up and get outta here."

Custus signed the freight receipt and Iggy and Stinson lifted two heavy crates filled with Winchester 1866's aboard the wagon and quickly covered them with a tarp to prevent prying eyes from seeing.

"Boys," Custus said when their work was done, "it's too

late to start our trip back to Black Arrow, so let's pull this wagon back behind Madame Rogers' place and spend the night. On my dollar."

"That's one thing I like about you, Custus," Iggy said. "You got a three-track mind."

Custus stared at him. "Just what do you mean by that remark?

"I didn't mean nothin' by it," Iggy said. "Fact, it's a compliment. What I'm a sayin' is that you can focus on money, rifles, and sex, all three at the same time."

The three men shared a laugh.

CHAPTER SEVEN

That evening Jones was west of Sidney sitting next to a fire watching Potter fry bacon to a crisp in a cast-iron skillet. "Bacon is one thing I can cook," Potter often said. "Pork and beans another. A man can live a long time on bacon, pork and beans, but ya don't want to be downwind of him," he'd say with a laugh.

A long day in the saddle had not brought Jones any closer to Custus. He was getting angrier by the minute thinking about how he was suckered in by Iggy's lies. "Iggy's one of few men I know who can look you right in the eye and lie to you," Jones said. He chucked a stick at the fire barely missing Potter's frying pan.

"Careful where you throw things, will ya?" Potter fired back.

"Should have listened to my gut. It told not to believe Iggy. Now I've spent days proving my gut instinct was right all along."

Cody's Pawnee scouts rode in. By the flickering light of the campfire, Jones watched the rapid exchange of sign language between Hook Nose and Bill Cody. Their shadows played amid the Sandhills near their campsite. Jones saw the mutual respect between the two and wondered how a man of Cody's young age could have earned such respect.

Cody confirmed Jones' worst fears.

"Hook Nose says there are no signs that Custus traveled this way. There are tracks, but only those made by many horses."

Cody signed once more, and Hook Nose nodded. "Jones, you are correct our friend Iggy has thrown us off their trail. Whatever Custus had planned, he's had plenty of time to do it without our interruption."

"You learned all that from those crazy hand signals? How'd you do that?" Potter asked, his bacon going from crisp to burnt right before their eyes.

Cody grimaced. "You're going to have to start over with that bacon. I've eaten a lot of strange things in my day, but I never could stomach somethin' burnt."

"After supper," Jones said, "I'm taking Potter with me and we're going to start back to Sidney. Meet us at Parson Abel's. We'll see if we can pick up Custus' trail from there."

A NOONDAY SUN beat down on the roof of the veranda in front of Abel's front door. The roof over the veranda kept it cooler on hot days like today. Jones stood at the front door. His knocking brought Sarah. She pulled back the curtains to find Jones standing there. Nimble fingers unbolted the lock. She flung her arms around Jesse's neck.

"Oh, Jesse, it's so good to see you," she said.

"It's good to see you too," he said. "What's with this sudden show of emotions?"

"You men are all alike," Sarah said without letting go.

"May I come in?" he asked.

"I'm sorry," she said. "I was just so glad to see you I lost all sense."

Jones stepped into the hallway. "Has Custus been around town? Iggy led us on a wild goose chase."

"I heard he and his men were at the depot yesterday, but that's the last I heard," Sarah replied. "Adeline told others about what happened to the Parson, so after you left a couple of men from his congregation have been watching over us."

"Good idea. They must be doing a pretty good job of hiding. I didn't see anyone when I rode up. How's the Parson doing?" Jones asked.

"You kin ask him yerself. Doc's been attendin' to him in the study. He's set up a makeshift bedroom in there."

Jones walked into the study.

"And the answer's no," Doc said to Jesse. "No, you can't ask him yerself." Doc began. "He can't talk or he'll tear out my stitches."

Parson Abel tried to sit up in his makeshift bed, but Doc forced him down. "Stay put."

Abel refused to lie back down.

"Alright," Doc said, looking right at Parson Abel. "If you're just gonna disobey my orders, what the heck am I doing here?"

Abel tried to smile, but his eyes showed that smiling hurt too much.

"Don't just stand there; get him a piece of paper and a pencil. He can't talk, but I'll betcha he can write," Doc said to Sarah.

Sarah drew out some paper and a pencil from Parson Abel's desk.

"Better grab a book 'er something, otherwise he'll just poke holes through the dad gum paper," Doc said.

Doc looked about the room for sympathy and found none. He slammed everything into his bag and headed for the door. "And no, I ain't grumpy," he fired off before slamming the door behind him.

"What was that all about?" Jones asked.

Everyone in the room shared a laugh, but Parson Abel, who couldn't for fear of ripped stitches.

"Ah, that's just Doc," Adeline said as she entered the room. "He and the Parson have been friends for a long time and they like to get under each other's skin. However, sometimes it sounds like they don't like each other very much."

"Kinda a peculiar way of showing a friendship," Jones said. "How ya feeling, Parson?"

Parson Abel scribbled down a few words and handed the paper to Jones. *Lots of pain*, the note read.

"Bet that laudanum helps," Jones interjected. Abel nodded. "You got cut up pretty good."

"We're doing a lot better," Adeline said, "now that we have Sarah to help. She's agreed to stick around at least for the next month or two." She glanced at Sarah. "I think Swede is looking for help. Let me see if he'll hire you. You can live here and walk the six blocks to Swede's."

"I can help around the house, too," Sarah said. "You have done a lot for me that I want to try to repay."

"Has anyone seen Custus other than at the depot yesterday?" Jones asked.

"Visitors have stopped in to see the Parson," Adeline related, "but none have seen Custus, not in this part of town, anyway."

"I sent Potter to a couple of Custus' favorite hangouts,

the bar and the brothel," Jones said. "Let's see what he comes up with."

THAT SATURDAY AFTERNOON, with the dishes cleared, Sarah and Jones sat at the kitchen table alone. Jones rolled a cigarette, struck a match, and sat back in his chair. "How are you feeling about this?"

"About livin' here?"

"Yeah. I mean, this is quite a change for you, ain't it?"

"I haven't felt this secure since before the war. It reminds me of when I was a little girl." She poured coffee. "I used to dream about lots of things then. Like getting older and havin' children. The war changed all that. Men came. Soldiers. Men like Custus. They killed my father."

She lost herself in thought for a long moment before she continued. "They stole my dream. I searched for it and discovered that all along I've searched in the wrong places. Staying here has given me new dreams." Sarah touched Jesse's hand. "I ain't had no one stand up for me the way you did except my pa. And for that, I thank you."

"No one should treat you like property," he said.

"Can I ask you a question? Hope this isn't too personal. Is there a Mrs. Jones somewhere?"

"Nope," he said, taking a drag on his cigarette. "I guess I've been running away, too. Never had time to think about it. I've traded one war for another. Travelin' from one place to another. Didn't want to drag a wife into it."

"What if she didn't mind?" Sarah said, looking into his eyes. "What would you say, then?"

"That would change everything," he said.

Sarah's eyes sparkled in a way Jones had not seen before.

A longing. A desire. It was not a desire he could resist, nor did he want to. A war had hurt them both physically and mentally, yet this same war had brought them together. He leaned over the table until her lips were close to his and kissed her.

"Oh, I'm so sorry," Adeline said entering the room. "I did not mean to interrupt."

Jones and Sarah separated like school children caught in some mischief or another. The room emptied of all passion.

"That's alright," Sarah said. "We were just talking about the War and the impact it made on our lives."

"Would you mind running upstairs and fetch the laudanum for me?" Adeline said. "The Parson's in terrible pain."

Sarah hurried upstairs.

"She's changed, hasn't she?" Adeline noted. "God does that. With His forgiveness we no longer remain the same."

"I'd like to talk to you about that sometime," Jones said. "With all the killin' I've done during the war. I chased down the colonel that killed Buddy Ransom, my best friend and strangled him to death. I took out my vengeance, even stole his gun. Can God forgive me for that?"

"You need to meet the God that forgives," Adeline said. "His heart is bigger than your sin. His Son said, 'Father, forgive them,' and He meant it for all of us. Even for you."

Potter stepped in and spun a chair around and straddled it. "I got a line on Custus," he said. "I ended up at the livery stable. Custus rented a wagon. He told them something about a shipment arriving on the train."

"What kind of shipment?" Jones asked.

"Search me, but there's a wagon parked in the alley behind Madame Rogers'. Been there several days, in fact. There's a big 'ol tarp over it. He's hiding something."

"Maybe we should go have a look-see. What do you think?"

"Maybe you should hold on a moment," Cody announced while he and Buntline entered the room. "I think it's time I let you hear why I recruited you."

When Sarah returned with the laudanum, Adeline excused them both and the women returned to Parson Abel.

Cody pulled up a chair and joined Jones and Potter at the table. "I've just received orders to ride north to Chartran Trading Post to check out reports of some white men crossing into Dakota Territory and upsetting the Sioux and the Cheyenne. Not sure what that's all about. What is known is that Custus isn't who he says he is. I'm guessing that whoever this is, maybe Custus, maybe not, thinks that there is gold in the Black Hills and is willing to take his life into his hands to find it. Ned and I are ordered to ride north and find out what the Sioux are upset about. For now I want you and Potter to stay in Sidney in case Custus shows up. Better still, maybe Potter here can do a little snooping."

"I already know Custus rented a wagon and was waiting at the depot for something arriving on the Omaha train. There's a wagon behind Madame Roger's. What if I tried to find out if this is the same wagon or not?"

"Ned and I are riding north," said Cody. "We'll be back in a week. In the meantime, you two stay here and keep an eye out for Custus and don't let him out of your sight. We don't want this trap sprung until we're ready to spring it."

Jones tapped his finger nervously against the tabletop. "Our situation gets more interesting by the minute."

"Yeah," Buntline said. "But, think of it this way; the more impossible the situation, the more readers will speculate that this is the end of Bill Cody," he said with a flourish.

"Meaning what?"

"Meaning readership will soar and money will roll in. Listen to the latest installment I telegraphed in earlier today."

Ned read aloud.

'The telegraph operator jotted down what appeared to be no more than chicken scratches as his telegraph clackity-clacked to the sounds of a message coming over the wires. Bill Cody stood at the window in silent amazement. He could speak and write several native languages, but he had no idea what these sounds meant.

When the telegraph operator finished he never looked up as he asked, "Help ya?"

"I'm Bill Cody and I'm expecting a telegraph," Cody said.

"Cody, huh? Let's see." The telegraph operator thumbed the day's stack of telegrams. "Cody, you said?" He searched deeper into the stack. "Ah, here we are. Bill Cody."

He pushed up his glasses and peered over them. "Well, I'll be. It is Bill Cody. Buffalo Bill Cody. I should have recognized you right away. I got yer latest 'dime novel' here somewhere." He searched another stack trying to find it.

Cody interrupted: "My telegraph, if you don't mind?"

"Yes. Yes, of course." He handed Cody the telegraph and continued to search. "I got it right here! Where did I lay it? My wife'll kill me if I don't get yer autograph, Mr. Buffalo Bill Cody. After a long search he handed Bill Cody a slip of paper to sign.

Cody signed his name with a flourish. Even when the Old West beckoned him into action, Bill Cody still had time to come to the aid of someone who needed his help, especially when it came to life and death in a man's own home.

At the bottom of the telegraph Cody noticed the 5th Cavalry Commander's name and realized the importance of the contents inside. He unfolded the telegram and studied it carefully.

It read: 'Essential you leave at once. Report to Chartran Trading Post, Nebraska. New information uncovered. Cheyenne raids imminent.' `

Buntline paused for a reaction to what he had read aloud.

Potter obliged. "Sounds like the start of another great adventure for Buffalo Bill Cody."

"Exactly what I thought," Buntline said and he closed his notepad.

CHAPTER EIGHT

Sunrise revealed Custus, Iggy and Stinson already hard at work preparing their wagon behind Madame Roger's. Ropes holding the tarp in place were undone and then removed altogether. Custus said, "We gave it a hurry up job the other day when we only had to drive the wagon a couple of blocks. Re-rope it and cinch it tighter, we got a long ride ahead of us and we don't want them crates bouncin' out and ruinin' our profit."

"Geez," Iggy said, "yer actin' like our lives depend on this or somethin'."

Custus grabbed him by the front of his shirt and pulled him closer. "Let me tell ya right now. Mess this up and your life won't be worth diddly-squat. Do I make myself clear? Not you, nor anyone else is gonna mess this up for me. Ya got that?"

When the ropes were secure, Custus made a trip around the wagon to inspect their work, lifting each rope to make sure it was in place and twanging it against the tarp to hear it snap.

"Mount up!" he commanded. "We have a long ride and Black Arrow ain't a patient man." He grabbed hold of the wagon and lifted his large frame aboard. "Far too many white men have lied to him in the past and that's dangerous. If we don't deliver as promised, there will be Hades to pay. The thought of vultures picking my bones clean turns me cold."

Stinson attempted to imitate Custus by grabbing the wagon and swinging into the 'shot-gun' position, but after several feeble attempts to haul his huge body aboard the wagon, he abandoned this idea.

Custus took great delight in watching Stinson struggle and let out a laugh that shook the wagon. "That's the funniest thing I've seen all morning," he said pointing to Stinson. "You can't haul yer fat butt aboard. Trade places with Iggy, why don't ya? He'll ride shotgun and you follow along on yer horse." He took a momentary pause and then added, "That is, if you can mount yer horse." He belly laughed again. "And before you mount up, get that old drunk out of the alley there or else we'll run him over."

Iggy climbed up the side of the wagon and soon occupied the seat Stinson had wanted; all the while Stinson ambled down the alley and kicked at the drunk laying there with bottle in hand.

"C'mon, old man, get outta the way or yer gonna get run over," he said. The drunk was unsteady and fell three times before crawling to the side of the building and pulling himself upright using the wall for support. He stumbled up the sidewalk.

It took Stinson an equal number of attempts to mount his horse, but mount he did.

"Ha-yeah!" Custus shouted at the two horses pulling the wagon and everything lunged forward down the alley and into the street. Custus thought he saw the drunken man poke his head around the building as Custus turned the wagon and headed north, but when he turned again to look, the drunk was gone.

JONES CINCHED his saddle and tucked his rifle in its scabbard while Cody and Buntline watched from the veranda. Their three horses shared the hitching rail in front of Parson Abel's, saddled and ready to ride.

"More coffee, boys?" Adeline called from behind the screen door.

"No thank you, ma'am," Cody replied. He took out his pocketwatch and noted the time.

"Six-fifteen?" Jones said.

"It's almost that now," Cody said.

"I told Potter to arrive at six-fifteen. He's got a couple minutes left."

On time, Potter ran up. Jones stared at his watch. "Yep. Six-fifteen right on the dot."

"I spent the night in the alley behind Madame Rogers' place just like I said I would," Potter reported. "They thought I was an old drunk layin' there in the alley so they gave me no never mind. The wagon we saw earlier is loaded with two crates of Winchesters. A hundred rifles. It's enough to arm a small army. Custus just left and headed east."

"Any idea where he's going?" Cody asked.

"I overheard them say that they're taking the guns to arm Black Arrow and his braves."

"That makes sense," Cody stated. "Black Arrow recently rebelled against Dull Knife and took several braves with him. Arming them with Winchesters makes them a threat to every white man in the area. Here's what we'll do. Ned and I will ride north to Chartran Trading Post as ordered. Hook Nose, you take the others and track Custus."

Hook Nose nodded.

"Let's meet back here three weeks from today. Stay out of sight. We don't want Custus to suspect anything and change his plans. Are we all agreed?"

"Yep," Jones said.

Jesse watched Cody and Buntline ride north knowing they would encounter overland markers guiding their way to Chartran Trading Post. Jones knew the area well. Court House Rock, Jail Rock, Chimney Rock, the North Platte River and Snake Creek. He also knew Buntline would take notes along the way for the dime novel he was writing titled 'Buffalo Bill, the King of the Border Men,' which the New York Weekly had agreed to publish. Jones couldn't wait to read excerpts of Cody's latest adventure. That is, if he lived that long.

Hook Nose led Jones and Potter east. Deep ruts told the three men of the heavy crates with Winchesters in them. Hook Nose easily verified Potter's account of a lone horse and rider on the left flank with two other horses in tow.

The party rested their horses when they feared their pace might lead them within eyesight of Custus. Hook Nose shook off any attempt to make a campfire while they rested. "Smoke tell story to Black Arrow's braves. His scouts are near. No smoke," he said.

Hook Nose gave good advice. Not long after they hid themselves in the trees near Lodgepole Creek, a small scouting party of Black Arrow's braves passed their hiding place. These braves continued their westward ride before angling north and riding along the top of the hills.

"Must be Custus' rear guard," Jones concluded.

Hook Nose changed tactics and soon led them only at night, with the first order of business being to intercept a scouting party to learn the whereabouts of Black Arrow's camp.

The men spent days sheltered by the trees at a cold camp. That meant nothing hot to eat. Mealtime was corn dodgers, buffalo jerky, and water drawn from Lodgepole Creek.

When the sun set, Jones and Potter stayed among the trees while Hook Nose scouted alone. He'd often disappear without a sound and return in like manner. This happened for several days in a row. On the third night, with a new moon overhead, Hook Nose returned with news of a camp a mile away.

"You come now," Hook Nose insisted. Jones and Potter followed.

"See," he said. Hook Nose pointed to five braves crowded around the campfire, speaking a language none but Hook Nose understood. "You wait," he said.

Hook Nose approached the fire. His presence caught the braves off-guard. The nearest one brandished his knife and lunged at Hook Nose but was no match for the old scout. Hook Nose plunged his knife into the brave's belly. The man's horrific scream echoed in the night.

From the bushes, Potter and Jones supported Hook Nose with pistol fire. Two braves collapsed dead in a heap near the fire. Two remained. These two ran for their horses and leaped on them. Lunging forward, they draped their arms around their horse's necks and rode away.

Bam! Potter fired and missed. "Dang it," he said.

One brave headed north, the other east.

Bam! Jones' LeMat roared to life. Like Potter, he missed on his first attempt.

Bam! Jones' gun again belched fire. The north-bound brave tumbled backward to the ground and didn't rise.

Hook Nose leaped on the back of one of the dead brave's horses, kicked its flank and sent it after the brave heading east. The distance between the two riders was about a quarter mile.

Soon the two horses were speeding along side-by-side. Hook Nose flung himself from his horse and the two men tumbled to the ground, rolled once and landed on their feet.

The brave drew a knife, the moon reflecting on the blade. Hook Nose drew his. The brave crouched and moved in. They circled each other. At arm's-length they slashed the air with their knives.

The brave opened a flesh wound on Hook Nose's right arm. He ignored the sting and the blood. The brave lunged again. Missed.

Hook Nose focused on the brave's eyes and noticed his pupils widen before he lunged. There. Again. The pupils widened. A lunge. A second miss.

Hook Nose transferred his knife to his left hand, lashing out to the brave's surprise. He fell forward and off-balance. Hook Nose thudded his right fist into the brave's face. The brave dropped unconscious in the dirt.

Hook Nose draped him over his shoulders and bore him back to camp.

"Dang," Potter said, watching Hook Nose carry the brave like he would any deer he had killed. "Is he dead?" he asked.

Hook Nose shook his head and plopped his prey near the campfire.

"Not dead," he said.

"Well, I'll be," Potter said.

"We wait," Hook Nose said, sitting cross-legged by the campfire.

Jones helped himself to the venison strips from the braves' knapsack and boiled coffee over the flames the braves had lit. Hook Nose took salve and rubbed it on his knife wound to relieve his pain.

LATER THAT NIGHT, the captured brave opened one eye and then the other to orient himself. He felt the place where Hooks Nose's fist connected with his jaw and rubbed in a vain attempt to lessen the pain. The brave knew at once that he was still outside because an evening breeze carried the familiar sound of locusts in the trees and the howling of coyotes in the not-so-distant hills. He also felt the warmth of the campfire.

Jones sat ten feet behind him watching his every move.

The brave did see Hook Nose sleeping cross-legged two yards away, his face illuminated by the fire. Believing himself alone except for Hook Nose, the brave slowly stood. He reached down to discover an empty sheath where his knife should be.

Jones cocked his pistol freezing the brave in his tracks.

"I wouldn't be thinkin' what 'yer thinkin'," Jones said. He leveled his LeMat at the brave's head and motioned him to sit back down. He did.

The clicking of Jones' revolver woke Hook Nose. He moved to the braves' side of the campfire and began speaking to him in his native tongue.

The brave sat crossed-armed, defiant and refused to answer. Hook Nose persisted. He reassured and cajoled, only to have the brave speak in a manner that sounded to Jones like pleading.

"No guns. Him say him not try to escape," Hook Nose said.

Jones and Potter thought this good news and holstered their guns.

"Watch him," Hook Nose said to Potter who stood in response to Hook Nose's request. Hook Nose took Jones aside to talk. "Him not want to help us," Hook Nose began.

"I gathered that much," he replied. "What do we do now?"

Hook Nose replied, "Him say him afraid of Black Arrow. Black Arrow a mighty warrior. Him have many braves. Him afraid if he takes us to Black Arrow's camp, Black Arrow will kill his woman."

"That complicates things a bit, don't it?" Jones replied. "We need something so fool proof that our friend here remains safe. And his woman, too."

"Me told him you a man of honor. A mighty warrior. You not let Black Arrow take her life."

"Well, I don't know about this mighty warrior bull, but I'll do everything in my power to help." Jones rubbed his unshaved chin.

"Him show us the way," Hook Nose said.

Nine

Custus received a hero's welcome in Black Arrow's camp when he and his men arrived with their wagon load of guns. He traded guns for gold and the promise of Black Arrow's braves if and when he needed them. Custus grinned. There were a lot of times extra men would come in handy. He could have the braves do all the killing in Sidney, and never come under suspicion. He liked that idea. "We'll stay here a couple of days and enjoy Black Arrow's hospitality," he told Iggy and Stinson.

A celebration broke out in Black Arrow's camp that lasted into the night. Custus and his men proudly took their places in a line in front of Black Arrow's tent.

"Now, we kill our enemies from far away!" Black Arrow said. Many Eagle Feathers translated for Custus. Sporadic rifle fire punctuated the night. Warriors danced and chanted war songs around the bonfire casting eerie shadows on faces and nearby tents.

A satisfied smile crept across Custus' lips. He looked past Black Arrow, past the braves dancing about the fire, to where the squaws stood. One squaw in particular caught his eye. She was petite, darker complexioned, and more beautiful than the others. He imagined touching her. Custus wanted to see more of her. All of her.

The sqauw noticed his gaze and turned away. Two braves stood emotionless on either side of her. *Were they guarding her?* Custus wondered.

"THE GUNFIRE MADE it a whole lot easier to find Black Arrow's camp," Potter said.

Jones and company looked upon the scene of dancing braves and Custus in the company of Black Arrow.

"And I'm not liking what I see," Jones said. "Black Arrow's braves are armed with Winchesters."

"Two Moons," Hook Nose said.

"What did you say?" Jones asked.

Hook Nose pointed toward a dark complexioned squaw

standing between two men. "Two Moons," he repeated. "Dull Knife's granddaughter."

"What's she doing here?" Potter asked.

Hook Nose asked the captured brave the same question and translated for Jones and Potter. "Him say Black Arrow took her. Black Arrow hold her hostage. Black Arrow kill her if Dull Knife try to stop him from killing white man. He kill her if we try to take her from him."

"What you're saying is that Two Moons is Black Arrow's hostage?" Jones said. "That changes things a bit."

"Yes," Hook Nose added. "Red Hand love Two Moons."

"Who's Red Hand?" Potter asked.

"I am Red Hand," the captured brave replied.

Jones inquired, "Why didn't you say something before?"

Red Hand shrugged.

"We're trying to prevent a massacre," Jones said. "The white man standing next to Two Moons bought the Winchesters and sold them to Black Arrow."

"I have seen him many times before," Red Hand said. "We call that white man 'Bad Medicine'."

"He's Bad Medicine alright," Jones said. "But that doesn't explain what you're doing here."

Red Hand said, "When Black Arrow leave Dull Knife, him take Two Moons. I rode with Black Arrow. Two Moons..." He stopped to think and continued in his native tongue.

Hook Nose translated. "Red Hand and Two Moons love in secret. Red Hand rode with Black Arrow to protect her."

"Now I protect her from Bad Medicine," Red Hand said. "Him stare at Two Moons. My blood turns cold. Him evil."

"But the good news is that Black Arrow isn't about to give up his greatest advantage over Dull Knife," Jones noted. "He's watching Bad Medicine."

From their hiding place among the undergrowth, the

men watched the braves. Early morning came before the gunfire and dancing died down. Braves walked Two Moons to her teepee and stood in front of it.

Custus followed Two Moons' every move. Black Arrow noticed and when Custus turned to leave, Black Arrow grabbed his arm. "Touch her and you die," he said without raising his voice.

A sleeping camp meant opportunity. Jones and Red Hand eased their way through the brush until they stood behind Two Moon's tent. Red Hand unsheathed his knife. The buffalo hide resisted his initial attempt to slit it open. His second try succeeded. The sound of ripping fabric woke Two Moons. She stirred. Jones unholstered his LeMat. From the brush Potter and Hook Nose kept an eye on the camp, especially Custus' tent.

Red Hand stepped through the severed fabric. Two Moons attacked him. Red Hand's gentle words calmed her. The commotion inside the tent aroused the braves outside. They entered the tent as Two Moons and Red Hand exited out the back.

Excited yells awakened the camp.

Hook Nose and Potter opened fire.

Bam! Bam! Their revolvers belched fire, sending death into the camp.

One brave stuck his head through the split in Two Moon's tent and found himself face to face with Jones' LeMat.

Bam!

"Get out of here!" Jones shouted. "Get to the horses."

He followed and covered their exit.

Potter discovered a makeshift corral and released Black Arrow's horses.

Pistol shots sent the horses off in every direction.

Custus stepped outside and into the fray. Iggy and Stinson stood at his side. He saw Red Hand leading Two Moons through the brush.

"Looks like Black Arrow has a traitor in his midst. Grab our horses," Custus commanded. Iggy raced toward their picket line.

Black Arrow's braves fired their new Winchesters sending bullets toward anything that moved, sometimes killing their own campmates.

Black Arrow shouted "Haliwista!" In the commotion, no one heard his order to stop.

With Red Hand and Two Moons mounted, Jones sent them into the night. He returned to Hook Nose and Potter.

Bam! Jones fired. He hit a brave near Custus.

A bullet from Custus' revolver whizzed between Jones and Potter and thudded into a tree.

"That was close," Potter said.

Black Arrow led a charge toward Two Moon's tent. Cross-fire whittled down the numbers. Black Arrow ducked inside and found a dead brave there.

Many Eagle Feathers joined Custus.

Black Arrow came out of Two Moons' tent and yelled a command.

"What's he saying?" Custus asked of Many Eagle Feathers.

"You'd better get out of here, my friend. Black Arrow say, 'Kill the white men!'"

Custus didn't wait for Iggy to bring the horses. He charged through the camp toward his picket line, killing as he went.

Braves fired at Custus and his men. A bullet grazed Stinson's left shoulder, tearing away a piece of his shirt. A thin line of blood appeared. Stinson returned fire. His revolver flamed forth death.

Bam! Bam!

"Come on," Custus yelled at Stinson. "This is no place for a gunfight." They found Iggy holding three sets of reins with horses attached, mounted and galloped east putting the gunfire behind them.

"What about the wagon? We can't forget the wagon" Iggy said.

"If you're worried about it, go back after it," Custus responded.

"I was just wonderin'."

If looks could kill, Custus' would have dropped Iggy dead in his tracks.

"Will you shut up," Custus yelled. "Forget about that dad-blamed wagon."

To the west a half mile or so, Jones was taking fire. He mounted and flipped the lever on his LeMat and the shotgun under the main barrel boomed to life.

BOOM!

Jones spurred his mount and the horse sprang to life carrying him away from hostile guns.

Hook Nose and Potter followed Jones out of range. They soon found Two Moons and Red Hand in a clearing.

"Good job back there," Jones said. "Is everyone ok?"

"Dang," Potter said.

Hook nose nodded that he was unhurt.

"What about you two?" Jones directed his question at Two Moons and Red Hand. Red Hand relayed the question to Two Moons who spoke no English. She responded.

"Two Moons is fine and so am I," answered Red Hand.

"Good," Jones replied.

"That was quite a fight back there," Potter noted.

"Better get used to it. It ain't over yet," Jones added. "You can bet that Custus and his men will come after us. If he returns Two Moons to Black Arrow, he can save his hide, and he knows it. The sooner we get Two Moons to her grandfather, the better. Hook Nose, you're awful quiet." Jones paused to reload. "What do you think?"

"Black Arrow follow," Hook Nose said. "Him need Two Moons to control her grandfather Dull Knife. Him plenty angry. Him kill white settlers. We warn Fort Sidney, then take Two Moons home."

"That's good advice, my friend," Jones said. He took out his pocket watch. "We'll rest the horses for another ten minutes. Everybody reload. We have the advantage. Let's not lose it."

About two miles east of Black Arrow's encampment, Custus spun his horse around. He was uncertain who had soured his relationship with Black Arrow, but he aimed to find out. The sun peeked over the Sandhills at the start of a new day. Thick smoke arose above the tree line.

"So much for the wagon," Iggy said. "How are we gonna explain that one?"

"Iggy, ya always gotta have somethin' to belly-ache about, don't ya?" Stinson chided.

Custus sneered at both of them. "Alright. Enough already. I want both of you to stop talkin' about the stupid wagon. You know, if I held both of yer brains hostage, I wouldn't get nothin' for 'em. We got ourselves a lot bigger problem than a two-bit wagon. Can we get around Black Arrow's braves without bein' seen? After that, we gotta find out who jumped our claim."

"What do ya mean? We ain't been north into Dakota Territory. 'Sides Pike's got our back at Chartran Trading Post," Iggy said.

Custus could not believe what he was hearing. "Geez. I'm talkin' about whoever shot up Black Arrow's camp and stole Two Moons. Whoever it was messed up our opportunity to sell more Winchesters. Don't 'cha get it? We supply Winchesters to the Cheyenne, they attack the settlers voiding the Laramie Treaty, and then the Feds come in and eliminate the Cheyenne and Dakota Sioux. With them out of the way, they'll open up Dakota Territory for 'investors' like us. But before we do that, we need leverage. We gotta get Two Moons back to patch things up with Black Arrow."

Jones saw the smoke from a distant fire behind them. He raised his right hand and shouted, "Whoa! Will ya look at that? Got a fire back there."

Everyone turned to see.

"Hope they got control of that thing. We don't need a prairie fire chasin' after us," Potter said. "Especially if the wind comes in outta the east."

"Better keep moving," Jones said. He turned his horse

toward Sidney. "We still got a couple of days' ride ahead of us."

Hook Nose rode point about a quarter mile ahead of the others. Red Hand and Two Moons rode side by side.

"Too bad Ned Buntline isn't here to record our adventures," Jones said. "What we experienced is equal to any adventures Bill Cody has encountered."

"Wonder what lies Buntline would put in print had he been here," Potter added. "Dime novelists sure know how to spin lies, don't they?"

"Yeah, and them city slickers back east can't wait to get their hands on them lies. A guy could get mighty rich sellin' novels at a dime a piece," Jones added.

CHAPTER NINE

Jones and party arrived at a point a mile east of Sidney in the early morning hours. Activities were already underway at the barracks at the top of the ridge. They steered their horses in that direction.

On the ridge a lone bugler sounded 'mess,' the sound echoing through the valley below where the townsfolk noted it and set their watches by it. Jones removed his pocket watch and nudged the minute hand forward, marking the time: seven-thirty a.m. He knew just ahead was breakfast, a hot breakfast with flapjacks, eggs, pork belly, and coffee. All of which would be far better than any cold camp could produce. Jones was looking forward to a hot meal and sleeping on a cot instead of the hard ground.

The saddle-weary riders dismounted in front of the mess tent and stepped inside. Lt. Col. Englewood arose from his chair, greeted them, and invited them to the officer's table.

"Jones, what news do you have for me? Did you find Custus?"

"Yes, sir, we did. We found him in Black Arrow's camp."

"Dead, I hope."

"No, sir. Very much alive. He's selling rifles."

There was a moment of startled silence when Red Hand and Two Moons entered the mess tent. Fingers pointed and tongues wagged.

"As you were, men," Englewood commanded. The men returned to their breakfasts, except for an occasional glance at the newcomers.

"So, that's what he's been up to, huh?" said Englewood.

"By the way that squaw is Dull Knife's granddaughter."

"Jumpin' Jehoshaphat," Englewood exclaimed. "What is she doing here?"

"Black Arrow kidnapped her as an insurance policy so her grandfather would leave him alone. Red Hand is her boyfriend. He helped us rescue her."

"She can't very well stay here. We haven't the troops to withstand an attack from Dull Knife and his braves."

"That's what I figured," Jones said. "That's why I need your help. I figure Custus will come gunnin' for us. We need to return Two Moons to her grandfather."

"That still leaves a huge unanswered question. Where did Custus get the money to buy guns?" Englewood said.

"Cody's got a lead that's taken him to Chartran Trading Post and that's not too far from Dakota Territory. I'm assuming, sir, and that's all this is an assumption, but maybe Custus is mining gold in the Dakotas and has some men up north guarding his backdoor," Jones said.

"So, what are your plans and how can I help?"

"I was thinking that you might order a couple of companies into town to guard against any attack from Custus or from Black Arrow. And then—."

Jones described an elaborate ruse. He would take Red

Hand and Two Moons to the Abel's. A change of clothes would hide their identities. Red Hand would dress as a trooper and Two Moons like his young wife. The end-game became one of hiding the two lovers in plain sight.

ADELINE ABEL WAS SURPRISED to see Jones, Potter, and the two Cheyenne. She darted upstairs to find 'white man's' clothing for Two Moons to wear.

Jones stepped into the parlor where Doc worked, removing Parson Abel's stitches.

"Owww! Ya old buzzard that hurt," Abel said.

"Look, if you're going to make such a fuss over this, I'm gonna leave the dad-blamed stitches in ya," Doc said.

"Alright, already. How many stitches you got left, anyway?" Abel asked. Not waiting for Doc's answer he reached up to count them himself.

"Keep yer hands off 'em," Doc said. "You'll get yer face infected."

"I already look like a chipmunk. What does it matter?"

Jones jumped into the conversation from the doorway. "Well, if this ain't a predictable sight. Two friends at each other's throat. It's like I never left."

Doc turned on him. "Now, don't you start in. I got enough trouble with one of ya."

"Doc, I want you two to meet some new friends of mine. This is Red Hand and Two Moons. By the way, Two Moons is Dull Knives' granddaughter," Jones said.

"Well, I'll be." Doc said staring up into the faces of the two Cheyenne. Red Hand was dressed in Army blue with his braids tucked under a broad-brimmed hat. Doc blinked twice when Jones' words sank in. "Did you say

Dull Knife's granddaughter? She's the grand-daughter—."

"She is," Potter added.

Jones explained the sequence of events that led up to his arrival. "Adeline's getting Two Moons a dress to wear so we can return her to Dull Knife," he said.

"Of course," Parson Abel said. "We'll do everything in the Lord's power to keep you safe."

"For added security, Colonel Englewood sent troops to cover the east side of town in case Black Arrow heads our direction. We're gonna set off for Wyoming Territory. Red Hand says he knows the location of Dull Knife's camp and can take us there. I borrowed a covered wagon from Sidney Barracks, so we can take these two home."

Doc closed his medical bag. "Well, I hope you'll excuse me. All your talk about the barracks reminded me that Mrs. Kelly is about to deliver her eighth, and I can't miss it. My company is expected, if you don't mind me saying so."

"Sergeant-Major Kelly's wife?" Potter asked.

"That's the one," Doc said. "Gotta get out to the barracks." He turned in the doorway to scold Abel one last time before leaving. "And you keep yer hands off your face. Ya hear me? I don't need you to get this wound infected."

Doc was gone.

"So, Jones," Abel said, "Your next move is to take this couple to Dull Knife. What if Custus finds you along the way? I can't imagine he'd take a liking to your plan."

Adeline entered the room. "Did Doc leave? I had a pie baked for him to take home to his wife."

"Addie, before you go," Abel said, "this is—."

"Red Hand," Potter said.

"We met already," Adeline said.

"Two Moons and Red Hand are going to stay tonight. I

thought we could put them in the upstairs guestrooms. Separate rooms, of course. Jones and Potter can sleep in the stable." He turned to them. "I'm thinking that sleeping there would be a lot softer than the ground and more generous than an Army cot."

"Not planning on staying long. We don't want to put you out any," Jones said.

Adeline shouted up the stairs. "Sarah, would you come here, please? We have guests."

"Be right down," Jones heard her say.

Adeline turned back to Jones. "She missed you, you know?"

Sarah arrived at the parlor door. The Abel's care had transformed Sarah and Jones noticed immediately. She looked radiant. Her long hair was braided and arranged in a bun on her head.

Adeline gave Jones a nod. "She looks beautiful, doesn't she?"

Jones couldn't reply before Sarah hugged him. "Oh, Jesse, I've missed you."

"I've missed you, too."

THERE WAS no sentimental reunion when Custus merged forces with Pike, a hardened frontiersman. Indian fighters by profession, he and his men had ridden hard to be here. They had a new tale to tell, an encounter with Bill Cody and his sidekick, a dime novelist named Ned Buntline.

Custus, however, was in no mood to swap war stories. Pike's narrow escape was but a Sunday afternoon stroll compared to him and his run in with Black Arrow.

"What you did was nothing compared with what we

did. Iggy, Stinson, and I made a wide arc around Black Arrow's camp. We were under constant fire from Black Arrow's braves. Had a running gun battle, too. Happened for over three miles before my Winchester dismounted the last brave. Besides," Custus said, "You had a job to do. Stay put at the trading post until we got there. And you didn't do it."

"Can't you understand?" a square-jawed man named Edwards said. "Cody made it too hot for us there. He kept asking if we knew you."

"They was asking if we knew anyone named Curtis Leaver, boss. What did ya want us to do?" Pike asked.

Custus worried his chin. "Word's out, ain't it? Someone's gonna start putting two and two together. We gotta get Two Moons back. She's our only bargaining chip."

"Then you can help me eliminate Cody," Pike said.

"There ya go again. Thinkin' only about yerself," Custus said.

"Listen, Custus," Pike insisted. "We was just playin' poker in the Chartran Tradin' Post when Cody came in. You remember that Bodeen fella, don't ya?"

"What about him?"

"Well, Cody and him got to talkin' about a missin' trooper named Curtis Leaver. I overheard Cody say that he had an order from General Sherman for his arrest for desertion. I knowed that was you."

"You did, did you?" Custus growled.

"Ya. But we didn't tell nobody. Not even when he came a-askin' about you at our table."

Miller butted in on the conversation. "Pike got all mad when Cody called him a liar. Cody said Pike was lyin', that he knew Curtis Leaver."

Edwards was not about to be outdone and joined in. "Yeah, why would Cody call Pike a liar?"

"To get a reaction," Custus said. "Pike's anger told Cody everything he needed to know." Custus shook his head. "How did I ever wind up with you three jokers in my deck of cards?"

Miller ignored Custus' comment. "Pike took a hostage so we could get outta there alive. And then there was this shootout, see? The bartender made a play first. He grabbed his shotgun and Pike blasted a hole in his forehead."

"I never got to make a play on Cody fer callin' me a liar. You owe me the chance to kill him, Custus," Pike said. "I wanna be writ up in one of them dime novels."

"You'll be writ up, alright," said Custus. "On yer headstone they'll write: Here lies Pike the man who called Buffalo Bill Cody a liar."

Sarah sat next to Jones at dinner, and an easy conversation occurred despite their time of separation. A new relationship was in bloom, and Sarah perceived it. *This is a different feeling. No other man makes me feel like this.*

Sarah smiled to herself and placed her right hand on top on his left and gave it a squeeze, eliciting a smile from Jones.

Something stirred within him, too, a feeling unlike any he'd felt before. He did not understand this emotion awakened within him. He had known women before as friends, but Sarah was different.

Abel and Potter retired to the parlor to enjoy a smoke after dinner. Adeline found this the perfect time to shuffle Jones and Sarah to the veranda. "It's too nice an evening to spend it indoors," she told Sarah with a wink.

The Abel's veranda overlooked the town. Sounds from the night's activities, the bars, the dancehall, the goings on outside Madame Rogers' brothel, were muted by the distance between the Abel's home and town proper.

Sarah reached for Jones' hand and led him to the porch swing. "Look at that moon," she said. "It seems nearer the earth than normal, like a lantern over Sidney." She snuggled closer. "Since I was a little girl, I dreamed of a night like this."

They both stared up at the moon. What are your plans?" Sarah asked.

"What?"

"I asked what your plans are after you return Two Moons to her grandfather."

Jones looked at Sarah. "I am not worried about that. I have you on my mind. I'm concerned that I may not come back to you."

They kissed.

CHAPTER TEN

Bill Cody and Ned Buntline arrived early in next morning. While everyone ate breakfast, Jones told them about the run-in with Custus and the plan to return Two Moons to her grandfather.

Afterward Cody filled Jones in on his adventure with Pike and his men at Chartram Trading Post. "Buntline's got it all written down and he's ready to telegraph my adventures to the folks back east," Cody said.

"So, we're looking for a former trooper then?" Jones asked while taking a large stack of pancakes.

"Yeah. A man named Leaver," Cody added.

"Seems coincidental that the guy comin' after Two Moons is named Leverette and you are looking for a man named Leaver," Jones noted.

Potter reached for the plate of sausages. "Dang, never thought of that."

Two Moons tapped Red Hands' shoulder. They talked. "Two Moons say the man you seek was in Black Arrow's camp," Red Hand said. "She say we name him Bad Medicine. Him drove wagon with white man's guns."

"That would be the wagon I seen parked behind Madame Rogers'." Potter said. He poured himself another cup of coffee. "Custus Leverette and Curtis Leaver are the same. We had him, but he got away."

"What we can't do," Jones said, "is stay here. If Custus returns, he'll find everyone he hates in the same place. I think it's time we taught Custus a lesson he'll never forget. We just can't do it here. Too many innocent people might get hurt."

"What are you thinkin'?" Cody asked.

"I'm thinking we hightail it to Fort Laramie and see if we can get Custus to chase after us. I still like the idea of putting Red Hand and Two Moons in a wagon."

"Are you crazy?" Potter interrupted. "A wagon is way too slow. We gotta travel fast. You ain't gonna hightail it if they're driving a wagon."

"Let me tell ya how this will work," Jones said. Everyone gathered around him.

THAT AFTERNOON, Custus and his men pulled up east of Sidney. He climbed down from his horse and let it nibble the stubble it found. "Give 'em a rest boys. Edwards, you get some kindling and boil some coffee. Leave yer saddles on, we ain't stayin' long."

Custus pulled Pike aside. They walked away from the rest. Custus took a tattered map from his shirt pocket. "As I figure it, whoever took Two Moons will wanna take her back to Dull Knife as soon as possible. Most likely they'll go to Fort Laramie, gather supplies and head north. Two Moons had a brave with her when I saw her running through the brush. Don't know who he is."

"Agreed," Pike replied, "I think they'll head to Ft. Laramie. The question is: Can we outrun 'em if they've got a head start on us?"

"I'm betting they're resting in Sidney. There ain't much civilization between here and Fort Laramie. They stopped in Sidney alright. And if they're stopped, it'll be a mistake."

"And if they didn't?" Pike asked.

"If they didn't, we got a lot of hard riding ahead," Custus said. He unfolded the map. "Let's say we do get ahead of 'em. Is there a good place for an ambush? Ah, here's one right here." He pointed to the spot on his map. "A ways north of Sidney there's a little place called Courthouse Rock."

"I know that spot. If we can get up into the rocks they'll never know what hit them."

"We just gotta be careful not to hit Two Moons. She's our only bargaining chip. Kill her and we're as good as dead."

JESSE HELD a meeting of his own in Parson Abel's kitchen. You gotta map Parson, one of Nebraska?" Jones asked.

"Don't know how accurate it is, but I've got one in my desk. I'll get it."

"You're not leaving me again, are you?" said Sarah.

"Soon. We need to end this. Dull Knife needs to have his granddaughter back, and that's not something Red Hand can do alone. If Custus and his men find them, they'll kill him and take Two Moons."

"I understand," she said, but her heart was not in her reply.

"Is this what you're looking for?" Abel asked showing the map to Jesse. Parson Abel unfolded it and spread it on the table.

"Adeline, dear. Would you make us some more coffee, please?" Abel said.

The men crowded around the table and Jones explained, "Here's the route we'll take to Fort Laramie. If I figure it right, it's about a five days ride. I'm wondering if there is a place on the way to Fort Laramie where we can set up an ambush. Lots of open prairie around here, but that doesn't give us an advantage. We need the safety of fighting behind a fortification, some rocks or a structure; something solid to fight behind."

"We can get some protection by blending in with pioneers heading west, can't we?" Potter pointed out.

"We can," Cody said. "But, if there's gunplay some innocent people might get hurt. Let's follow the trail north of Sidney and see what we find."

They traced the trail on the map to the northwest of Sidney until they settled on a rock formation.

Courthouse Rock.

EARLY ON THE morning of Tuesday, September 14, 1869. Jones placed Red Hand in charge of driving the covered wagon. Dressed in a borrowed Army uniform with customary blue pants with yellow stripe down the side and blue shirt with red bandana, Red Hand looked the part of a soldier. Adeline supplied Two Moons with a blue gingham checked dress and braided her hair.

"Ever driven a wagon like this before?" Jones asked. Red Hand shook his head. "Well, the old man in the livery said he selected four horses that were gentle and easy to manage. So, we'll see, won't we? Climb up and have Two Moons sit next to you. Thanks to a Colonel Englewood," Jones continued, "this is no ordinary covered wagon. This wagon comes with weapons, ammunition, and five troopers from Sidney Barracks under the care of Sergeant Major Kelly." Jones lifted a side flap so all could see the men and equipment. "This here conestoga's got all the extra firepower we'll ever need."

Bill Cody and Ned Buntline mounted and pulled up near the wagon. Hook Nose and his pony, a paint, moved into position in front of the wagon to scout the road ahead.

Potter untied his horse from in front of Parson Abel's home and waited for Jesse to say his goodbyes.

"I'll miss you," said Sarah. She held Jones tight, not wanting to let him go.

"I'll miss you, too."

Their lips met in a passionate kiss that promised more than either could deliver right now.

"I'll see you in a month," he said.

"God willing," she replied.

THAT AFTERNOON, Custus and his men stopped in Sidney. It didn't take long for them to learn that Jones had left for Ft. Laramie with a newly married trooper and his wife.

"They left Sidney this morning," Iggy reported after a visit to the Lodgepole Saloon. "Jones has two other men with him and they borrowed a Conestoga from the fort."

"A conestoga? What is that all about?" Pike asked.

"Supplies and trinkets for Dull Knife most likely," Custus

said. "I like it. A Conestoga slows them down some. Let's ride boys. I figure we'll ride west of the trail and get ahead of that wagon. We can hide out among the rocks and crevices at Courthouse Rock. They'll never know what hit 'em. We'll swoop in, get Two Moons and have her back to Black Arrow in a week."

"And what if they get to Dull Knife first?" Stinson said.

"If it's you that lags and causes us to miss our chance," Custus drew his Bowie knife, "You will answer to this. Do I make myself clear?"

Courthouse Rock and Jail Rock rise above the plain along the Pumpkin Creek, marking the route west along the Oregon-California trail. Miles to the north, Chimney Rock and Scotts Bluff, pointed travelers westward into Wyoming Territory and Fort Laramie.

Hook Nose turned in his saddle. To his left he saw the dust of faraway horses. These horses were not on the trail, but west of it. He pointed out the dust to Jones and Cody.

"Many horses come," Hook Nose shouted.

Jones sprang into action. He spurred his horse back about fifty yards and ordered Red Hand to stop the wagon.

"Why are we stoppin'?" Sergeant Major Kelly asked.

"Sergeant Major, we got company," Jones announced. "Riders. Swift ones, too."

"Now, don't ya be a worryin'. Me and the men are ready for 'em," Kelly said.

Jones had Red Hand climb down from the wagon. "Take Two Moons and a horse. Ride to the base of Courthouse Rock. You two should be safe there."

In moments Red Hand and Two Moons were on their way.

Jesse pointed north. "Alright, Sergeant Major, drive this rig off the trail and follow 'em. Custus is close enough."

White smoke bursting from Custus' rifles and the whizz of bullets brought a flashback of Jones' Civil War days. "You guys in the wagon. Don't fire 'til they're in range. You're our ace in the hole," Jones shouted.

"Better hang on to the sides, boys, 'er you'll find yerself on yer backsides. Yehaaa!" shouted Sergeant Major Kelly. He steered the wagon off the trail behind Red Hand to block the shots of the hard-charging men.

Cody and Buntline protected the wagon by drawing Custus' gunfire away from it.

In the rocks and safely out of range, Red Hand and Two Moons dismounted. With Custus' men charging toward them, they wouldn't be out of range for long. Red Hand slapped the rump of the horse, sending it away.

Hook Nose joined them. His 1862 Henry offered some protection. With smooth lever action, he chambered and fired round after round. His shots dismounted one rider, but still the others came.

Four hundred yards and closing fast.

"Easy boys. Stay down, don't let 'em see ya." Kelly parked the wagon in front of a pile of rocks and ducked inside.

Cody and Buntline joined Hook Nose among the rocks and opened fire.

Potter joined them, sending his mount scurrying away after the other horses. Two bullets kicked up dirt near him.

"Dang," he shouted, "is it hot around here, or is it just me?"

"Yeah, it's hot around here," Jones said scrambling into

the rocks. "Get your butt up further into those rocks. I'll cover ya."

Potter scrambled to safety, with Jones right behind. This move placed rifles to the left and Red Hand and company to the right with the wagon in between. The rocks secured their positions, except for the five troopers and the Sergeant Major sheltered in the wagon.

Three hundred yards.

Two hundred.

At one-hundred fifty yards, Custus raised his right hand to order a halt.

"Hand me the field glasses," he said. Custus used the glasses to survey the scene at the base of Courthouse Rock. After a moment's thought, he decided on a two-prong attack. Two-thirds of his men would concentrate on the rocks where only one rifle returned fire. The other third would seek to draw fire away from the others. It was not clear to Custus what the wagon was doing between the two groups hiding in the rocks, but since no one was firing from it, Custus assumed it was trinkets for Dull Knife.

An uneasy cease-fire hung over the parties separated by a scant one-hundred fifty yards. Jones maneuvered from his spot to a position much nearer Hook Nose and the unarmed Red Hand.

"Red Hand," Jones asked, "can you fire this Sharps?"

"Yes."

Jones snaked across the ground until he was safely behind the rocks protecting Red Hand, Hook Nose, and Two Moons. He handed Red Hand his Sharps and a box of ammunition. "She shoots a tad low, so aim a little over their heads."

Custus' men discharged a volley that ricocheted like a swarm of angry bees among the rocks.

"Sergeant Major, are you ready?" Jones yelled. "Wait until they get closer and then let 'em have it."

"Yes, sir," Kelly said.

Custus restarted his charge and the Sergeant Major lifted the side flap of the wagon and commanded his men to fire at will.

Bullets flew from the wagon like tiny wasps with stingers of death.

Bullets slammed into Edwards' head and chest to unsaddle him. He thudded to the ground.

Iggy's fire rattled off the rocks near where Red Hand sheltered Two Moons.

"Stay down!" Red Hand yelled at Two Moons in their native Cheyenne. "You don't need to see."

Gunfire erupted from the right side of Courthouse Rock. Potter, Cody and Buntline picked out targets on horseback at seventy-five yards and closing fast.

Stinson's large frame provided a magnificent target. Size was a disadvantage in this case. A bullet found him. He remained mounted and continued to fire.

Near Hook Nose, Jones drew his LeMat. He placed three bullets into Miller from forty yards away, unhorsing him. Then Pike fell, dropped in his tracks by Cody's rifle, the Buffalo gun he affectionately called Lucretia Borga.

Custus halted. This was a deathtrap. He was beaten. He'd been tricked into what he thought was an uneven fight with the odds in his favor. It wasn't. He counted his losses at three—Edwards, Miller and Pike.

That wagon. Whose idea was that? He settled on Jones. Custus jerked the reins to the left and rode away.

Jones saw Custus' rifle scabbard on the right and he knew without a doubt that Custus Leverette and Curtis Leaver were one and the same.

CHAPTER ELEVEN

Jones was content. The rest of the ride to Fort Laramie was uneventful His little troupe fell in with a wagon train headed west after the 'Incident at Courthouse Rock' as it was later called in the lore of Buffalo Bill Cody.

When they reached the Wyoming border Sergeant Major Kelly left them, taking wagon, troops and all back to Sidney Barracks. That left Jones, Potter, Cody and Buntline, and Red Hand to protect Two Moons.

Fort Laramie sat along the east bank of the Laramie River in the river's crook before its waters meandered to the southeast.

The aroma of fresh bread welcomed Jones and his weary travelers. Evening mess was a welcomed hot alternative to the slim pickings of life on the trail, particularly the horrible coffee Potter was in the habit of brewing. "This stuff is so strong," Jones told him with great frequency, "that any spill hitting the ground will march around your campfire."

Commander Colonel William Dye sat across from Jones in the mess hall.

Red Hand and Two Moons joined him there. Curious eyes scrutinized their every move. The battle hardened men were leery of strangers in their midst, and certainly strangers who dressed as whites, but were obviously Cheyenne.

"So, you want to return Two Moons to her people, is that it?" Dye asked while cutting his steak.

"Yep," Jones said.

Dye looked across the table at the beautiful young Cheyenne woman, carrying on a private conversation with Red Hand. "Where did you find her?" he said.

"In Black Arrow's camp, three days ride east of Sidney," Jones said. "We raided the camp and Red Hand here, helped us rescue her."

Red Hand turned his head toward Jones when he heard his name mentioned.

"It's alright, son," Jones said. "You make sure Two Moons eats something. We've got a hard ride ahead."

"Colonel," Cody said, "they also found out who is putting Winchesters in the hands of Black Arrow's braves. It's the same man I've been ordered to find and bring to justice. Curtis Leaver. Only he's changed his name to Custus Leverette."

"Leaver, huh? I remember him. He disappeared like a rattler among the rocks after last year's treaty was signed. Are you sure you've found him?" Dye asked.

"We've found him, alright," Jones said. "He and his men trailed us to Courthouse Rock. Some of 'em didn't survive. Leaver is buying the guns and selling them to Black Arrow."

"And I have a report that Leaver, or Leverette, is after gold in the Black Hills," Cody said. "If Black Arrow can keep our troops pinned down protecting settlers, Leverette's gang has free rein to steal gold from the Dakota Territory."

"We've got to have Dull Knife involved in shutting down Black Arrow. Two Moons' safe return means Dull Knife doesn't have to worry that Black Arrow will kill her," Jones said.

"How can I help you arrange a little family reunion?" Dye asked.

"Here's what I'm thinking," Jones replied.

The others leaned in to hear.

CUSTUS LIMPED NORTH with what was left of his men. The Black Hills would provide a place to lick his wounds like a wounded cur. But the Black Hills were two days ride from where Custus was now.

Custus cursed. He was angry, and he let the world around him hear it. "I let myself get into an ambush. Dang it all," he said. "It cost me three good men, too. I'm gonna get Jones, if it's the last thing I do. And when I do," he unsheathed his Bowie Knife, "I'm gonna cut him and watch him bleed to death." He clenched and unclenched his fists around his knife and paraded about the camp.

On this third pass he turned and attacked Iggy, grabbing him by the collar and tossing him to the ground. "Find some wood and start a fire. We're staying here tonight."

Iggy hesitated, tucked in his shirttail and tried a half-hearted attempt to stare Custus down.

Custus laughed. "Yeah, don't try that stuff on me. All I'll say is that you better not buck me." He pulled his knife again and stared back. Iggy squirmed and hightailed it into the woods.

Custus yelled after him. "Get a fire going for my coffee. I

want to be back in the saddle in two hours. Two hours. Do you get me?"

Iggy stopped and turned back to face Custus. "But a minute ago, you said overnight. Which is it—two hours or overnight?"

"Get the gall-darned wood or I'll carve my initials into your hide." Custus yelled. He turned to Stinson who was trying to nurse his wounded arm. "We're going to pay a little visit to the Black Hills. Then, we've got unfinished business to take care of in Sidney."

Custus studied his Bowie Knife, and then used the blade tip to clean his fingernails.

SARAH WAS certain Madame Rogers had unfinished business, too. She knew Madame Rogers disliked the notion that one of her girls had walked out on her. Sarah heard from her friend Brandy that Madam Rogers had discussed sending a couple of thugs to storm the Parson's home and drag Sarah back.

A HUNDRED PEOPLE crammed into the pews on the parson's first Sunday back in the pulpit. Others stood outside the church in a show of support. Madame Rogers was not there and did not hear that sermon, but Sarah was certain reports reached her brothel. The parson spoke about a dying man who forgave those who killed him saying: 'Father, forgive them, they don't know what they're doing.' At this point in his sermon, Parson Abel removed the bandages to reveal his wound and said, "I forgive the man who did this."

How is this possible? Sarah wondered.

THE FRONT DOOR of Swede's closed.

"I'll be with you in a moment," Sarah said. She had her back to the front door stacking a new supply of blue jeans. "Look around. If you find anything you like, holler."

Sarah heard footsteps coming closer.

"So, this is where you work now?" Madame Roger's alto voice startled Sarah and she knocked over a neatly stacked pile of jeans.

"Well, aren't you somethin'? The girls told me you worked here. I doubted 'em, and had to see it for myself. Can you make money in this type of retail sales? I mean, can you make the amount of money you're used to making?"

She came so near Sarah heard her breathe in before saying, "You don't want this life. You can't be serious."

"I don't work for you anymore," Sarah said.

"Sarah, you're regulars are asking for you," Madame Rogers said. "You can't make that kind of money working for Swede."

Madame Rogers took hold of Sarah's hand and pulled her toward the door.

"I'm not going anywhere with you!" Sarah shouted.

"You don't want this, do you? This isn't what you told me you wanted. You told me you wanted lots of money and servants, like you had before the war."

"I've changed my mind. I've met someone that I want to marry and settle down with. I want a different life. I want a husband and children. I'm going to be Mrs. Jesse Jones, if he'll have me."

"Well, if your soldier boy disappoints you, don't crawl

back to me. If I leave today without you, that's the end." After a long, hard look, she added, "Admit it. You're a prostitute and that's all you'll ever be."

Sarah slapped her, but before she could draw back her hand a second time, Madame Rogers grabbed her wrist. "That'll be the last time you ever slap me. Custus will make sure of that. You heard about One-Eyed Mary, haven't ya? She tried Custus' patience and look where it got her."

Madame Rogers stormed out the door.

Swede returned from the storeroom. "I see a tear on your cheek. What did dat voman do to upset you?" Swede asked.

Sarah buried her head in her hands. "It ain't nothin'," she said. Sarah tried to make light of the situation, but the stack of blue jeans she was rearranging did not cooperate.

"Yer hands are shaking," Swede said. "Yer upset."

Madame Rogers had threatened her before, but the possibility of Custus' involvement scared her. Custus had hacked One-Eyed Mary to death and the thought of it chilled her soul.

She looked around her. She felt trapped.

The room was spinning.

Memories flooded in to whisk her back to the time when soldiers tried to rape her. Memories. Horrible memories flashed in her mind. She had to escape, to run away. She bolted for the door and into the arms of Parson Abel.

"Mmmmmph!" The impact stole his breath away.

"I'm sorry, Parson," Sarah said. "But I've got to get away from here."

Parson Abel held Sarah in a secure embrace. "What is it, child?" Why are you so upset?"

She looked into his face where bandages still hid the wound Custus had carved into the skin with his Bowie knife.

"I gotta go, Parson. I gotta go back or she'll send Custus. I'm a prostitute, that's all I'll ever be."

"Not true," Parson Abel said. He held Sarah at arm's length so he could peer into her eyes. "People change all the time. God still transforms hearts."

Sarah struggled to turn away. Her heart knew he spoke the truth, but the years of physical and mental abuse would not release their grip.

"I wanna believe you, but it's so hard," Sarah responded.

"That's where prayer comes in," he said. "Look at me. Take a good look at me."

Their eyes met.

"My wife and I are sure God can change you, and because of that, we have taken you into our own home. It hasn't been easy. The scar on my face proves it. You are safe. You are no longer alone. You don't have to go back to the life of a prostitute. You are special. It's time you buried your past with all its heartache and pain."

Tears welled up in Sarah's eyes and overflowed down her cheeks. "I want to. I really do. I want to start over, but how can I?"

"It starts with Jesus, Sarah. Jesus died to make you into His new creation. In Baptism, he made forgiveness a reality and gives you a new identity. Have you been baptized?"

"There's no one left to tell me one way or the other," she said.

"Then Baptism is a good place to start over. Would you like that?"

"Can Jesus forgive me?"

Parson Abel nodded. "He can and He will," he said.

CHAPTER TWELVE

It took a few days to outfit fifty soldiers to escort Two Moons to her grandfather. Jones used these days to rest and to learn more about the man he knew as Custus Leverette.

Colonel Dye supplied the party with Custus' military record. It included several demerits for fighting and the account of Custus' Court Martial. In this case a witness had disappeared before he could testify against him.

"Don't know much about Custus' upbringing, but we do know that before coming west," Dye continued, "Custus was part of Quantrill's raiders based out of Stilwell, Kansas. He learned to kill from one of the most notorious killers the Confederates ever produced, Bloody Bill Anderson. He took part in the raid of Lawrence, Kansas back in '63 where an estimated one hundred sixty to a hundred ninety men and boys were slaughtered. The next year when Anderson was ambushed and killed, Custus hid out for a time before heading west and signing on as a private in the Union Army keeping the peace here at Ft. Laramie."

"You knew all this and yet you let him sign-up? That's inviting trouble, like opening the chicken coup and sending in a fox," Cody interrupted.

"Now, hold on a second," Dye fired back. "Custus falsified his record and we didn't find out about his history until after he deserted last year. We sent his desertion papers back east and got his true record back in return."

"To his exploits we can add the murder of One-Eyed Mary and the malicious cutting of Parson Abel's face in Sidney," Cody said.

Dye continued, "According to our report, his weapon of choice is a Bowie Knife which he keeps in a sheath and stuffed behind his belt. We've since learned that he's riding with two men on a regular basis. They go by the names of Iggy and Stinson. Iggy's rail thin and Stinson is so big he can hardly pull himself up into the saddle."

"We know 'em," Jones said.

"We shot up a couple more of his gang at Courthouse rock," Potter said.

"Don't think we're gonna run into them in a while. We shot 'em up pretty bad," Jones said.

"Someone's got to put a stop to him." Colonel Dye looked into the faces of the men gathered there—Jones, Cody, Potter and Buntline. "It's just a matter of time."

"And right now," Jones said, "ain't the time. First, we gotta get Two Moons safely home. Then we can think about bringing Custus in."

"Bring him back to me and a military tribunal will see to it that he gets a fair trial before he's hanged," Dye said.

At sunrise next morning, Red Hand led the contingent of fifty troopers out of Fort Laramie to travel north along the Bozeman Trail, a route that had once taken treasure hunters to the gold fields of Montana. Although calm now, the

Bozeman Trail had seen its share of hostilities. Jones recalled that eighty-one soldiers from Fort Phil Kearny had been surrounded by Northern Plains Indians and slaughtered. An Indian by the name of Crazy Horse had made a name for himself that day.

Today Red Hand was leading the group on a mission of peace, not war, traveling into Indian Territory to return Dull Knife's granddaughter in hopes of preventing further bloodshed.

Where the Tongue River intersected the trail, Red Hand reined his pony to the northeast and followed the Tongue toward the Yellowstone River.

"Dull Knife's encampment is near where the two rivers meet so our people have fresh water and an abundance of wild game," Red Hand said. "The trail is there if you know how to look for it."

Red Hand dismounted and walked his horse in order to keep on the trail made by Cheyenne moccasins. Jones walked his horse about five yards behind. The others followed.

Two Moons sat on a makeshirt wooden bench on the wagon Potter drove. Loaded with supplies and trinkets from Fort Laramie, staying seated aboard the wagon was no easy task. The wooden wheels found every half-buried rock, bouncing Two Moons and Potter around like a rag dolls. Two Moons sat with a stoic expression on her face despite all the jostling.

Buntline remained mounted and flanked the rear of the wagon on the right side; Hook Nose flanked the left side with Colonel Dye and his men bringing up the rear.

For nearly five hours the group zigzagged through tall prairie grass and sloshed through meandering springs. At last they reached the place where the Tongue River took a jog to the left and the trail disappeared behind a grove of oaks. Here the party rested and made camp.

Hook Nose did not rest preferring instead to know what lay beyond the trees. He'd felt eyes watching his every move since the party had passed the charred remains of old Fort Phil Kearny.

Even though Hook Nose knew he was being watched, he was still taken from behind by a pair of Dull Knive's braves. One pressed a knife against Hook Nose's jugular.

"Not welcome here," the brave said.

"We come in peace," Hook Nose said. "We bring Two Moons. Return her to Dull Knife."

"How we know what you say is true?"

"I am Hook Nose, chief scout for one named Buffalo Bill. We come in peace."

The brave loosened his grip and shoved Hook Nose forward. His knife pressed against Hook Nose's back. "Show me," he said.

Hook Nose led Dull Knife's braves to where Cody sat a stone's throw away from the dismounted troops. Jones, who had stepped into the bushes to relieve himself, watched the silent party pass by. He drew his LeMat and prayed no one heard him cock it.

Buntline was the first to notice Hook Nose's approach; then Potter who slipped between the horses along the picket line. He unsheathed his rifle and chambered a round before taking aim across his saddle. He hoped the display of firepower was enough to end the threat.

Three braves followed Hook Nose. Nerves were on edge. Some of the troopers noticed the small procession. They stood and drew their weapons. Bodies tensed for battle.

Red Hand rose to his feet. "White Feather," he shouted.

A smile crossed the face of the brave behind Hook Nose .

He sheathed his knife and signalled for the other braves to lower their bows. "Red Hand?" the brave replied. "Me thought I'd never see you again."

"This is White Feather," Red Hand said as a means of introduction.

"You two know each other?" Jones asked tromping through the brush. He holstered his LeMat.

Potter eased the hammer down on his rifle and slid it back in its scabbard.

"For many years," said White Feather. He and Red Hand embraced.

"White Feather is my brother," Red Hand said.

"Dang, who'd a thunk that?" Potter said.

DULL KNIFE's village was where Red Hand remembered it; between the Tongue and Yellowstone rivers. The village was large with hundreds of teepees.

White Feather sent one brave ahead to insure everyone's safety. It was decided that only Jones, Potter, and Colonel Dye could accompany Red Hand and Two Moons into Dull Knife's village.

Nearly a year had passed since Dull Knife last looked upon his granddaughter. Her return, unharmed, was an occasion to celebrate.

Proud warriors danced around a central campfire that night. Bodies pulsed to the beat of many drums. Firelight cast shadows on the ground and nearby teepees. Jones sat to the left of Dull Knife with a new Indian blanket across his lap. It was a personal gift from the Dull Knife. Two Moons sat at his right with Red Hand, her husband to be. Dull Knife rewarded those who cared for his family.

Buntline sat near Cody scribbling down notes. This account would find its way back east as part of the legend of Buffalo Bill Cody.

THAT EVENING IN SIDNEY, miles away from campfires, dancing braves and Buntline's note taking, Sarah Fitzpatrick sat across the table from Parson Abel and Adeline. Doc was there, too. A candelabra in the center of the table provided the room's only light.

The evening meal of potatoes and sweet corn from Abel's ample garden, served alongside a pork chop supplied by a thankful parishioner, left everyone in good humor.

Sarah rose to clear the table. It was her way of repaying the kindness the Abel's had shown her. She was living in the Abel's upstairs guestroom: Ever so much nicer than her accomodations in Madame Roger's brothel.

"Leave them, Sarah. I'll help you with them later," Adeline said.

Parson Abel refreshed everyone's wine. "Tonight is a special night," he said. "Sarah asked me to baptize her in the spring. Tonight we celebrate what God has done in her life."

Sarah's life had indeed changed since the incident in Swede's Mercantile. Not the everyday circumstances, but her attitude toward them. Madame Rogers still came in to shop and belittled her, yet somehow, Sarah remained calm. She never crumbled in tears or struck back in anger. She did not understand her new demeanor but knew it had come about through evenings with the Abel's who read and talked about the Bible. Somehow, in this change of routine, God had worked a miracle. He had transformed her, smoothing the rough edges of her personality like sandpaper smooths rough hewn wood.

"There is only one thing missing," Abel said. He looked at Doc. "We've got a young lady ready for baptism when the weather warms up. We've got the water. Lodgepole Creek will do just fine."

"Kinda muddy, if you ask me," Doc said.

"It'll do just fine, Doc," Abel said. "We've got a place to hold the meal after the baptism. Adeline has seen to that."

She smiled.

"But, there is on thing missing."

All eyes turned toward Doc.

"Why is everyone looking at me? What are you all up to?"

"Sarah needs a sponsor," Abel said.

"Oh, so you cut the deck, and I got the low card, huh?" Doc said. "Is that it? I won't say it, but I sure am a thinkin' it. You railroaded me into this. You've been tryin' to get me into yer church for years and I told ya I wasn't comin'. Now, you pull these shenanigans."

Sarah laughed at Doc's mock outrage.

"Sarah, did you put him up to this? Is this all your doin'?" Doc asked.

"I can't imagine a better sponsor," she said.

"I've got half a mind to tell ya no. I can't remember the last time I was in a church. And I ain't a gonna start now."

Doc saw only smiling faces around him.

"Oh, well, I give up," he said to the delight of everyone present.

CHAPTER THIRTEEN

Custus squatted near the fire adding kindling to the embers. He blew on these embers and grinned to himself. He delighted in watching the flames dart from one twig to another, bringing dying coals of last evening's fire to life again. As the flames reached higher, Custus added pieces of dry wood Iggy had collected and stretched out his hands to warm them. It was a chilly morning and that meant that the sleeves of his shirt, which he liked to wear rolled up about halfway up his arms, were unrolled and buttoned at his wrists. The pale hint of early morning gave promise of a sunny day as Custus poked the flames and brought it out to watch the fire dance on the end of his stick.

Iggy and Stinson were sleeping under their saddle blankets and Custus decided to let them sleep longer. The quiet was good for thinking. For planning.

He thought back to the signing ceremony for last year's treaty at Fort Laramie that deeded the Black Hills to the Indians of the Northern Plains, the Sioux, Cheyenne and

Arapaho. And white men were expected to honor and respect this arrangement.

The Indians saw it as law. In the Black Hills they had the freedom to hunt and live without interference. But treaties were only good if both parties stuck to them. As far as Custus was concerned there was an exception written into this treaty in invisible ink. The exception that there was gold there and he wanted it.

Custus didn't care if these hills belonged to the natives who lived there. Gold made him wealthy. That wealth bought him everything he wanted. Whiskey. Women.

Custus limited to two the number of men who rode with him into the Black Hills. His forays had remained undetected. But Custus knew that soon Native eyes, Cheyenne eyes, would discover him. Then, these eyes would report his every move back to Dull Knife. Custus may have shaken off the dust of a cavalryman and turned highwayman, prospector, and king over his own dreams, maker and ruler over his own legend, possessing the stuff dreams are made of—gold taken from the Black Hills. But to the natives he was a trespasser and interloper.

Custus withdrew his pan and sieve from the saddlebag, along with a small Ames shovel and shouted over his shoulder as he made his way to the nearby creek, "Get yerselves down here and help me. Time's a wastin'."

Iggy rubbed the sleep from his eyes and complied, but not without a curse under his breath. There would be further commands. And he had ridden with Custus long enough to know to obey him or suffer the consequences.

Stinson took longer to stand up. His weight made it difficult to stand up, so he used a nearby log for support. "Be there in a minute," he said. "Gotta get moving first."

"Getting tired of you slowing me down," Custus said.

"And that poor horse of yers is getting more swayback every time you ride her. One of these times she's just gonna collapse and drop dead."

Iggy sniggered. Stinson did not.

"Let's get what we need, and get out," Custus said. "This place always gives me the creeps; like someone's watching."

He gouged the earth with his shovel and dumped the contents into the sieve on top of his pan before kneeling on the riverbank to allow a gentle flow of water over the sieve. He sifted the bigger stones by hand and tossed them into the water, took off the sieve, and studied what remained by shaking the pan from side-to-side.

"Gold is heavy and sinks to the bottom of the pan," he said. Behind his back, Iggy and Stinson rolled their eyes. This was the umpteenth time they heard him repeat the words.

Custus dipped the pan, filled it with water and washed the mud away. Again and again he repeated the process until only the black sand remained. "See it, boys? There's the gold on the bottom of the pan in the black sand. Iggy, get me my little pouch, will ya?"

Iggy went up the creek bank in fulfillment of Custus' command.

"The stuff of dreams," Custus said and snatched the pouch from Iggy. He coaxed the gold into it, careful not to lose even one tiny gold crumb, like a child guarding a precious toy. "Dig in, boys, we ain't got all day."

Stinson found it difficult to bend because of the wound he sustained at Courthouse Rock, so he flung himself to the ground backside first and slid toward the bank. His chubby legs dangled as he slid.

"Hand me the shovel, will ya, Iggy?" he said. With effort,

Stinson placed the sieve in the pan and dug while nursing his arm.

"Got just one question for ya, Stinson," Custus said

"I know what it is," Iggy interrupted with a laugh. "How will you get up the bank again?"

"One thing at a time," Stinson said. "One thing at a time."

Stinson went to work searching for gold the best he could.

A BRISK WIND blew through Dull Knife's encampment, the harbinger of a change in the weather. Jones sat alone inside a tent Dull Knife had provided, contenting himself in the important task of cleaning his gun. Sitting spread-eagle on the ground with his LeMat in pieces he whisked his cleaning rag in and out of the nine empty chambers and two gun barrels. Within the span of about forty-five minutes everything was cleaned, inspected and certified by Jones himself as fit for action. Only then did he snap the pieces back together and fill the nine chambers with .42 cartridges and a 20-gauge shell.

A clean gun is a reliable gun was what Jones knew to be true. He'd seen numerous times when a gun misfired or failed to fire because it was not properly cared for. He spun the cylinder and gave one final inspection before sliding the weapon into its holster and strapping the gun belt around his waist. Through the years he'd grown so accustomed to wearing a gun that he felt naked without it.

The tent flap opened and Potter poked his face through the opening. "You about ready?" he asked.

"Almost," Jones said.

"Everyone's waiting for you," Potter said.

"I'm sure they are," Jones answered. "But you know what I always say…"

"Yea, I know. 'A clean gun is a reliable gun.'"

From outside his tent he watched Dye lead his men away from Dull Knife's encampment. Dye carried a beaded necklace from the Chief to secure their safe passage through Cheyenne territory if stopped on the way back to Fort Laramie.

Jones grabbed his saddle horn and with a smooth continuous motion swung himself into the saddle and squirmed a bit to get comfortable before lifting his right hand in the air to signal his readiness.

Dull Knife and his many braves had turned out to send Jones and his men riding in pursuit of Custus, wherever his trail took them, but their departure was delayed by the arrival of one of the braves Dull Knife sent as his eyes in the Black Hills. The brave had ridden through the night to deliver his message and slid down from his saddle-less mount and raced to his Chief.

Red Hand stood in the company of the great Chief and heard every word the newcomer said.

"White men have entered the sacred hills," Red Hand translated for Cody who was yet to mount. "Three men dig gold."

"Can he describe them?" Cody asked.

Red Hand whispered the question to Dull Knife and waited for him to ask his brave, who answered at once.

"Him speak of a white man with large knife, a man too fat to ride, and another," Red Hand said.

"Custus," Cody said. "I wondered if he'd ride to the hills or double-back and return to Sidney. I've got my answer."

Red Hand returned to Dull Knife's conversation with the

brave, but soon returned with a message for Cody. "Before you go, Dull Knife want speak to you."

The Chief spoke and Red Hand translated. "Long ago my people came. We hunt buffalo. We live free. White men come. Kill buffalo. Tell us we no longer hunt. We sign treaty with Great White Father. He gave back our sacred hills. Him say no more white men come. I tell the Great White Father that I want peace. Still white men come. Now white men return to the hills."

Cody nodded his understanding.

Dull Knife continued. "What white men say is not true. Men still come. Where there are few, many follow. Take hills. Kill my people. Shed much blood. I am old. Have seen many days. I say, 'Peace.' Young braves say, 'War.' Black Arrow say, 'Kill all white men!' Him take many braves and kidnap Two Moons. You come. Bring her back to me."

Dull Knife stopped.

Cody surveyed the surrounding braves. He saw the grit in their eyes, a determination to restore what was stolen from Dull Knife, the trust that a white man's word was his bond.

"Red Hand," Cody said, "tell him that we do come in peace. We know others have spoken with forked tongue. We cannot change that. We ride to find the men who violated the treaty and bring them to justice. Dull Knife must know that not all white men lie."

Red Hand spoke all these words to Dull Knife and then brought his reply to Cody and the others.

"Your words speak wisdom. Your actions speak the same words," Dull Knife extended his right arm in fellowship to Cody. The two men grasped each other's forearms to signify their unity of purpose.

Cody grabbed his saddle horn and mounted. "Gentlemen, we've got work to do. What do ya say, we get started?"

"I'll ride with you," Red Hand said.

"Stay home with your new bride," Jones said.

"Dang right," said Potter.

Custus and his men dug and panned for three days and the earth yielded all the gold Custus needed. For now. He was not satisfied with the take but feared spending too much time in a place where he was considered a trespasser.

"Time to leave before anyone knows we've been here," Custus said. "Besides, I'm tired of sleeping on hard ground."

"You need a feather mattress and a woman's touch," Iggy said.

"I know where we can find both. Madame Rogers' brothel," Stinson said with a contented look upon his face.

Custus agreed. "Mount up."

"That's easy for you to say," Stinson mumbled under his breath with the hope that Custus hadn't heard. Thankfully for him, Custus hadn't.

"Mount up," Custus yelled. "We're riding south now that our business is complete. I got some pleasure waiting for me in Sidney. I'm tired a sleepin' by myself."

His laugh substantiated the darker side of his desire.

Stinson fought his way into his saddle to the jeers of Iggy, who asked him if he needed a stepstool to help him get his foot high enough to reach the stirrups. Stinson's undersized horse seemed to disagree with his mounting, and refused to stand still.

Custus took the lead and headed south but abandoned the usual trail leading through the Black Hills back to

Sidney. Instead he sauntered to the southeast some eight miles east of the main trail.

"I'm taking no chances. I'm thinking that with Two Moons safely in her grandfather's village, Jones will try to pick up our trail and I don't want to make it too easy for him. Or have him find us out in the open."

Where he took his men was filled with undulating hills where valleys and deeply cut gullies provided ample shelter. What he risked by traveling this route was discovery by a random Sioux or Cheyenne hunting party. These hills belonged to them and he knew it. The Treaty of Laramie said so.

"Treaties," Custus explained to his companions, "are only paper unless backed by the threat of action. And how could there be any action? There are too few troops to keep squatters and miners out of an area the size of the Black Hills; especially where god-forsaken gullies justified the name 'Badlands.'"

What Custus liked was the ample cover of these gullies had for illegal activities, such as panning gold. Yes, Custus liked his chances. Mentally, he had weighed all the odds, and the odds weighed in his favor. So Custus and his men rode southeast.

Custus was correct about one thing. Jones was after him and it was, indeed, hard to pick up his trail. Dull Knife's braves led Jones and company east from Dull Knife's encampment, splashed through the Laramie River and made their way into Dakota Territory. Dull Knife's braves who'd seen Custus pan for the yellow stones led the way. They soon stood on the banks of the slough where it was obvious that spade, screen and pan had yielded gold to pour into Custus' pouch.

Hook Nose kicked at the remains of a campfire and then squatted to put his hand over the place where fire had burned. No warmth remained. No embers glowed to fan into flame. Dull Knife's braves discovered footprints and followed them to where Custus' horses once stood and nibbled the prairie grass.

Hook Nose interpreted the brave's words. "He say, 'three horses stood here. One horse bears a heavy man.'"

"Custus and his men," Jones announced. All eyes watched the brave lead his horse along the path left by Custus and his men. The path suddenly veered to the southeast.

"How far ahead are they?" Cody asked Hook Nose.

"Him say two, maybe three days," Hook Nose said.

"Any idea where they're heading?"

Hook Nose shrugged his shoulders.

CHAPTER FOURTEEN

Jones and party splashed across Elk Creek that afternoon, but lost Custus' trail on the opposite side. They backtracked in an attempt to find it.

"Looks like Custus anticipated we'd be coming after him and used the creek to throw us off," Jones said.

The group separated. The braves under Hook Nose riding east in the creek; Cody, Potter and the others riding west. They searched in vain for the exit point where Custus and his men had climbed out of the the creek.

Potter found prints in the steep embankment a half mile west.

"Over here," Potter yelled.

"Buntline and I will go get Hook Nose and tell him you found the spot," Cody said.

"Good idea," Jones said. "I'll take a look at what Potter's found here." He dismounted midstream and walked toward the bank to find mud-caked hoof prints.

"Two horses climbed the ridge without incident, the third did not," Potter noted.

"Looks like the third horse stumbled. A heavier man rides one horse," Jones said. "That's what Hook Nose said."

He examined further. "This horse stumbled and threw his rider. The man's butt print is visible in the mud."

Jones climbed to the top of the ridge and looked for tell-tale signs of Custus and found a horseshoe. He held the shoe for all to see. "This'll slow 'em down a bit. With the combination of a big man on his back and the muddy bank, this shoe came off. By the look of the tracks, this man's on foot now."

Potter joined Jones on the high side of the creek. "What are you thinkin'? Did this come off the front leg?" Potter asked.

"Most likely." Jones put the horseshoe into his saddlebag. "We've got us a horse with a gimpy leg unable to carry his rider, so we've got a fat man on foot. Custus' head start will shrink unless they find a blacksmith fast. And the best blacksmith in the area is at Chartran Trading Post."

Potter shook his head. "Bad part is men who know Custus shot up the place the last time they were there. I'm bettin' that if he shows up, nobody there will help him unless it's at the point of a gun."

"Or at knife point," said Jones.

The rest of the company arrived within minutes. After a brief discussion with Cody they set out for Chartran thinking any advantage Custus' had had melted like snow on a fifty degree day.

To the southwest, storm clouds gathered with the sound of distant thunder rumbling like off-beat native drums. One of Dull Knife's braves was the first to hear it. As a matter of life or death, his trained ears heard the slightest rustle among blades of grass. He stood erect beside his horse, his arm raised to point toward the rising storm, urgency clear in his gestures.

What had been a cool, clear day suddenly turned cloudy and cold. Buntline removed a ratty coat from his saddle bag and put it on, an added layer against the cold. Others did the same to keep warm while the temperature swiftly dropped.

"One of the braves say falling temperature mean bad weather come from rocky mass," Hook Nose told Cody with Jones listening in.

"That 'rocky mass' is what the natives call the Rockies," Jones said.

"A storm is coming," Cody said. "We need a place to ride out the weather."

Cody removed his slicker from behind his saddle and the others did likewise to put another layer between skin and the cold rain. A gully in the rolling terrain where the end of one hill kissed the start of another offered the shelter they sought when the earliest snow pellets pounded down on hats, slickers and any other exposed surface. Fierce winds drove the pellets like watery gnats to soak everything. And wash away the tracks they followed.

Custus laughed. He looked upward and didn't mind the cold and wet splattering against his face. Instead he welcomed the change of weather as a natural way of hiding his tracks. Now he didn't have to cut a huge branch off a tree and drag it behind his horse. Mother Nature did everything for him.

"Son of a gun," he said. "This is the best thing that could happen. It's gonna take a tracker far better than anyone Jonzie has with him to find us now."

He looked around him and spotted Iggy close behind. A

half mile or so back Stinson walked his lame horse, battling the elements which Custus had so recently praised. The fat man trudged along, one arm bandaged while the other gripped the reins of his horse. Even from this distance Custus heard Stinson muttering curses under his breath. When he heard his own name proclaimed in one of those curses, Custus' blood boiled over. He reeled his horse around and drove his spurs into its side, pulling up alongside Stinson in a heartbeat. Iggy followed.

"Stinson," he said, "you're as worthless as teats on a boar. You're slowing us down."

"Ya know, I don't really give a dang anymore. I'm tired of walkin' and I'm tired of your mouth. Why don't ya just shoot me and be done with it?"

Custus dismounted and handed Iggy his reins. He got in Stinson's face, pushed him to his knees, drew his six-shooter and pressed the cold steel barrel against Stinson's forehead. The hammer clicked in place.

Iggy was horrified. He and Stinson had ridden together since boyhood. Now he could only watch his best friend's brains blown out, splattered across the prairie, shot dead like a rabid dog. If he intervened, Custus would kill him too. When it came to his own death, Iggy was a coward.

Time stood still. Stinson's eyes glazed waiting for the gunshot—the last sound he'd ever hear.

Custus laughed.

"Ah-ha-ha-ha. Look at you. You really thought that 'ole Custus would blow your head off. You should see your eyes. You're so scared you probably peed your pants."

Custus gave no apology. He uncocked and holstered his pistol. He helped Stinson stand and gave him three pats on his cheek, like a parent might do to a small child caught with a hand in the cookie jar. Then Custus looked at Iggy.

Maybe Stinson hadn't peed his pants, but Iggy had. The tension was so great that he'd relieved himself on the spot.

Custus chuckled and looked first at Stinson, then at Iggy, and then to the hobbled horse whose reins Stinson held. He blew out a frustrated breath.

"Against my better judgment, we're splittin' up," he said. "Stinson, you can't ride and you can't keep up. That means sooner 'er later we're gonna have someone nippin' at our rear, if I know Jones and them other fellers. The rain and snow gave us a break, 'cuz now they don't have tracks to follow. Stinson, I want ya to head west and make yer way to Chartran Trading Post. Trade that horse for a better mount or have a new shoe put on him or somethin'; after that ride on ahead to Sidney. Iggy and I will ride east. Black Arrow's got to be about out of ammunition. That's a need I can fill. Iggy and I are goin' lookin' for him. Then we'll join you in Sidney."

Lesson learned, Stinson made no sass. He and his lame horse walked westward without a whimper, while Custus led Iggy, wet pants and all, in search of Black Arrow. Custus needed assets, not liabilities like Stinson.

In the morning, Jones found tracking impossible after the snow squall and led his party back to the main trail and headed south to Chartran Trading Post. It was early afternoon when they rode in. The grounds were littered with fur trappers and Indians hawking beads, pelts and blankets, bustling about like ants on a sweet cake.

Hook Nose noticed a swayback horse tied to the hitchin' rail. He dismounted his paint and made a wide arc around the backside of the animal, knowing sometimes horses hate being snuck up on, and they'll kick back a rear hoof in return for that sneak. Not this time. Hook Nose patted the steed. He reassured the creature in his native tongue. The animal whinnied in response. Hook Nose examined the right front leg and found the hoof without a shoe.

Cody and Jones approached the trading post when a heavy hand swung Jones around. Jones' left arm rose to block an imagined swing while his right drew his LeMat.

"You want blanket?" The heavy hand belonged to a squaw. She stood four feet tall and was four feet around.

"No, Ma'am," Jones replied. "Right now, I'd just like a little somethin' to wet my whistle."

"Feels like we've been here before," Buntline chided Cody as they stepped inside.

"Very funny," was Cody's reply.

"There, at the end of the bar," said Jones, "is the rider of the swayback horse. Custus calls him Stinson."

The man never looked up. He was too busy making love to his beer and that love required all of his attention. He gazed into the glass and sipped on the amber liquid as if it was his only friend.

Taking advantage of Stinson's preoccupation was easy. Jones and Cody maneuvered their way past a group of men playing five card stud at a small table. Cigarette smoke clouded the air. A bluish haze bathed the players and gave the inside of the bar a trance-like appearance, making it easy for Cody and Jones to find a table with their backs to the bar so Stinson could not see their faces. Cody searched in vain for Bodeen, the owner of the place while a sleazy barmaid took their order.

"Two beers," Jones said. He thought to himself how similar the barmaid was to the horses. Ridden hard and put away wet. It was plain to see she had once possessed a dignity about her, but no more.

Outside Potter kept his eye on Stinson's horse while the Indians roamed the grounds and talked. Once or twice Jones saw Potter press his face against the glass to peer inside. Jones was sure the unwashed window yielded little.

It wasn't long before the barmaid brought two luke-warm beers with a huge head of foam on top. That bitter foam was all they tasted when they took their first few sips.

"Remind me to order whisky next time," Cody said.

Jones nodded in agreement. "Not the best beer I've ever drank."

"So, what do we do next?" Cody asked between sips.

"We wait for the fat man to make his move."

"He doesn't seem to be in a hurry."

"Makes me think that he and Custus have parted company, at least for a while," Jones said.

They watched Stinson attempt to roll a cigarette, an impossibility with a shoulder wound. He removed the tobacco pouch from his shirt pocket, untied it, and poured. His fill was good, but he failed on the roll up, and spilled tobacco all over the bar. He swore at his mistake, crushed the paper and brushed the mess onto the sawdust floor. He tried to stand, but with his weight and amount of beer he had sloshed down, he stumbled.

"Whoa, partner, I think you need a hand," a man at the bar said. He caught Stinson and stood him upright. "You look a little unsteady."

Stinson pushed himself free, staggered to the door and went outside. Jones stood to follow him.

Cody stood as well.

"Easy does it," Jones said. "I've got this."

Cody grabbed another sip of his lukewarm beer.

Potter raised the brow of his hat a quarter of an inch when the door banged open and Stinson tumbled through with Jones right on his heels. They stood together watching Stinson lead his horse down the sloppy street to the blacksmith shop.

The smithy was hard at work. Tongs held hot metal and placed it on the anvil where his muscular right arm brought hammer strokes down on hot metal. Sparks like tiny fireflies flew in all directions. He quenched the metal in a water bucket. The metal hissed like a chorus of snakes. Sweat soaked his long-sleeved shirt that bore scorch marks where sparks had set it afire. A leather apron protected his chest. The man never looked up when Stinson approached. "What can I do fer ya?" he said.

"Need a shoe."

"For yer horse, 'er fer you?" the smithy said. He followed his words with a loud guffaw that spooked Stinson.

"Horse," he said.

"Tie 'em up over there." The smithy pointed to a nearby hitching rail. "Come back in a while and I'll have him ready 'fer ya. Now, go away." he barked.

"So, what's it gonna cost me?"

"Don't know fer sure. I ain't even looked at 'yer horse yet." He returned to work. "Let's say six bits."

When he turned to Stinson, the smithy found the large man hadn't moved. "And if yer gonna stand there a-watchin' me while I'm workin', it's gonna be an even dollar. Now, get outta here. I got work to do. Come back about three."

With a mighty blow, the smithy brought his hammer down causing hot sparks to fly everywhere. He spat part of his chaw onto the ground. The tabacco splattered like a filthy brown raindrop.

This conversation sobered Stinson up. "I need another beer," he said. Stinson withdrew his pocket watch from his breast pocket. "I got until three."

Stinson tied his horse in front of the blacksmith shop and waddled back to the bar where he asked the bartender if his favorite spot was still available at the other end of the bar. It was and he pushed his way to it.

"I like the view," he said. "I can see people coming in and out of the place."

Stinson was soon too preoccupied with his beer to notice those coming in and out or that Bill Cody and Jesse Jones were sitting right under his nose watching his every move.

CHAPTER FIFTEEN

In Sidney early on the evening of September sixteenth Sarah assisted Doc Hardesty while he removed the last stitches that held Parson Abel's cheek together.

"There's going to be a pronounced scar," Doc said. "Over time the scar will lessen, but there will always be a scar. The redness will lessen, too, but the wound Custus carved into your face will always look back at you in your mirror."

After letting his words sink in, Doc continued: "It's normal for the scar to ooze when sutures come out. That's why you keep a bottle of alcohol handy. Wet a piece of cloth with the alcohol and wipe the wound to clean it. You'll feel some pain when you do, that just tells you the alcohol is disinfecting. If the pain gets too intense, take a shot or two of some different alcohol. Take it internally, not externally, before you begin. For medicinal purposes only, of course."

A bit of a struggle ensued as Doc removed the last stitch.

"Hold still, will ya? I'm almost done," Doc barked. Abel winced and tried to bark back, but Doc interrupted. "And don't ya talk back. I'm about done and I don't need any of 'yer sass."

Sarah watched Doc finish his work. He walked to the washbasin to wash up.

"I'm gonna put a bandage over that wound to protect it from infection. I want you to change it every day for the next week. Put some goose grease on the wound to decrease the scarring."

"You did that on purpose," Abel said.

"Did what 'on purpose?'"

"Caused me pain."

"Why would I do that?" Doc asked.

"'Cuz you like to see people suffer, 'ya ole coot."

"That's the shot of whisky I gave you talkin'. You know better than that."

Doc wiped his hands with a towel and turned to Abel. "'Sides, I swore an oath when I became a doctor to do no harm. Why would I intentionally hurt 'ya?"

"Oh, 'yer talkin' about the hypothetical oath," Abel said in his stupor.

"Hypocritical oath," Doc said then paused in thought. "Wait a minute, let me correct myself. It's the Hippocratic oath. Hippocratic."

"You old buzzard. You were right the first time. Hypo-critical. It's the hypocritical oath, and that makes you a hypocrite."

"I will not argue with you." Doc wagged his finger in Parson Abel's face. "I never argue with a fool or anyone who has had too much to drink."

He paused a moment and said, "This would be a good time for you to take a nap. You'll feel a lot better after you wake up. You don't have to remember what I said to you about wound care. Sarah will remember it for you. Won't you Sarah?"

He closed his satchel but couldn't help getting in one last barb. "She will remember a lot more than you will when you wake up."

Parson Abel wanted to respond but thought better of it. Besides, his face hurt and a nap appealed to him.

"WE'LL HEAD to the spot along Lodgepole Creek where we last saw Black Arrow and see if we can pick up his trail from there," Custus had told Iggy. They were in the saddle all day and finally arrived just before nightfall. He and Iggy made camp and bedded down for the night. It was a dark night, so dark their campfire provided the only illumination, except for the sliver of a moon overhead. Not far away a coyote screamed like a banshee at the veil of clouds passing in front of the moon. The howling sent cold shivers down Iggy's spine but brought a delighted squeal from Custus.

Custus tossed a final log on the fire and lay down for a few hours of sleep. His head rested on his saddle. To his right, just a clod-kick away, Iggy was already snoring.

"I never snore," Iggy had once said, but Custus knew those words for what they were—a lie. Iggy's snoring wasn't the loud kind of snoring like a rasp makes when scraped over metal, but more like the faint sound made by distant thunder. Custus pulled his blanket over his arms to cover himself. He held his Colt close to his chest with a vise-like grip. He pitied anyone who arrived uninvited into his camp. Custus drew in a breath, held it and listened. *Had he just heard something?* He wasn't sure.

There it was again. The sound of a twig snapping.

He pointed his hidden revolver in the direction of the sound—and waited. The sound came closer. A careful step. Deliberate. Patient.

"Drop the knife or I'll blow 'yer head clean off," Custus said. He tossed off the blanket and rolled over to face Many Eagle Feathers. Custus pointed his pistol at the brave's chest.

Many Eagle Feathers dropped his knife. He had no other choice. "Ah, Custus, my friend," he said.

"Many Eagle Feathers, we've been looking for you," Custus said. He holstered his gun. The commotion roused Iggy from his sleep and he sat up, rubbing the back of his neck.

"And I you." Many Eagle Feathers stooped to retrieve his fallen knife.

"Why are you looking for me?" Custus asked. He did not wait for Many Eagle Feathers to answer. Instead he yelled at Iggy: "Iggy, get 'yer lazy butt up and stoke the fire."

Iggy sat and tried very hard to wake up.

"Me see to it Black Arrow know you not steal two Moons. Him no longer want your scalp. Want bullets," Many Eagle Feathers said. "Or braves soon return to old ways of fighting."

"Black Arrow doesn't like the odds, eh? Well, we can help each other out. Ammo for the use of a few braves," Custus said. "There's this store in Sidney I can raid and get all the ammo he needs. Need to pay that town a little visit anyhow. There's this soldier there givin' me all kinds of reasons to hate him. Stinson's on the way there now."

"Ah, fat man who ride sway back pony," Many Eagle Feathers said.

Custus laughed a hearty laugh. "Yes, that's right. The fat man who ride sway back pony."

THE DINNER DISHES sat untouched in the Abel household. The after dinner conversation had stalled like good conversations sometimes do. For weeks, a question lingered, gnawing at Sarah, and tonight she concluded this gnaw would linger as long as her question remained unasked.

"Parson, have you ever—?" Sarah hesitated. She felt self-conscious and afraid to continue.

"Have I ever what?" Abel asked.

She demurred.

"It's alright, child. Ask anything you'd like. You are among friends."

Adeline smiled at Sarah. "It's alright, dear," she said.

"Have you wanted to avenge the wrong done to you? Have you ever wished that someone would bring Custus to justice for what he did to you? I mean, every day you look in the mirror and see the harm he has done. Don't you want to do something to make it right?"

"Those are good questions. And the answer to both is yes. I have had thoughts of revenge. Adeline can attest, thirty years ago I would have done just that. I had a hair-trigger temper back then. I believed I had a right to seek revenge and I would have planned out my revenge meticulously, in the same manner Adeline plans our meals."

Adeline patted his right hand, letting him know it was alright to continue. He looked into her eyes and smiled.

"So, what changed?" Sarah continued. "What is it that makes you different today than thirty years ago?"

"I have changed, but it isn't because of anything I've done to make change happen. I've changed because, by the grace of God, He changed me." Adeline smiled at him before he continued. "The Bible says an eye for an eye, and a tooth for a tooth. That's the credo I lived by back then."

He turned to look at Sarah. His passion scared her, so he tempered his words, but continued. "Anyone or anything that hurt me or my family became the centerpiece of my hatred."

He paused and reflected. "Then this pastor rode into St. Louis: One of those circuit riders who rode from town to town. He saved me when I was near death. Adeline somehow talked me into it and I went to hear him preach. He looked at Adeline and winked. "I let my guard down, didn't I?"

Adeline nodded.

"The preacher spoke of God's love for His creatures, of how hate and violence only begets more hate and violence. Then, he spoke the words that forever changed my heart— 'vengeance is mine, saith the Lord.' He preached about hearts and minds turned to Jesus. About how Jesus soothes all their hurts and pains. He forgives. It says in John's Gospel that Jesus did not come to condemn, but to save."

He took Sarah's hand. "Those words transformed me. They will transform you, too."

Stinson rode south from Chartran Trading Post, not knowing Jones and his men followed. Stinson had tried to shake off his stupor by dunking his head in one of the horse troughs in front of the blacksmith's shop but found the more the beer flushed from his system, the angrier he became about the way the smithy had treated him.

"That buzzard had the advantage over me," he muttered. "He knew I wasn't going anywhere with a lame horse. The only good to come of it was that my horse was done at three like he promised." Stinson replayed the encounter with the blacksmith in his mind.

"No one talks to me like that. No one." He paused. "Been around Custus so much, I'm beginnin' to sound like him."

Stinson's preoccupation with the smithy, much like his preoccupation with his beer earlier that afternoon, played right into Jones' hands as he, Potter, Cody and Buntline rode single file a half mile or so behind the fat man. In fact, while Stinson replayed the scene, he never looked back as his horse ambled on, coming to a halt only when the sun and the moon traded places in the sky.

"I'm thinkin' that one of us ought to ride into his camp to find out what he's up to," Jones said. "Maybe Potter and me. He's been drinking all afternoon and probably won't know either of us. But he will recognize Cody from the illustrations in Buntline's dime novels."

"Think he's riding back to Sidney?" Cody asked.

"I'm guessin' so," Potter said. He sat up a little on the boulder serving him as his chair. "Only one way to find out. Ride in and ask him."

"I'm in favor if the two of you go. I'm not in favor if it's only one. Too risky. Hook Nose," Cody said. "Why don't you sneak in close to the camp? We'll give you an hour and then Jones and Potter will ride out. That'll get them a little extra fire-power if somethin' goes wrong."

Hook Nose nodded his approval. He soon vanished into the night.

Jones and Potter waited an hour to climb into the saddle and ride south on a well-used trail. Their approach to Stinson's camp was noted by Hook Nose, whose owl hoot acknowledgement was indistinguishable from the real thing.

"Hello in the camp," Potter called.

"Watta ya want?" Stinson asked, readjusting the bandage on his wounded shoulder.

"Just passing by," Potter said. "Wondering if ya got any coffee left? Sure smells good from where I'm sitting."

"Climb on down and help yourself. But don't settle in 'cuz ya ain't stayin'."

It was obvious to Jones and Potter that Stinson enjoyed being alone, so his hospitality, or lack thereof, showed. There would be no pleasantries.

"You here by yourself?" Jones asked.

"That's none of yer business," Stinson said. He stared at Jones. "Don't I know you?"

Jones ignored the question and picked up a cloth near the fire, removed the coffee pot, and poured himself a cup.

Then Potter helped himself to the cloth and the coffee. "Can I pour you a cup while I'm at it?"

"Nope," Stinson said. "And it's not because I don't like the coffee I made, nor that I don't want some. It's because you ain't stayin' that long."

Potter reached inside his jacket pocket and removed a small flask and uncorked it to pour some of its contents into his coffee. The flask attracted Stinson's attention like a worm attracts fish. He held his cup in both hands and extended it toward Potter like a beggar asking for alms. Stinson's eyes followed Potter's flask wherever he moved it. "Now, I could go for what ya got in yer pocket. Don't need no coffee, but I sure could use a drink."

"Two fingers or one?" Potter asked.

"Since yer offering, I'll take two."

Potter poured the hooch out slowly, like snow melting on an early spring morning. Stinson eyed Potter's flask. His tongue darted in and out between closed lips in anticipation and a soft squeal of delight slipped through his closed lips.

When Potter finished the pour, he placed the cup back into Stinson's hands. He quivered with delight. It had been two days since Stinson had his last drink, and he felt it. He tried to resist temptation but failed. He emptied the cup in one gulp. Ecstasy. His eyes rolled back in his head and then closed. A delighted grin erupted.

Stinson brought the sleeve of his dirty chambray shirt across his lips to wipe away any evidence.

Stinson's eyes opened. "Who did you say you were?"

"We didn't," Jones said.

Consternation replaced ecstasy on Stinson's face. Jones couldn't tell the direction this conversation was going, so his gun hand drifted downward until even with his LeMat.

A moment later, Stinson roared with laughter. "Names don't matter," he said. "We're drinking buddies now, ain't we? And drinking buddies don't ask stupid questions like names and stuff. Sit down already, yer makin' me nervous hovering there like a couple of vultures."

Jones pulled up a log and sat on it while Potter offered Stinson another two fingers. He gulped down the second cup like he had the first. In a lapse of memory, he asked again for their names. Potter got the better of him.

"We already told ya that. Don't ya remember?"

Stinson looked dumbfounded, thought for a moment and then answered, "Oh, yeah. I asked that before, didn't I? Ya told me yer names already, so I guess it's my turn. The name's Stinson. Howard Stinson. Sure glad you two came along to keep me company. I've bin riding with a couple of guys and they took off on me. Headed off to find a Cheyenne named Black... 'er somethin', and told me to spy out Sidney ahead of an Indian raid."

He realized what he had just said and halted then restarted his conversation. "I wasn't supposed to tell you that. Ahhh, shoot. I dun told ya somethin' I shouldn't have. You won't tell nobody, will ya?" Stinson fumbled around until he found his revolver and held it in front of him. "Cuz, if ya do, I'm gonna have to kill ya. Swear it. Do you hear me? 'Swear it."

An awkward silence followed until Jones broke it.

"We're drinking buddies, remember? Drinking buddies keep each other's secrets." He motioned for Potter to refresh Stinson's cup.

"Ain't you two drinking?" Stinson said. He held the third cup of "two fingers," and waited for an answer.

Jones added some dry branches to the fire and looked over at Potter. "We've been drinking right along with ya," Potter said. "Haven't ya noticed? C'mon, drink up."

Stinson did.

CHAPTER SIXTEEN

There was a chill on the afternoon breeze when Jones, Potter, Cody, Buntline, and the Indian scout Hook Nose rode into Sidney. Dull Knife's braves had left them to return home once they reached Chartran Trading Post. The five men rode in from the north, passed Boot Hill Cemetery, where two men shoveled dirt on a new grave.

Jones reminisced with Potter who rode stride for stride with him. "I remember when the first grave was dug back in early sixty-eight. Life on the plains was harsh then, in many ways harsher than today. Seems to me that tombstones and freshly dug graves are a reminder to all who passed this way that it does not matter who you are, rich or poor, military or civilian, the trail of life always ends in death. Here in Boot Hill everyone is equal. Death is the great equalizer."

A half mile south the construction of Fort Sidney continued and encompassed a huge rectangle that measured six hundred feet by sixteen hundred feet, with the shorter sides on the north and south and the longer on the east and west. Construction was also underway on the infantry quarters on the north side of the rectangle, a structure giving more shelter to the enlisted men than the tents at the top of the hill two miles further south.

"They are far enough along with construction that they're working inside today," Potter noted.

"Wouldn't like it," Cody said from behind him. "Don't like being confined. They've done a lot of work since I last rode by." Cody pointed further south. "The stable's done and the saddle house and I'm guessing over yonder is the quarter master's stable butting up against Lodgepole Creek."

The five rode a path between the northern and southernmost buildings to the spot where four buildings faced east. Three were officers' quarters and the fourth already housed the commanding officer quarters, in front of which stood a freshly painted sign with the name *Lt. Colonel Englewood*. Here they reined up, dismounted, and tied off their horses.

Their entrance into the bulding caught Englewood midsentence. "... and tell the men that they can begin moving into their barracks early next week."

Sergeant Major Kelly saluted. "Yes, sir. I'll be a tellin' them to start packin,' sir." He turned toward the door, running into the men who stood in the doorway.

"'Scuse me, gentlemen," Kelly said. "Why if it ain't Jones. How ya doin' Jonzie, me boy? I hardly recognized you with all that dust on ya."

"Fine, sir. And how's the misses and all the kids?" Jones said.

"All fine," he said.

Colonel Englewood interrupted him, "Sergeant Major,

move out of the way, and let the men in. And stick around. You may want to hear this."

"Aye, sir. As you wish." He stood at parade rest near the door.

Jones and Potter each saluted, while Cody and Buntline removed their hats and dusted them off. Hook Nose stood there taking all this in, seeing no value whatsoever in military etiquette. It mattered little to Cody as well. Cody worked for the army but always remained a civilian.

"At ease, gentlemen. What do you have for me?" Englewood said.

"Sir," Jones began, "we believe the citizens of Sidney are in danger. After we returned Two Moons to Dull Knife, we tracked the men who attacked us at Castle Rock into the Black Hills. Only three of them survived. We found their camp and it appeared to all of us that they were panning gold."

"I thought as much," Englewood said.

"They split up. Custus and Iggy rode to the southeast and Stinson is on his way to Sidney on a reconnaissance mission."

"And how do you know that?" Englewood inquired.

"We caught up with Stinson awhile back and got him liquored up," Potter answered. "He was so drunk he didn't recognize us. I'm guessing he'll be here tomorrow."

"Sergeant Major," Englewood said.

Kelly snapped to attention. "Yes, sir?"

"Ride out to the barracks and bring a company of men into town tonight. They can stay in the new barracks for a few days, but make it plain to them they are on duty and I don't want any candles to light the place up like a Christmas tree. Have them walk into town with their horses on leads and keep them canteens quiet. Do you understand, Mr. Kelly?"

"Aye, sir. Is there anythin' else, sir?"

"No. That will be all, Sergeant Major. You are dismissed." Kelly saluted and was gone.

"So, what are we expecting anyway?" the Colonel asked.

"We're not sure," Cody said. "If Custus is heading where I'm thinking, he's looking for reinforcements. We shot 'em up pretty bad at Castle Rock."

"My bet is that he's lookin' to link up with Black Arrow for some additional firepower," Jones noted.

"Black Arrow's responsible for a couple of raids into Kansas," said Englewood. "Not sure where he launched his raids from. Killed a couple of homesteaders just across the border." Englewood took a map off a shelf, unfolded it on his desk and pointed to a spot near the Kansas Nebraska border. The men crowded around the map. "I'm thinking it was right about here."

"Dang," Potter said. "There are a lot of places Black Arrow could hide. It will be difficult to find him, even when we have a general idea of where he might be."

Buntline silently noted all this in his notebook.

LATER THAT AFTERNOON the aroma of the stew Adeline was teaching Sarah how to make caught Abel's attention.

"Mmmm, smells good," he said and grabbed a spoon to sample. It tasted as good as it smelled and he kissed his wife's forehead. "Jones is back in town," he pronounced.

"When did he get back?" Adeline asked. She took the wooden spoon from his hand and stirred the mixture. Not waiting for his answer she spoke a reassuring word to Sarah. "It's difficult to master the technique with wood fired stoves since it's hard to know how much wood is needed to maintain the correct temperature. Too much wood means too much heat, and we scorch the stew. Too little wood and it takes forever for the stew to get done. Don't worry you'll get used to it."

"Jones rode in earlier this afternoon," Abel said. "Just ran into him in the barbershop."

"Did you invite him to supper?"

"No. Was I supposed to?"

Adeline gave Sarah a glance. "Sometimes men just don't know what to do."

"How was I to know?" he asked. He grabbed Adeline around her waist and swung her around for a passionate kiss.

"Mama always said that it's a good idea to keep men guessin'. How am I doin' so far?" Adeline said.

"Yer doin' just fine."

"Now you skedaddle back over to the barbershop and invite him. He doesn't need to be eating that stuff they serve at the fort, if he's got somethin' better."

"And it don't get any better than when the two of you make homemade beef stew and fresh biscuits." He looked around for evidence that Adeline was making biscuits. "You are making biscuits, aren't you?"

"Of course. Now, skedaddle. I can't get any biscuits made if you hold on to me."

THE MANTEL CLOCK in the parlor chimed five times. Adeline and Sarah stepped into the parlor to find Parson Abel in his chair with a newspaper propped up in front of him, masking his true intentions. He was sound asleep.

Adeline grinned fondly. "He figured that I'd peek in and think he's wide awake reading the newspaper," she said to Sarah. "Ever since Custus cut him up so bad, he's been taking a little nap before supper. He doesn't want me to know that he's tired, so he props the paper up so it looks like he's reading."

Adeline cleared her throat and announced from the doorway. "Time to dress for dinner!"

"I was just catching up with the news," Abel said from behind the newspaper.

"I know dear," Adeline replied with a chuckle.

Parson Abel put down his newspaper and saw that his wife had traded in her house dress for something more formal. "You look lovely this evening, dear."

"Thank you," she said. "Hurry along, he'll be here any moment and I want you dressed for dinner tonight."

Abel examined Adeline framed in the doorway. "What are you up to?" he asked. "You don't normally wear that dress for dinner. Why tonight?"

"Whatever do you mean?" Adeline replied. "I wear this old taffeta dress all the time to dinner. Don't tell me you've forgotten."

"I don't mind it when you play the innocent with me. We're married after all, but now is not the time." He turned and saw Sarah and a grin lit his face. "What are you up to, my little match-maker? I invited Jones for dinner and you scurry about the house like a church mouse," Abel said.

"You heard me scurry? I don't believe that. In fact, you were snoring."

"I don't snore. Oh, I get it. You want to change the subject, don't you?"

She kissed him. "Now, will you hurry and get dressed?"

"Yes, ma'am. You win. I won't ask any more questions. I'll just toddle along upstairs like a good boy and get dressed for dinner." He mounted the steps.

"Don't patronize. It doesn't sound good coming from you," she fired after him.

"Yes, ma'am. I won't do that again, ma'am," Abel said. He closed the bedroom door.

ADELINE HAD SET the perfect table using her good Bavarian dinner plates with hand-painted roses interlocked with dainty green vines. She'd told Sarah the story behind the plates. "My mother brought these plates with her from 'the old country.' How pieces so delicate survived the harsh Atlantic journey while my mother did not remains a mystery known but to God," she remarked.

Adeline's father had given gifts to all of his seven children. These plates he'd given to her, his eldest daughter. She remembered his words. "Addie, these dishes belonged to your mother. If she were here now, she would want you to have them."

Adeline fought back tears every time she looked at the plates. Her father's stoic German background kept his emotions in check regardless of the circumstance, but still she cried.

Adeline set these dishes when she wanted to bring civility to an uncivil frontier. Tonight was such an occasion. Jones was coming. This night was extra special.

She'd told Sarah a woman always knew when another woman has eyes for a certain man. "I'm not a match-maker," she told her. "I've just arranged for you and Jones to be together. What happens happens."

SARAH FITZPATRICK CAME DOWN the stairs with her long blonde hair clean, brushed, and draped over her shoulders. She wore a blue gingham dress she'd mail-ordered from Chicago, but had never had a reason to wear it until tonight. Her beauty belied her work at Madam Rogers' brothel.

"Oh, Sarah, dear. You look lovely tonight. We're gathering in the dining room." Adeline removed her tiny pocket watch. "Dinner is at seven. You'll sit opposite our special guest this evening. After which the Parson and I will make ourselves scarce."

"Are you sure this will work?" Sarah asked.

"Of course, my dear. Haven't you heard that the easiest way to a man's heart is through his stomach?" She laughed.

Parson Abel entered the room. "Would you mind buttoning this cuff, Adeline? I can't seem to get it."

"Men," Adeline announced. "I don't know how they ever get along without us. What do you think, Sarah?"

"Don't answer that, Sarah," Parson Abel said. "That's a trick question. You both look radiant this evening."

Both ladies blushed and the parson chuckled. "Haven't you heard, Sarah, the easiest way to a woman's heart is through a sincere compliment?"

"With these formalities out of the way, all we have left is to wait for Mr. Jones," Adeline announced.

A knock announced his arrival.

"I'll answer the door," Abel said. "This will give me an opportunity to let the man know he's stepping into a trap. He needs to know that this whole evening is a conspiracy. If

I was an attorney, I'd call this entrapment," Abel said, nearing the door.

"Jonathan! Don't you dare," Adeline said.

"Jonathan? Did you just call me Jonathan?" he asked.

Adeline nodded.

"Well, I'll be. You haven't called me Jonathan in years. This *is* serious, isn't it?"

Again she nodded but this time she choked back a laugh. "Very serious."

"Alright then, *Adeline,* I'll play along."

A second knock sounded.

"Answer it, will you?" Adeline said. "Don't leave the groom-to-be standing at the front door."

"Oh, what a tangled web we weave, when first we practice to deceive," he announced from the hallway.

"Let Shakespeare out and let Mr. Jones in," she called after him.

"Come in. Come in. Glad you could make it," Abel said. He led Jones down the hall and into the dining room. "We have a lovely evening planned. We will start with dinner. It's one of our family favorites. Beef stew and biscuits."

"Sounds wonderful compared to what the barracks is serving tonight—chipped beef with cream sauce over toasted bread. It's so bad we've started calling it shit on a shingle. Pardon me, ladies."

Sarah did her best to stifle a laugh. For some reason, the phrase 'shit on a shingle' struck her as funny. She turned her head away and bit her tongue to minimize her response.

"No offense taken," said Adeline. "I heard talk like this in the years before the parson became the parson."

"All right, let's be seated for dinner, shall we?" Parson Abel indicated the finely set table.

THE ABEL'S veranda was perfect for an after-dinner smoke. The two men could see the town from there. It was a cool, quiet evening except for the distant tinny piano at the Lodgepole Saloon. Stars flickered overhead.

"Wonderful to see the town grow," Parson Abel said. "So, what's next for you? Would you like a cigar?"

"Not sure what's next," said Jones. He took the cigar and accepted a light from Abel's match. "Depends on what Custus does. If he comes here, we're ready for him. The Colonel brought some men into town. Tomorrow, he'll spread them out across town and we'll wait to find out if what Stinson told us is true."

"Are you up for a little brandy? Got some in the house if you're interested."

Jones nodded, and Abel ducked back into the house. He was met by Adeline and Sarah.

"That's your cue," Adeline whispered to Sarah. "Head on out."

"Wish me luck," Sarah said. She wrapped a shawl around her shoulders to protect her from the evening chill and stepped outside.

"I still don't like what you two have planned." Abel said.

Adeline took him away from the front door and further into the house. "Sometimes Cupid needs a little help, that's all," Adeline replied.

"COOL EVENING, ISN'T IT?" Sarah said. She perched on the

porch swing. "The parson said he would be out in a bit with the brandy. Care to join me in the meantime?"

Adeline was right, Sarah thought as she set the swing in a gentle movement with her foot. *Sometimes Cupid needs a little help.*

"You know, I never thanked you for all the times you protected me," she said.

He sat next to her on the swing and looked into her eyes. In that instant they both realized what they'd missed on all those lonely nights.

They kissed the passionate kiss of new love.

CHAPTER SEVENTEEN

Across town a rifle butt smashed glass sending shards flying every which way. Custus' gloved hand reached through the broken glass to unlock the front door of Swede's Mercantile. He heard stirring upstairs.

"Careful," Custus whispered. "It sounds like we woke Swede. I hear noises upstairs, so keep it down, will ya? I've been told that Swede keeps a scattergun up there and I just don't feel like being blown to smithereens today."

Iggy and Custus entered the store. Stinson stayed outside. With a motion of his hand, Custus and Iggy split up with Custus walking to the right of Iggy.

The door to Swede's upstairs rooms opened with a loud creak. Custus could hear Swede's rapid breathing. *He's scared.* Custus stopped and motioned Iggy to do the same. "Shhhh," he said barely above a whisper.

After a few moments of silence, Custus gave the signal to start walking again. Glass crackled under their feet as they moved to the back of the store. Custus could just make out the outline of the stairway ahead. He motioned Iggy to walk toward it while he moved a bit to his right to catch Swede in a crossfire.

"By golly, dats far enough," Swede commanded. "I see you so don't take another step or dat'll be the last step you'll take." Swede pulled back the hammer on both barrels with an audible click and started down the stairs, shotgun pointed right at Iggy.

That was all Custus needed. From his vantage point, he could see Swede, but Swede could not see him. In the darkness Custus threw his Bowie Knife. It hit home with a distinctive thud, embedding the blade deep in Swede's chest with such force it spun Swede around.

Both barrels of Swede's scattergun roared to life. Buckshot blasted through the door at the top of the stairs. A woman screamed. Swede's bloody body fell lifeless on the stairs. Another thud of a falling body sounded from upstairs.

"Let's git what we came fer," Custus said. "Iggy, bring the wagon around back. Hurry."

THE SHOTGUN BLAST brought a halt to any thought of romance on the cool fall evening. Before the echoes died, Jones was on his feet and bounding down the steps and into the heart of town. He joined others racing toward where shots had been fired, arriving at Swede's with Sheriff Blanton and one of his deputies roused from their evening game of checkers.

Those who arrived first found busted glass in Swede's front door and the door ajar. Afraid of what they might discover inside, they gathered in the street, refusing to enter the building. They didn't want any part of gunplay. That was the sheriff's job.

Sheriff Blanton sent his deputy around back to cover the

alley. He lit a kerosene lantern, drew his revolver, and he and Jones stepped inside. They listened. Only silence answered. Then, from deep inside the building the two men heard a weak moan. Blanton opened the shutter on the lantern and held it high so the light snaked across the room to reveal the features of a man collapsed on the stairs.

"Send for Doc," Blanton yelled. "Swede's been hurt bad."

Glass cracked underfoot as Jones and Blanton inched through the dimly lit store. Swede laid draped across the stairs, a Bowie knife protruding from his chest. Swede wheezed each time he drew breath, and that wasn't very often.

"Ella," Swede said, his voice barely audible.

Blanton leaned closer. "What, Swede?"

"Ella."

Blanton's deputy burst in through the storeroom door. "The back door is wide open," he said. "There are wagon tracks in the alley. Whoever did this is gone."

"Well, don't just stand there. Round up a posse and get started after 'em. If they're in a wagon, they won't outrun you," Sheriff Blanton said. The deputy ran into the street to gather the men.

Townsfolk peppered the deputy for information.

"We can talk about that later," the deputy said. "I need a few men to go after the ones who hurt Swede. Get your horses and meet me back here in ten minutes. We're riding hard."

Doc arrived and the growing mob parted to let him through. Jones used the sheriff's lantern light to direct the doctor to where he knelt beside Swede on the stairs.

"Help me get Swede to my office. I can't work on him here," Doc said. Jones recruited a couple of men to carry Swede the two blocks to Doc's office.

"Careful with him. Easy does it," Doc commanded while pushing on-lookers out of his way. "Go home," Doc said. "You're in my way. Scram."

Swede tried to talk, but no one could make out his words. His voice was too weak.

"What did you say, Swede?" Doc asked as the men paused a moment for Doc to listen.

"El...la."

"Ella?" Doc asked. Swede nodded.

"Has anyone seen Swede's wife, Ella?" Doc yelled back at Jones. "He's asking for her. Someone go look for Ella. Swede's not gonna last much longer."

Parson Abel pushed through the crowd in time to accompany Doc and the four men carrying Swede down the street to Doc's office.

Potter rushed in to the merchantile. "What's going on?" he asked Jones.

"Swede's heading for Doc's office, dying from a knife wound. A posse is on the trail of the scum who broke into his place, and I'm headed to find Swede's wife, Ella."

Sheriff Blanton had already taken the lantern and climbed the stairs to the apartment above the store where Swede and Ella lived. Jones and Potter followed right behind him. Finding the door slightly ajar, the sheriff pushed, but the door resisted.

"Hold this lantern a little to the right. I think I see something," Blanton said handing the lantern to Potter. In the lantern's flickering light he could just make out the shape of a foot. After looking around, Blanton used the hallway window to crawl out onto the ledge and inched his way to the window of Swede's apartment. His gun butt smashed the glass and he crawled inside.

Jones and Potter heard the sound of something being

moved away from the door and opened it. Ella lay in a crumpled heap.

"She fell and wedged herself between the wall and the door," Blanton said.

"Is she. . .?" Potter asked.

"Dead? Yes," Blanton said and pointed to a spray of small holes in the wooden door. "Hit by buckshot. She must have been at the door when the knife struck Swede. Swede's shotgun was beside him on the stairs. Both barrels were fired. I'm thinking that when the knife hit Swede, it spun him around and he fired his scattergun. The buckshot penetrated the door killing Ella instantly." He entreated Jones. "Do you have any idea who or why someone would do this?"

"Don't know the why, but I think I know who," Jones said. "The knife sticking out of Swede's chest belongs to Custus. It's the same knife he threatened me with, and the same knife that cut up Parson Abel's face."

Blanton stood. "Got a posse after whoever it was. Let's get Ella outta here. Somebody's gonna have to tell Swede. And unfortunately, I am that somebody."

Jones removed the covers from Swede's bed and the three of them covered Ella in a cotton shroud and carried her down the stairs. At the bottom of the stairs, the sheriff drafted some townsmen to carry Ella to the undertaker's while he made his way to Doc's office.

"What are you gonna say to Swede?" Potter asked.

"Not sure. This is the part of my job I hate the most," he said.

Swede had willed himself to live while he waited for news of his beloved Ella. When the sheriff told him she was dead, he could no longer bear living. Swede exhaled, never to inhale again.

Doc noted the time and scrawled down Swede's cause of death in his ledger.

"You guys might want to step outside for a minute. I'm just gonna pull out this knife and patch the hole the best I can. Then you can take Swede down the street to join his wife. As the town's coroner and only quack, I'll need *Ella's* cause of death." Doc looked expectantly at Sheriff Blanton.

"Multiple buckshot wounds," Blanton said. "Swede shot her through the door when the knife plunged into his chest."

"Ah, what is this world coming to?" Doc sighed.

Parson Abel made the sign of the cross on Swede's forehead and commended him into the hands of Almighty God.

Custus and his men rode hard to outrun any posse, not an easy thing to do with a wagon load of ammunition stolen from Swede's storeroom. The wagon ride was not a pleasant one because of the rough terrain, but the full moon helped by lighting their way on a narrow path. The theft was part of the deal Custus had worked out with Black Arrow. Supplying cartridges for the Indians' Winchesters and he was back in Black Arrow's good graces. True to his word, Custus had the cartridges.

"Get out in front of the wagon and watch for Many Eagle Feathers," Custus yelled at Stinson, who rode his swayback horse beside the wagon. Stinson did what he was told.

Iggy rode shotgun in the wagon with Custus. The wooden seat he shared with Custus sat on springs, but the springs did little to cushion the ride. Iggy's thin body bore the worst of it.

"Where did ya say the braves'll meet us?" Iggy asked.

"Out here somewhere. They're supposed to meet us about three miles out. They'll close the back door in case somebody comes after us," Custus said. "Ya know I wish I hadn't killed Swede back there. I kinda liked him. He talked funny an' all, but I kinda liked him."

What Custus wanted more than anything else was to have his Bowie knife back. If Swede hadn't come down the stairs, this whole thing would have ended peacefully. *It's a shame. It was a good knife, and now its evidence in the hands of the law. Evidence that could get a man hanged.*

The men rode on in silence for another mile before finding Many Eagle Feathers and a handful of braves in the middle of the road. The braves split apart and allowed the wagon to drive between them.

"We did our job and Black Arrow will be pleased," Custus said to Many Eagle Feathers. "Now its yer turn to stop the posse in our rear."

SARAH CRIED AT THE NEWS. She could not understand why anyone would want to hurt Swede and Ella. When Madame Rogers and her 'ladies' had mocked her when she wanted to be something other than a prostitute, Swede had given her a job in his store. As part of Parson Abel's little congregation, Swede and Ella provided Sarah with clothes at their own expense. They lived their faith. In fact, the Parson often said Swede was the first person he baptized in Sidney. Swede had been baptized in Lodgepole Creek, like Sarah would be come spring. Now Sarah sat at the same table where, just two hours ago, she ate and fell in love.

Adeline met Jones at the front door. "She's at the table.

She hasn't moved nor quit crying since she heard about Swede."

Jones nodded and proceeded down the hall. He gently knocked on the door frame to announce his arrival. "Is it okay for me to come in?" he asked.

"Only if you tell me why?" she said.

He held his hat in his hands and walked to the table, spun the chair around, straddled it, and sat down. "I can't answer that question. That's probably one of those questions ya need to ask somebody else. The Parson, maybe. He's good at stuff like that. I'm a soldier and I don't know answers for questions like that." He took her hand.

She slid her chair closer and hugged him. "Can you hold me for a while? I feel so alone."

He held her close. She'd never felt this way before. She found herself in the warm embrace of a man who cared for her, who truly cared for her. She heard Parson Abel come through the front door.

"Where is Jones? I've got to talk to him for a minute," he said.

Adeline halted him in his tracks with a tender word. "You don't want to go in there right now, you might interrupt something."

"What would I be interrupting?" Abel asked. "Oh, I get it. Sometimes I'm a little slow on the uptake."

"Sometimes?" Adeline asked.

She was right, Sarah thought. The Parson would interrupt if he charged in at this instance. She didn't want any interruptions, not now, not ever, as long as she could be with Jones.

She lifted her head up and Jones responded to her. Soon her tear-stained lips met his. This was a kiss that sent sparks through her system like a Fourth of July fireworks display.

"When I'm with you, I don't feel alone anymore," Sarah said.

"I never want you to feel alone again. You've been alone a lot, haven't you?"

"Yes, I have," she said. "It's difficult to outrun loneliness."

They held each other tight.

CHAPTER EIGHTEEN

Jesse Jones had no answer for Sarah's tears or her persistent "Why did this have to happen?" She turned to Parson Abel.

"We may never know that answer this side of Heaven," Parson Abel told her. "There are just some things that God keeps to Himself."

Townsfolk crowded into Parson Abel's little church to say their goodbyes. A small wood-burning stove gave off enough heat for those sitting next to it, but offered no warmth at all for those sitting where a strong north wind drove the cold in through drafty windows. Sarah listened as Parson Abel spoke of Swede and Ella's tragic murders. He spoke of a kindly man defending his property against intruders, of a Christ-like sacrifice. "This message, however, is not all about Swede and Ella," he said. "It is all about Jesus Christ and His promise of eternal life."

The assemblage sloshed through snow and slush that coated trousers and hemlines with mud as they walked behind the two black hearses with black drapes carrying two bodies to their resting place. A temporary burial vault built in Boot Hill Cemetery relieved workmen of the impossible task of digging graves in the mud. Fresh graves would be dug to lay Swede Larsen and his wife Ella to rest later.

At the burial vault, Abel recited familiar words, "Ashes to ashes and dust to dust," and pall bearers carried Swede and Ella's caskets inside to await their burial and what the Parson called, "The great resurrection of the dead."

That evening, with a few people still gathered in Parson Abel's home, Sarah and Jones secreted themselves in the kitchen where Jones spoke his true intentions with the words,"Sarah, will you marry me?"

Sarah's tears of sorrow turned to tears of joy. She had waited years for someone to ask that question. Her reply came in an instant.

"Yes," Sarah said and held Jones tight.

SNOW FELL on Sidney and wrapped everything in a white blanket. With the snow came big changes for Jesse and Sarah. Jesses retired from the military and purchased Swede's Mercantile with the help of Parson Abel and the town's cantankerous old doctor. When January 1870 appeared on the calendar, Jones and Sarah started renovations to Swede's store.

Sarah had overheard Doc in conversation with the Parson.

"I still can't believe that Sarah talked Jones into a business venture and a home in the Sandhills," Doc said.

"Doc, you did the same thing, didn't you?" Parson Abel asked.

"Ya, but that was different." Doc said.

"Nope. It was the same. You settled here and put down roots."

"It was different. I was older and kept a lot of my freedoms. Jones'll be tied down like a calf ready fer branding."

"Is that really what you think of marriage—a guy's all tied up ready for branding?'"

"That's the way it is, and you know it."

"'Your wife might say that it's different."

"Don't think so," Doc said.

While for some, peace returned to Sidney. For Doc and Parson Abel, it was business as usual.

IN FEBRUARY, Jones watched Bill Cody take Ned Buntline, Hook Nose and Major Frank North, recently assigned to Fort Sidney as a guide and interpreter, and ride east to North Platte. The army sent them to track down Custus. Like a chameleon he and his men had blended into the Sandhills.

CUSTUS HAD NOT ATTEMPTED to camouflage himself. He migrated to North Platte for the winter. "Bigger town, more opportunities. 'Sides," he'd said, "there ain't much use in freezing to death when a warm bed and a warm body can prevent it."

He doled out some of the money Black Arrow paid him for the ammunition to Stinson and Iggy but kept the largest portion for himself.

One particular brothel attracted Custus' attention. He liked their turn of phrase in an advertisement hanging on the door *It's a business doing pleasure with you.*

With ammunition in hand, Black Arrow went on a murderous rampage in February 1870. He attacked sod houses along the tracks first. He was aided in his success by the decommissioning of Fort Kearney. No fort. No protection.

Custus never hid his contempt for Jones. He spoke of it in the local taverns while he recruited new men to ride with him. He paid them in advance out of his share. North Platte was a favorable place to recruit.

The only thing that bothered Custus was what to do about Bill Cody and Ned Buntline. "I'm not ready to deal with them yet," Custus told Stinson one evening at the poker table. "So keep yer fat butt out of sight."

Iggy laughed out loud, but Stinson didn't appreciate the reprimand.

Custus was content to wait it out. Black Arrow's raids gave him the perfect cover. "When the time is right," Custus said, "we'll ride to Sidney. We've got all the money we need and if we need more, the gold fields of Dakota Territory aren't that far away. When the time is right, we'll ride in and catch Jones off guard."

Stinson and Iggy followed Custus' lead like two marionettes who moved at his beck and call. They found themselves little dogs in a big fight but they were little dogs content with the scraps Custus tossed them.

SUNDAY MORNING DAWNED with an uncertain promise. In late March, the weather can change in an instant as Sarah knew very well. Near the banks of Lodgepole Creek, south of town, Parson Abel assembled his small congregation. Six members, including Sarah, welcomed their Baptism day.

"I want each of you to wade into the water," Abel said. "I'll say a few words and dip you backwards into the creek."

Dressed like the others in a white robe, Sarah Fitzpatrick waited her turn. Jones and Potter stood nearby.

"These robes symbolize the purity given to you by God's Word in these waters," Abel said.

Sarah wondered how this could be. She had no purity of her own. That she once worked for Madame Rogers attested to that. She recognized the Murphy twins, John and William. At fifteen, they already stood a head taller than Sarah. They also wore white robes. Were they pure? Isaac Watson and his wife Elizabeth joined the others on the banks of the Lodgepole, also robed in white. The sixth member of the baptismal party, Jeremiah Cotton, was not robed at all. At fifty-six, and a lifelong bachelor, he was by far the oldest stepping down into the waters this morning.

Adeline offered Jeremiah his white robe.

"I ain't a gonna wear no dress," he said in a voice loud enough for everyone in Cheyenne County to hear. Men laughed. The women didn't.

One by one, the participants came to the water, women first.

"Elizabeth Watson," Parson Abel called out.

Elizabeth slipped on the muddy bank. Elders stationed along the bank caught her and kept her upright. Parson Abel tilted her backward into the chilly water. As he did, Elizabeth grabbed her nose to pinch her nostrils shut.

"Elizabeth Watson, I baptize you in the name of the Father, and of the Son, and of the Holy Spirit. Amen," Parson Abel said.

Elizabeth gasped and sputtered for breath after Parson Abel lifted her out of the water. The Elders standing sentinel helped her climb up the creek bank again. Adeline furnished a towel to dry her off.

"Sarah Fitzpatrick," Doc said.

Sarah heard her name, but hesitated.

"It's alright, child," said Adeline. "This is your special day when God reaches down to take a hold of you, never to let you go again."

"You don't have to do this today, ya know? You can wait 'til you're more comfortable," Doc said.

"Doc," one elder of the congregation said. "You ain't helpin' things out. Instead of blabbin' why don't ya give her a hand?"

"No, sir," Doc said. "It would be my luck that I'd slip and the next thing you know, it would be me getting baptized. I ain't havin' my day ruined. If I want to get wet, I'll step outside next time it rains."

Doc's comment drew laughter, not unlike the laughter given Jeremiah Cotton's comment. And like Jeremiah's comment, the men thought it funny, the women did not.

Parson Abel's smile reassured Sarah enough to coax her into the water. "Close your eyes and hold your nose," he said. "Sarah Fitzpatrick, I baptize you in the Name of the Father, and of the Son, and of the Holy Spirit."

THE SIDNEY SOCIAL HALL was festooned for the occasion. Buntings and banners of bright colors welcomed those who entered the joyous celebration for the six newly baptized. Parson Abel used the festivities to invite many of those he seldom saw in church.

"Yer just luring them in," Doc complained, "with a Midwest favorite, a church potluck."

Several of the church ladies had spent the entire day before this affair in their kitchens. The Drapers brought fried chicken; the Newberry's furnished mashed potatoes and gravy. Home-made biscuits and rye bread with caraway seeds were the specialty of the Lodl's. And there were pies, too many to count, lining the wooden tables put up for the day.

Abel introduced the baptized, now in fresh, dry clothes. "By Baptism God's Kingdom has expanded by six, and hell has depopulated by the same number," Abel said.

RUMORS OF GOLD in the Black Hills drew speculators. Although their operations remained covert, their true intentions became obvious by the supplies they needed.

"The Union Pacific chugs into Sidney on a daily basis," Parson Abel said. "The trains off-load an odd mixture of businessmen, homesteaders, land speculators, fortune hunters, gamblers, and prostitutes. Sidney, Nebraska, now boasts of eighty saloons, many gaming halls, and an ever larger number of houses of ill repute. We are getting quite a reputation, but not one I am very proud of. Have you heard the names they call us? Magic City on the Plains, Hardest Hole, Sinful Sidney, Toughest Town on the Tracks, and Wickedest Town in the West. None of these are very flattering if you want a sustainable community."

PARSON ABEL'S church was filled on a Wednesday afternoon. The wedding of Jesse Jones and Sarah Fitzpatrick was a welcomed oasis, calm amid the frantic population growth Sidney had experienced since the first of the year.

Sarah followed the custom for women and wore a black dress that draped all the way to the top of her black laced boots.

Jesse Jones had borrowed a suit from Potter that was a size too small. He found it quite impossible to button the vest to the top, so it hung open. This was the first time he was without his gun in years. That morning he'd stowed his LeMat at Parson Abel's.

Parson Abel addressed the couple in front of him, and by their presence there, those seated in the pews. He talked about God's intent in marriage and how it was God who was bringing this couple together. After an exchange of vows he pronounced them 'man and wife.'

Sidney's Social Hall was the site of a reception, a wedding reception, and this time liquor flowed and inhibitions melted like ice on a summer's day. Off to one side, the wedded couple stood motionless while the town photographer took their picture.

The community band played music for the reception. The band wasn't impressive by any stretch of the imagination, with two ill-tuned fiddles, three trumpets, and the tinny piano from the Lodgepole Saloon, wheeled in from two doors down. The piano came as a package deal, a polite way of saying the bar's piano player, Billie, was thrown in with the rental of the piano.

"If anyone had aspirations of celebrity, Billie does," Doc said to Jones.

Billie was rail thin with a face that somehow made it difficult to pin down his age. Red garters kept his ruffled shirt sleeves away from his nimble fingers as they pounced upon the piano keys, every note played fortissimo. His face remained oddly cocked toward the crowd, and he paid no attention to the fiddlers. It was as though his piano lifted him out of the ordinary and into some sort of piano player's fantasy, much to the chagrin of those attempting to dance to a cacophony of beats.

The social hall door sprang open. Custus, Stinson, and Iggy strolled in. Billie, was the first to see them enter. He stopped playing. The trumpets and fiddlers kept on without him at first, but then one of the fiddlers looked up and his fiddle screeched to a halt. All eyes migrated to the door and the three men who stood there. They feared for what might come next.

"Pardon me, ladies," Custus said. He doffed his hat and looked around the room and spotted someone he knew; Billie the piano player.

"Billie, who told you that you could play the piano? You sound awful," Custus said.

Billie flashed back a toothless grin from behind the piano.

"It's this here, piana," Billie said. "Ain't been tuned since I got here, and that's nigh on to ten years now."

Custus drew his revolver. "Step aside, Billie, and I'll tune it fer ya."

Billie didn't move. He just sat on the chair that served as his piano stool and looked down the muzzle of Custus' six-shooter. Custus motioned for him to move out of the way. Iggy and Stinson chuckled.

"Are ya really gonna do what I think yer gonna do?" Iggy laughed out the words.

"I am," Custus' replied. "I'd be a moving if I was you, Billie, 'er this slug'll find you instead of yer piano."

Jones and Sarah stood near the makeshift bar. Instinct moved Jones' right hand down to his LeMat. He looked down. His eyes confirmed what his right hand had told him. No gun.

Custus cocked the hammer of his revolver. "I mean it, Billie. It's you or yer piano. What's it gonna be?"

Still Billie failed to move. He spread out his arms to cover his beloved piano. Custus' revolver spit lead and a thumb-sized hole of splintered wood appeared in the piano where the bullet thudded inches under Billie's outstretched left arm.

That's one. Jones thought to himself.

Billie let forth a scream that could have stripped the bark from a tree. "Look whatcha done to my piana!"

Custus' revolver belched fire three more times. Each round pelted the piano like a giant woodpecker. A splinter pierced Billie's left hand. He pulled out the slim piece of wood.

"I ain't never killed me a pie-an-a," Custus said, mocking Billie's way of talking. Stinson and Iggy laughed.

That's four shots. Jones thought.

In anger, Billie latched onto his half-full beer mug and readied it to throw at Custus.

"Custus, you cantankerous cuss," Billie screamed.

A fifth shot rang out. The glass mug shattered in Billie's hand, showering him with glass and warm beer.

Stinson and Iggy doubled over in laughter.

"You can't shoot any better than that, Custus," Iggy said.

"No. No, you can't," chortled Stinson. "That beer mug never had a chance." He laughed at his own joke.

"And now, Billie, how about a little dance for us?" Custus said, pointing the gun at Billie's feet.

Thinking the episode was over, Billie mopped his face and hands with a bar rag. That was a mistake. He wheeled about to look down the barrel of Custus' Colt.

"Well, looky here, boys," Custus said. He lowered his weapon so his companions could see. "If I ain't got just one slug left."

Dang. Potter thought. He also had been counting shots like Jones.

With the three intruders' attention diverted, the bartender crept closer to the shotgun he placed behind the makeshift bar. He raised it and the distinctive click of both hammers locking into place was heard above the laughter.

"Ah, Seth," Custus said. He gave the barkeep his full attention. "Why did ya have to do that? I was only funnin'. I ain't gonna kill nobody tonight. I came to give the wedding couple something to remember me by. C'mon now, Seth, put the scatter gun down."

Custus took no chances. He fired his last bullet through Seth's arm. The bone shattered, and the scattergun discharged nearly hitting some innocent party-goers.

Jones and Potter sprang upon Custus and his men like wildcats. Custus went for his new Bowie knife, but Jones knocked it free. He plunged his right hand into Custus' mid-section, causing him to double over in pain.

Potter pushed Stinson out of his way, and into the arms of Sheriff Blanton, who held him secure. Stinson struggled to free himself, but unlike Jones, the sheriff had not come to the dance without backup, his Navy revolver was tucked in his belt hidden behind his coat. The gun came out to meet Stinson's ribs. Stinson lifted his uninjured arm in the air.

Potter grasped Iggy by his shirtsleeve. He'd hoped for more substance in his grip, but Iggy moved too fast and anticipated Potter's move. Iggy took a poke at him and landed a blow that glanced off Potter's jawbone. From the sting it created, Potter was glad that Iggy hadn't landed the haymaker. Iggy was a powerful man for his size, wiry, scrappy, and slippery like an eel.

The crowd stampeded toward the only exit in the place.

The fighting men grunted and tumbled to the floor. Fists flew. Doc came to Seth's aid. He covered the wound with a bar rag to staunch the blood that spurted everywhere. All the while Billie screamed over and over, "My piana! My piana!" He felt each of the bullet holes Custus had shot in it.

At the gift table, Sarah stood crying. "Custus ruined by wedding day," she sobbed. Adeline tried her best to comfort her.

Custus attempted to rise, but Jones spun him around and, with a swift kick in the backside, booted him outside. Potter's punch did the same to Iggy. Somehow Stinson broke free, stumbled out the door after them.

Custus shouted, "I'll be back! When you least expect it, I'll be back!"

CHAPTER NINETEEN

In the fall of 1871 reports of Black Arrow's attacks continued, but none of these attacks came within a hundred miles of Sidney.

Along the banks of Lodgepole Creek, some six miles west of Sidney, Jones erected a cabin for his new bride. The long, straight boards he used for construction came from the splendid Lodgepole Pines along the creek itself. Jones allowed troopers to harvest the timber for additional buildings needed at Fort Sidney with the condition that a few men helped him erect his home. Nearby a newly constructed sawmill converted tree trunks into planks. Planks not used by Jones or the army were loaded on wagons and driven to Sidney, where old man Higgins sold them to build homes and businesses as Sidney grew and expanded.

Jones liked this arrangement. It meant he had troops nearby to protect Sarah against Custus and his promised return.

The house Jones built did not look like much from the

outside. The design was simple and Jesse often commented that it lacked the elegance found in Abels' home.

"It's sufficient," Sarah answered him. And when asked by townsfolk to describe the interior décor of the place she would say 'Newly married.'"

The front door opened to the south to protect the house from the prairie winds that would blow snow against the north side. In addition Jones left several pines uncut to form a windbreak there, putting only one window on that side of the house to allow some sunshine into their bedroom.

When one entered the place, they entered the kitchen. In this area, Jones placed a wooden table and four pine chairs made by hand, a cooking stove, and a small pantry for storing everyday food items.

There were rooms on the north side of the cabin, the larger of the two had a window, while the second was set aside as a nursery 'when the time comes,' as Sarah put it.

"We must have a garden," Sarah had insisted. "I remember my mother's love of the soil. It's one of my most cherished memories of home before the war, holding the warm earth in my hands."

With his bare hands, Jones tilled the ground to scratch in the garden Sarah wanted.

Sarah loved watching her husband work. She delighted in it. His sinewy body took on a bronze tint when he toiled shirtless in the August sun. At day's end, his manly aroma comforted her when she readied for sleep. Some nights she'd trace her index finger in a lazy line down Jones' chest while they lay together wearing nothing but their smiles.

The couple took Adam Potter on as partner in their mercantile business. Potter oversaw the daily operations of the store. In Swede's honor, they kept his name over the place. Potter made his home in the apartment Swede and his wife once occupied.

Sidney grew and with that growth there were more 'incidents'. People were shot, there were robberies, bar fights, domestic disputes, all associated with that growth. There were too many incidents each day for Sheriff Blanton to manage. So the town hired additional deputies; Jones and Potter.

Still there remained no signs of Custus' promised return and his threats were nearly forgotten.

LIKE A MAD DOG once bested in a fight, Custus licked his wounds and growled that he'd made a mistake at Jones' wedding reception. He'd arrived without sufficient back-up. He knew it, and it hurt his pride to remember that night when, against his better judgment, he took only Stinson and Iggy with him to the wedding reception. He wouldn't make that mistake again.

He had gone in half-cocked. His reputation had been kicked in the posterior, as he had, and he didn't like it. Yet, here he was alone in the Nebraska Sandhills with only Iggy and Stinson to help him. "I won't make that mistake again. I had back-up but I left men behind in North Platte thinking that I could handle Jones myself," he said under his breath.

Custus tossed another log on the campfire and pondered how close they were to Sidney. From what he could gather they were only four miles east of town, as the crow flies.

"You two were worthless. Worse than useless. Why do I let you two ride with me?"

"We don't know," Stinson said, "but thought it was 'cuz ya liked us."

"Ya," Iggy said.

"Well, right now I'd as soon gut ya as look at ya," Custus said.

"Yer kidding, right?" Stinson asked.

Custus made sure that his expression told Stinson not to press the issue or he'd regret it. He glared at the pair for what seemed an eternity to Iggy and Stinson and then erupted in laughter. This time neither man knew whether or not to join him. They looked at each other, with no idea of what to expect—more laughter, or perhaps a bullet.

"Ha! Ha! You guys are alright, ya know that? C'mon, don't look so glum. I got me an idea." Custus motioned his minions to sit. "We're gonna ride back to North Platte tomorrow morning."

"What for?" Stinson asked. He tucked his chambray shirt behind his belt for the hundredth time today. He realized the sassy tone of his question and cowered in anticipation of Custus' reprisal. But it did not come.

"Well, Stinson, if ya wanna know, yer gonna have to ride along and see. I got somethin' a brewin' that'll be hotter than this cow manure you call coffee." Custus cast the last of his coffee to the wind.

A succession of wispy clouds swept across the moon. Stinson and Iggy needed no blankets tonight. It was too hot. They laid their heads against their saddles. Coyotes howled.

"I hate that sound," Stinson said.

"I don't," Custus responded. "Especially the howl coyotes make when they have somethin' cornered, 'cuz I'm looking forward to cornering something."

Custus stayed awake to clean his revolver and hone a new Bowie knife. The sound of blade gliding over the whetstone made a *sssshhhht* sound while it slid. Time after time, he traced the pattern. Once Custus stopped to thumb the blade to test its edge and winced when he cut himself. He smiled and squeezed the wound so more blood oozed out. Custus set his knife in his lap, stuck his bleeding thumb in his mouth and sucked and then squeezed his thumb again so he could watch the blood drop grow bigger. This time he wiped his thumb on his filthy pants.

The look on Custus' face was one of satanic, sadistic, delight. He looked at his sleeping men and laughed to himself and then resumed honing his blade. Custus muttered under his breath words that would have given every living creature goose bumps.

"Death is coming," he muttered in time with the sssshh-hhht of his blade and the coyotes' howls. "Death is coming. It won't be long before death rides to Lodgepole Creek."

Swede's Mercantile had a different look. With Sarah, Jones, and Potter in charge it became a little less cluttered, although not entirely so. The three new owners compart-mentalized, giving special attention to gender and age of their customers instead of randomly placing merchandise throughout the store. Grocery items were moved nearest the service counter, with guns and ammo stored behind the counter in glass cases.

"Did we get everything in we ordered?" Sarah asked.

Jones stopped in the doorway to the storeroom door. "Looks like we got shorted a barrel of flour."

"That's the second time in the last few months," Potter noted. "Don't know what's wrong in Omaha, but it looks like they lack basic math skills."

"So, did they bill us for it this time?" Sarah asked, never

turning from the pile of calico fabric on the counter she was folding for Mrs. Graham.

Mrs. Graham was a woman of forty who looked much older. She had three ornery children in tow. An occasional slap of their hands helped her maintain discipline.

Jones thumbed through the invoices. "Nope. At least this time we won't have to telegraph them and ask for a refund."

"I have in mind to sew Millie here a new dress," Mrs. Graham said. "She's gettin' old enough to have a dress of her own instead of hand-me-downs from her cousins in North Platte."

"Do you mean it, Mama, a new dress?" Millie asked. It was only after Mrs. Graham removed the child's straw hat that Sarah could distinguish the girl from her two younger brothers. Her long auburn hair tumbled in ringlets around her face.

"You heard me, child," Mrs. Graham added. "Lemme have about six yards of that gingham ya got there."

Sarah unpinned the bolt of fabric and stretched it between her shoulder and the end of her fingers to measure out a yard at a time. With scissors in hand, she cut the fabric, pinned it and gave it to Mrs. Graham.

"Do you need thread to match?"

"Yes, please," Mrs. Graham said, following Sarah to the notions. Millie traipsed after her; however her disinterested brothers made their way to the stick candy in eager anticipation of what usually followed.

"Help yerselves, boys," Jones said. They did.

"Snaps or buttons?" Sarah asked.

"Snaps," Mrs. Graham answered. "Never got the hang of sewin' button holes, my fingers seem too big for that."

"I can teach you how to sew button holes when you are

ready to try them," Sarah said. "What else do you need, Mrs. Graham?"

"Suppose I ought to get Pa some coffee and I'm gonna need sugar if I'm gonna bake a pie. Make it five pounds of each."

"Don't confuse the two or you'd never forgive yerself," Sarah said with a laugh.

"I would, but Pa wouldn't," Mrs. Graham said in all seriousness.

"That'll be fifty cents for the sugar, sixty cents for the coffee and another sixty cents for six yards of gingham. That's a dollar-seventy total. No charge for the snaps."

"How much fer four apples?" she asked.

"They're two for a nickel, so ten cents will cover it," Sarah said.

"Then I'd better take a couple home for Pa to chew on. I'm givin' ya two dollars and takin' all six of yer apples."

Mrs. Graham slapped two silver dollars on the counter. Sarah neatly wrapped the purchases in brown paper torn off the spool behind the counter and tied the two packages securely with string. The Graham children pounced on the apples like sweets. They bit through peel, flesh, seeds and core, and left only a bit of apple juice on their fingers, which they promptly licked off.

Mrs. Graham sauntered to the front door followed by her three children, who traipsed along like goslings behind a mother goose. The last in line closed the door.

A moment later, the door opened and Mrs. Graham poked her head in. "Thanks for the snaps," she said and was gone.

Potter chuckled aloud. "Think I'll head over to the telegraph office to notify the warehouse in Omaha that they shorted us on the flour again. It's one of those things if I don't do now, I won't remember to do it," Potter said.

Sarah watched Jones move about the store. His lethargy was obvious. Call it women's intuition, she knew her man. She knew he was unsettled long before he ever did.

She moved toward him and broke the silence with her words. "Are you alright?"

"Why wouldn't I be?"

"Oh, I don't know, but you've been going about the store today like a caged animal. Kinda reminds me of a fenced in bronc, not quite willing to jump the fence, but thinkin' about it." She paused and then asked, "Is it the store or is it me?"

Jesse thought before he answered. "Neither," he hesitated again. "It's me. I'm not sure what it is. There's this itchin' inside of me and I can't scratch it. You're gonna think that I don't love you and that's not it at all."

He took hold of her hands and looked into her blue eyes, which reflected his image back to him. "I love you," he said before they kissed.

"Do you want to catch up with Bill Cody?" she asked. "Is that it?"

"I was thinkin' we need the money Custus' reward would supply. I could support you better bein' on the trail than I can standin' behind a counter."

"I'm glad yer thinkin' ahead, 'cuz there's gonna be another one to consider," Sarah added.

"You're pregnant?"

"Doc confirmed what I already suspected."

"Maybe this isn't the time."

"Maybe it's the perfect time."

She drew him close and kissed him.

CHAPTER TWENTY

Dawn arrived to light the road in front of the Jones cabin to reveal Adam Potter. He had ridden through the early morning. The breeze whistled through the trees along the banks of Lodgepole Creek. With no woman to tie him down, Potter wriggled free from his responsibilities at Swede's to ride with Jones in his quest to bring in Custus Leverette.

Sarah had promised Jesse that she would stay with Parson Abel and Adeline until his return. In Potter's absence Doc had moved his medical practice into Potter's apartment above Swede's. With these arrangements in place Jesse was comfortable leaving Sarah behind.

Yesterday Jesse had helped pack what meager belongings he and Sarah possessed into the wagon and covered them with a tarp against the elements. Before their lone rooster crowed this morning, he had hitched a team of mules to the wagon and pulled it around front. Sarah would complete what little packing remained, finish loading the wagon, and follow Jones and Potter into town.

All that was left was to say, "Goodbye."

Sarah held Jesse tight.

"When we get to North Platte, I'll telegraph our arrival," Jones said, reluctant to free himself from her embrace.

"Everything will be fine," Sarah said. "Adeline will open the store. I've got a couple things to pack and I'll be on my way. Don't worry, things will be fine." They kissed.

Jones put his left foot in the stirrup and swung his right leg over the saddle. It felt good to him to see the world from atop his horse instead of the wooden seat of a buckboard.

"There's a warm day a coming, no doubt about it, so don't stay out in the sun too long today," Jesse said. One more look into Sarah's eyes brought peacefulness, a peacefulness he could not describe. He returned her smile. He wanted to stay, but the five hundred dollar reward for Custus, dead or alive, lured him away.

Jones had shown Sarah the wanted poster with the sketch of Custus on it. He remembered the conversation that went with it.

"They're offerin' a reward for Custus," he said, laying the poster on the table.

"There ain't much to talk about, is there?"

"Five hundred dollars is a lot of money."

"You don't have to convince me. We knew there'd come a time like this. I already gave you permission, remember? You need to be in the saddle. Don't worry. I'm not goin' anywhere, Jesse Jones. I'll wait in town fer ya to come back to me. We've got a family comin' and it'll take the two of us to handle it. I don't want you lookin' over your shoulder the rest of our lives. I will be alright. Put Custus in jail and we won't have to worry anymore."

"I just hope he gives me an opportunity to shoot first

and ask questions later, then we really won't have to keep looking over our shoulders wondering where he is."

Jones pulled the reins taunt. His horse knew what to do and trotted down the road to town. Potter followed behind, but it wasn't long before they rode side-by-side. About a quarter mile down the path, Jones turned, pulled up his horse, removed his hat, and gave Sarah a long goodbye salute. He watched until she hiked up her dress and went inside.

THAT WAS what Custus hoped would happen. Neither Jesse nor Sarah suspected any danger.

Custus made his way back to camp, where six members of his gang awaited his next move. His trip to North Platte had added four desperados eager for easy money—Hoover, Lynch, Estes, and Cooper. These men were fresh off the cattle trail. By their own estimates, to ride with Custus was a lot easier than driving cattle, if for no other reason than they'd likely have a roof over their heads when it rained. Last night had been an exception.

"Mount up, we're goin' calling," Custus said. "I wasn't invited to the wedding, and got kicked out of the reception, but that don't mean that I can't deliver a present. I waited a long time to kiss the bride and I ain't gonna miss it."

The response was instantaneous. His men mounted and splashed across Lodgepole Creek.

SARAH HEARD FOOTSTEPS OUTSIDE. "What did you forget?" she asked.

Custus burst in. "I forgot to give you a kiss on yer weddin' day and I came collectin'." Custus pushed his way into the house while Stinson and Iggy blocked the doorway. The rest of the gang spread out across the yard to watch in case Jones and Potter returned.

"My husband will be back at any time," Sarah said.

"Yer bluffing. I saw him ride off with that Potter fella. They were headin' toward town, and my guess is they'll keep riding. That's a bad thing for you, but a good thing fer me."

He grabbed Sarah and drew her toward him. His breath was hot on her neck. "We ain't had any time together lately. I thought we could make like old times. What do ya say?"

"I can't. I'm pregnant!"

"That don't mean nothin' to me. I can make this private if ya want." He pointed toward the bedroom. "We can go in there and close the door, if ya don't want no one watchin'. But just lettin' ya know, it don't matter to me."

Twisting against his tight grip, Sarah freed herself. With all her might she raked his face with her fingernails. A defiant smile crossed her lips.

Custus' left hand went to his cheek and returned bloody. "I like it when you play rough," he chuckled. "This is just like old times."

He dragged her into the bedroom and kicked the door closed. "Two can play yer little game of rough-n-tumble." He tossed Sarah onto the bed like a sack of flour. The sun squeezed through the narrow cracks in the red gingham curtains, the light reflecting off the blade of Custus' Bowie knife. "This here says I win!" he yelled. "Don't fight me or I cut ya. Do ya hear me? So help me, I'll cut ya."

Sarah heard the insane laughter of Custus' men. Instead of helping her, they reveled in her terror. Sarah resisted, but her efforts were in vain against a man of Custus' stature. He was as unthinking and brutal as a buffalo during rut.

He took her.

She pounded his face in anger, but found it of little use. In pain, she lost consciousness under his weight.

When she came to, Custus stood in the doorway. Sarah struggled to stand in defiance.

"Alright, let's mount up," he said to his men. "We're goin' after Jones and Hades is riding with us."

Sarah grabbed the only thing she could reach and threw it. A book smacked the back of Custus' head. Now the Bible Parson Abel and Adeline had given her lay in a heap on the floor amid ripped pages. She screamed. "You leave my husband alone!"

"Do you hear that, boys?" Custus said. "She ain't near done fighting, is she?"

He swung around.

Fire sparked from her eyes and she dove into Custus with clenched fists. He stood there unmoved while she flailed at his chest and shoulders.

"Ha. Ha. Ha," he laughed when at last she stood exhausted before him. She spit in his face and the spittle hung there like a wet souvenir. In Custus' mind, the spittle was a testament to his fortitude and manhood. Stinson and Iggy left their posts to help Custus.

He waved them off.

"Shoot boys," he said, "I've had feistier women than this. She ain't nothin'. Go on; get back to your posts. Ol' Custus can take care of hisself."

He shoved Sarah with all his might.

She stumbled and fell backwards into the bedroom, hitting the floor like a cast-off rag-doll. She laid on the floor wheezing to catch her breath.

"Ya know," Custus said, "I thought we had this here discussion afore. You ain't a goin' to interfere in my business. And I got business with yer old man. I'm a goin' to keep my appointment come heck or high water."

He moved to tower over her.

Sarah tried to scoot out of his reach, but in two quick steps Custus was bent over her again.

"Don't do this. Please don't hurt me anymore," Sarah pleaded for her life.

Custus' sinister voice answered, the words running together and impossible to understand. Sarah knew the intent, and that was enough.

Sarah's screams ended and all was still within the little cabin on Lodgepole Creek.

"Death has come," Custus said softly, making his way to the front door. "Death has come."

No one moved. No one dared. Even the birds were silent.

The doorknob turned. Custus emerged. Spittle clung to his face like a badge of honor and three blood tracks from Sarah's fingernails evidenced the struggle that had taken place. He felt the sting of these wounds when his senses broke through and his anger abated. Custus grabbed a rag from his jeans and wiped spit and blood from his face before wadding the rag and stuffing it back in his jeans.

"Doggone it," Custus muttered. "I wish she hadn't done that. I hadn't planned to kill her. Just rough her up a bit. It's her man I'm after."

He walked to his horse and mounted. "Alright, boys, we still got work to do. Jones is lookin' fer us, but he ain't got no idea that we're lookin' fer him. We know where he is but he don't know where we are and that puts the odds in our favor. So mount up."

COPPER PUSHED his way past Stinson and entered the bloody bedroom. He knelt beside a heap that once was a living human being. To his amazement, it still was. Sarah moaned at his touch. She peered at him through swollen eyes. "Bible," she mouthed.

Cooper bent his ear to her lips to hear. "What did you say, ma'am?"

"Bible. I want my Bible."

Cooper looked about the room. He saw ripped pages everywhere. In the melee, Sarah's Bible had been torn apart. After she'd smashed Custus' head with it, she had held the Bible tightly while Custus' beat her. Custus had pried it from her hands and thrown it against a wall scattering the pages everywhere about the room.

The hardened hands of Cooper, a hired gunman, closed on the remnants of Sarah's Bible and placed it in her dying hands.

She clutched it to her breast and mouthed the words, "Thank you."

"Cooper, get yer butt out here!" Custus yelled.

Cooper did what he was told.

CHAPTER TWENTY-ONE

It was six-thirty a.m. when Jones and Potter rode into town to find activities well underway for a Saturday morning.

"Saturday means business," Swede had often said, and if the number of wagons and people milling about were any indication this was going to be a good day. Jones also recalled Swede saying that most frontier families came into town just once a week, and some only once a month, so when those two occasions, the once-a-weekers and the once-a-monthers, happened on the same Saturday, you could count on a very good retail day.

"This must be one of those Saturdays that Swede talked about before he died," Jones said to Potter. "There will be long lines at the barbershops, Higgins Lumber, and at Swede's."

"And at the bars," Potter added. "We're going to miss out on all the fun when those who ran up a tab in the store come in to settle their accounts. No one wants to go into the weekend with unpaid bills."

"Cowboys will come to town with money burning a hole in their pockets after eating dust all week on the ranches. And the womenfolk will gather at places like Swede's to renew conversations, buy supplies, or gawk at the latest creations from back east, or shake their heads in disgust when their men folk leave them behind to wash down the trail dust," Jones said pulling up his horse in front of Swede's.

As they hitched their horses, Adeline arrived, removed a key from her purse, and found the keyhole in the front door with it.

Jones noted that the latch was stiff and made a mental note to ask Parson Abel to take the oil can to it. After several tries, the lock yielded access through the front door of Swede's.

Adeline turned the sign on the door from CLOSED to OPEN with the flick of her wrist and then waved to Parson Abel and Doc who were eating breakfast while watching her arrival through the café window across the street.

It was Parson's new routine to breakfast with Doc on Saturday mornings, and then help Adeline in the store for an hour or two before he returned home to finish his Sunday sermon.

Doc usually went to his office after breakfast to make ready for the day. When a busy community migrated to town on Saturday, as they would today, there would be broken bones to set, bullets to dig out, stab wounds to stitch, social diseases to treat and babies to deliver. Doc said when it came to practicing medicine he was a jack of all trades and a master of none.

"Mornin,' Adeline," Jones said. "We stopped in for supplies before we start for North Platte. We're heading over to the telegraph office to let Bill Cody know we're on the way."

"Thought I'd see you before you left town," Adeline answered. "How's Sarah this morning?"

"She'll be along in a bit," he answered. "Got a touch of morning sickness. Other than that, she's fine."

"Had that when I carried my young ones, too. But the worst part of my pregnancies was the fear that I could die during childbirth. Don't think I ever really got past that fear." She pondered a moment. "That was a long time ago and my children have children of their own. What do you need today?" Adeline asked.

JESSE JONES SENT Buffalo Bill a telegraph. Ned Buntline recorded this entry in his journal.

Buffalo Bill read the telegram dated September 10, 1871 and smiled. It read: Making our way east. Thought we might pick up Custus' trail from our end. J. Jones

"Well, that's good news," Cody said at last. "Jones and Potter are on their way. Didn't take him long to realize that five hundred dollars is a lot of money. I'd like to have been a mouse to hear that conversation. I thought he was happy as a storekeeper."

"Runnin' a business like that robs a man of his manhood," added Frank North, a rail-thin man with a broad mustache. He and Cody were fast friends and often spoke about two major business ventures together, a scout rest ranch and a Wild West show.

"That show will bring the American West to the world," North had promised.

"It's a grand idea," Cody said. "But I doubt if either has any great potential."

"This is an opportunity to sell more dime novels with you available for public appearances," North added.

"I'll think on it," said Cody. "Now, let's get down to business. If there's one thing I like about this Jones fella, it's his sense of duty; regardless of circumstances. How many guys would leave their young wife and a new business to ride to put an end to all the unrest? Few, I'll tell you. There's a sense of duty in Jones matched by only a handful of others. Time to put out our feelers and see if we can get a lead on where Custus is."

"I've heard some talk about a man who seems to match Custus' description here in North Platte," North interjected.

"Well, then, this will be easy," Cody said. "Find Custus and wait 'til Jones and Potter get here and we'll have enough men to bring him to justice."

Cody sent North on a mission to track down Custus without drawing attention to himself.

Frank North mingled with the ruffians at the local whiskey bars, each filled to the brim with the Saturday trade. He first heard Custus' name mentioned in the Red Dog Tavern. Five men seated around a table played Five-Card Stud. North grabbed his whisky and wandered in their direction. One man at the table boasted that he'd like to win back some of the money Custus won from him, even if it meant that he had to kill him.

A second man chided him. "There is no way you'll win yer money back," he said. "Custus' has more lives than an ol' tom cat. 'Sides he's out a town for a couple days. I overheard him say he was going to Sidney to take care of unfinished business."

That was all North needed, and he relayed it to Cody.

"Head back down to the telegraph office, Frank, and let Jones know Custus is headed his way." Cody said.

"I hope we aren't too late."

DOC AND PARSON ABEL watched through the front door of Swede's as Custus and his men road in from the west, right down the main street of Sidney. The two men had an uneasy feeling about the situation and cut their breakfast short.

When an hour had passed and still Sarah had not reported to work, their concern became panic. Any moment the Abel's expected the bell over the front door of Swede's to mark Sarah's arrival. Her arrival never came and the wall clock chimed nine times. Parson Abel gave a hopeless stare at his pocket watch before he put it away in his vest pocket.

"Something's not right. Sarah's never been late before."

"Get Doc and a couple others and ride on out to Sarah's place," Adeline said. Before she could complete the sentence, Abel was already at the door of Doc's upstairs office.

The two men were of like mind. "I'll get a buckboard hitched and be right with ya!" Doc said.

Sheriff Blanton's office was two doors down. Parson Abel opened the door and stuck his head in. "Think we got trouble, Wade. Sarah's late and Doc and I saw Custus pass through town a while ago."

Wade put a deputy in charge, grabbed a rifle and a box of shells from the gun rack. "So much fer a quiet Saturday," Sheriff Blanton said.

Doc rounded the corner aboard his buckboard.

Sergeant Major Kelly watched the crowd gather in front of the Sheriff's office through the barber's window. Whatever was going on, he was not about to miss it. "I'd appreciate it if you'd finish this later," he said, squirming in the barber chair. "Times 'a wastin." He raced out the door still wiping the shaving cream from his face.

"That'll be two-bits," the barber shouted after him.

"Put it on my tab," Kelly shouted back. He dropped the barber's cloth and the towel on the sidewalk, neared the others and made his presence known. "What's got everyone of ya so riled up that ya be a takin' me away from my Saturday shave?"

Abel drew a deep breath. "Sarah hasn't come into work yet and we saw Custus ride by. Adeline says there's trouble and I've learned to trust womans' intuition. We're about to ride over to the Jones' place."

"Not without me, ya ain't," Kelly added as he mounted his horse and joined Sheriff Blanton riding single file behind Doc and Parson Abel aboard Doc's buckboard.

OUTSIDE THE JONES' cabin, things appeared normal except for the silence; deadly silence. Doc drew his buckboard near the front door and tied it off. Kelly and the Sheriff followed suit.

"Somethin's not right," Kelly said and pointed to the ground. "Just look at all these tracks. I'd say there were several riders in a small area in front of the house. 'Sides that, it's way too quiet."

"Sarah. Sarah, are you alright?" Abel shouted. There was no answer. He knocked on the front door. No answer.

"Look around back, will ya, Sergeant Major?" Parson Abel said. "See what you can find."

Kelly ran for the back of the cabin. He wiped the prairie

dust off the north window and squinted to see inside. There in a heap he saw Sarah.

"She's on the floor in the bedroom. There's no movement."

Sheriff Blanton barged through the door, and Doc and Parson Abel charged into the bedroom, nearly stumbling over Sarah's body.

"I was afraid this would happen," Abel pronounced.

Doc bent over Sarah. "We're too late," he said. "She's gone."

Sarah lay face down on the floor. Doc rolled her over. She clutched an object to her breast. It was her beloved Bible; torn, shredded and without its cover.

"Look at this, will you?" Abel knelt at her side to peer at the bloodied pages. "With her dying breath and with her own precious blood, Sarah circled these words 'Vengeance is mine, I will repay,' says the Lord.'"

"I'll be darned," Doc said.

Abel shot Doc a glare.

"Sorry, it just came out. I didn't mean any disrespect."

"She must have hoped Jones would find her. She knows how this will eat at him."

"It sure will," Doc said.

"'Vengeance is mine,' says the Lord,'" Parson Abel whispered. He stood with the Bible in his hands.

"Those are hard words to live by, I'm a thinkin," Sergeant Major Kelly said.

"Even harder when someone takes the life of your young wife and unborn baby. This is gonna tear Jones apart and drive him mad," Doc said.

"It will, if he lets it," Abel added. "I pray he won't."

"Let's lay Sarah in my buckboard and take her back into town," Doc said. "No one needs to see her like this."

The four men placed Sarah's body into the buckboard and covered her with Jones' Indian blanket. Doc carefully drove his horses slower than usual. Sheriff Blanton and Sergeant Major Kelly rode single file behind.

It was a long, solemn, dusty ride along the banks of Lodgepole Creek and into Sidney.

CHAPTER TWENTY-TWO

Adeline waited anxiously inside Swede's Mercantile. Her eyes wet with tears. It was hard to concentrate on business from worry over Sarah and her unborn baby. Under her breath she prayed over and over for the well-being of both, but with customers packing the place, it was hard for her to break free and watch from the front window as often as she wanted for the men's return.

Just when the anguish was about to overtake her and her worries grew beyond containment, a buckboard turned onto the street two blocks away. Ignoring the questions of impatient customers, Adeline opened the front door to get a better look. Everything else faded to the background. At this moment all that mattered to her came rumbling down the street.

Adeline knew there was trouble. Even from a distance she saw that her husband never looked up, staring at an object in his lap. *That's not a good sign. Something's happened. Something terrible has happened*, she thought.

Ignoring good manners, she hiked up her skirt and darted up the street, stopping horse and buckboard a half block short of Swede's. Something was covered by an Indian blanket in the back and she started for it.

"Adeline! No!" Parson Abel cried. He met her before she could pull back the blanket and turned her from the wagon. "Adeline," he spoke softly, yet somehow his voice penetrated her psyche. "Don't sweetheart. She's gone and you don't want to see her now."

He handed her the torn and shattered Bible. She took it, buried her head against her husband's chest and cried.

"We don't know why these things happen," Abel continued, "but we do know that God has promised never to leave us nor forsake us."

"I know," she stammered through her tears. "But why does it have to hurt so much?"

"Loving as we are called to love does hurt." Abel sheltered Adeline in his arms.

In the street in front of Swede's a crowd gathered.

"Ain't you Jesse Jones?" The words stopped Jones in his tracks and he turned toward the voice which belonged to the local telegraph operator in North Platte.

"I am."

"Got a telegraph fer ya. Been holding it a day or two."

Jones unfolded the telegram and read the contents:

Sarah murdered. Suspect Custus.
Urge restraint. Abel

The weight of the information dropped Jones to his

knees, pelting him like a summer's hailstorm sent directly from Hades. Shock. Disbelief. Hatred. Loathing. Mourning. Panic. Helplessness. Hopelessness. Nothingness.

"I should have killed him when I had a chance," he muttered.

"Who?" Potter asked. "What's going on?"

Jones handed the telegram to Potter to read.

"Now he's taken everything from me. My wife. My baby. My reason for living." Jesse's voice grew hard. "I'll kill him. I swear to God that I will. I'll kill him for the dog he is!"

When he stood Potter held him fast.

"You can't go flying off half-cocked," Potter said. "Custus could be anywhere. What if he's riding this way with a plan to ambush us? We'd be riding into a trap."

Jones tried to free himself from Potter's grasp but could not."Let me go. Let me go." Jones shouted in desperation.

"Not until we think this through. I don't want to lose a friend."

"Is everything alright?" a stranger asked.

Jones turned his head and lit into the concerned man. "No, things are not alright."

The stranger walked away.

Potter wondered aloud about the fastest way back to Sidney. "What if we rode the train back to Sidney? At least then we'd have a train car between us if they have an ambush planned. And if they don't, we can get behind Custus. We can get word to Cody to bring our horses along with him. What do ya think?"

Jones' voice was low and rumbled with anger. "I think I want to kill him right now."

"I know you do. I want to give you that chance, but you won't get that chance if you do something stupid."

Those words hit home and Jones nodded. "You're right," he said.

"I'm gonna let you go now," said Potter.

Jones nodded. Potter turned Jones loose.

"We'll ride the train. That's the fastest." Jones drew his LeMat and counted the cartridges. "One of these has Custus' name on it. It'll just take one."

SIX HOURS LATER, the locomotive steamed into Sidney, covering the distance between the two cities at an average speed of twenty miles per hour, trading hours for days. If Custus was indeed at Jones' rear only hours ago, their roles had been reversed now.

Jones and Potter carried their saddles and waited for their horses shipped in the livestock car.

No one met them. The evening sun already had poked its head between the cracks of the western hills, bringing all the promises of a beautiful evening. An evening not unlike the evening when he had proposed to Sarah.

They mounted.

"I like the familiar. Like my horse," Jones said.

"It's like sleeping in your own bed," Potter said.

From the fort, a lone trumpeter sounded mess call.

A short ride later Jones and Potter stood on the veranda in front of the Abel's. They knocked and waited until Parson Abel pushed aside the curtains. When he saw Potter and Jones standing there, he unbolted the lock and let them in.

"Where's Custus?" Jones began.

"Haven't seen him lately," Abel said. "We think he's gunning for you. He was last seen heading east with a bunch of men. It was the day we discovered Sarah."

"Can I fix you two anything?" Adeline asked as she hugged Jones.

"Just coffee for me, but I'll betcha Potter will eat something," Jesse said.

Potter nodded. Adeline led the way toward the kitchen, while Abel ducked into his study to retrieve Sarah's tattered Bible.

In the kitchen, Adeline stood in front of a wood-burning stove with hot pad in one hand and a large fork in the other, turning bacon, which sizzled and popped in the cast-iron skillet. She paused long enough to give Jones another hug and whisper, "I'm so sorry," in his ear.

The men sat around the kitchen table while Abel poured coffee. "I can tell by your voice that you're going after Custus the minute Sarah's funeral is finished tomorrow," Abel said. "Before you do, I want you to look at what Sarah circled in blood in her Bible as she died."

Parson Abel shuffled through the pages and laid the Bible open before Jones, reading the words aloud. "'Vengeance is mine,' says the Lord.'" Abel paused. "Sarah didn't want violence in return for what happened that day. She circled the words in her own blood."

Jones looked up to meet Parson Abel's compassionate gaze. "The Bible also says, 'an eye fer an eye, and a tooth for a tooth.'"

In silence, Jones returned to his coffee.

A SOLEMN PROCESSION snaked its way north to Boothill Cemetery. Townsfolk surrounded the horse-drawn hearse bedecked in black. Lt. Colonel Englewood and five troopers served as pallbearers to carry the simple wooden coffin containing the mortal remains of Sarah Jones from the hearse to its final resting place.

Handkerchiefs wet with tears daubed at the misty eyes of the ladies from Madame Roger's brothel. They remembered Sarah's sweet innocence and friendly manner despite the contentious nature of her vocation.

Parson Abel wiped the sweat from his brow. He looked into the mourning faces of those gathered on the lonely hill a few blocks from town. Adeline, who had befriended Sarah and made her part of their family, stood nearest him.

Abel put his hands into the air to silence the personal conversations that punctuated the occasion.

"Friends, we do not know for what purpose God chose now to call two people home—Sarah and her unborn baby," Abel began. "Here we stand seeking answers and finding none. What we know is Sarah was baptized, and that she had a commitment by God that at her death she would be in His presence forever. Sarah believed in that promise and God kept His word." He paused for a moment to let his words settle in.

"Our God is a just God. He will not let sin go unpunished." He continued after an "Amen" spread among the mourners. "But God's Word is very specific when it says, 'Vengeance is mine,' says the Lord.' It is not for us to take a life in return for the two lives we bury today. Vengeance belongs to God and He will repay."

"'Vengeance is mine,' says the Lord' are the last words Sarah read in her Bible before she died. She circled them on the page with her own blood. We honor her wishes, no matter how difficult this might be. We allow room for God to work. Remembering Sarah's dying wishes, we commit her into the hands of God. Ashes to ashes. Dust to dust."

Parson Abel picked up a handful of dirt and sprinkled the dry dust on the casket. "In the sure and certain hope of the resurrection of the dead," Abel said while making the sign of the cross. "In the Name of the Father and of the Son and of the Holy Ghost. Amen."

He looked up. Jones and Potter were gone.

The pallbearers assisted the undertaker. Together they lowered the casket into the hole workers had created in the ground. Mourners walked away shaking their heads. The murder of a young wife and her unborn child disturbed them. "How could a just God allow such things?" they wondered aloud.

Walking from the grave gave Doc a chance to get in his two-cents' worth with Parson Abel. "You weren't serious back there, were ya?"

"What do you mean?"

"I mean about that leaving vengeance to God business."

"Yes. I was serious."

"There ain't no way a person can do that," Doc said.

"You are right. A person can't, but God is in the changing business. I know that sounds preachy, but there it is."

The two elder statesmen walked side-by-side. There was no requirement for every minute of a conversation be filled with words. For them, pauses were permissible while they thought about what to say next.

"Yer livin' that out, ain't ya? You didn't take out your vengeance after Custus cut up yer face." Doc stopped and turned to face the Parson.

"It isn't easy living it out," Abel said. "Sometimes I just want to strike out in anger. You think I enjoy looking at my face every morning and seeing a scar slashed across it? But how can I take revenge and be obedient to the life God has called me to lead? Boothill is already full of gunfighters and revenge seekers. If we're going to have a civilized town, the gun play has got to stop and the hatred's got to end."

"So what yer saying," Doc added, "is that yer trying to put me out of business?"

CHAPTER TWENTY-THREE

Jones rode southwest toward the bank of Lodgepole Creek and then turned right with Potter trailing after. He wanted none of Abel's talk of forgiveness. He could not, he would not forgive Custus.

Potter had tried to restrain him but thought better of it. Flush with anger, Jones reined in his horse at the cabin he'd built for Sarah with his bare hands. He gently removed Sarah's Bible from his saddlebag; and found a match. Jones entered and made his way to the bedroom and lit a single candle.

"Sarah died here," he said under his breath. "Oh, God, and I wasn't here." Memories played in his mind. He heard her laughter, remembered the joy in her eyes when she told him how much she loved him.

"Sarah," he moaned.

No one answered. Anger crowded out happy memories. There would be no more memories made here in this cabin. His mind filled with 'What ifs?'

"What if I hadn't ridden after Custus in the first place?"

"What if I'd have settled down like Sarah wanted me to?"

"What if Custus had drawn his gun the first time we met?"

"You've got to quit second guessing yourself," Potter reassured him.

Jesse's mind would not let him hear his words. He was confident how that gunfight would have ended.

His mind pulled him back to reality, but like a fly in summer, his mind had too many places to land, and never stayed on one thought, flying on to the next.

Jones thought of the finality of the grave. All that was left of his beloved Sarah was her Bible. He treasured her Bible torn and abused in the final battle of Sarah's life. Those torn pages were a living testament she had lived and loved. Her Bible furnished tangible evidence of the influence of Parson Abel and Adeline. He thumbed the pages until he found Sarah's name inside the front flap and then searched in vain for her blood encircled words that spoke to him from beyond the grave.

"Where are they?" He pawed through the pages, giving no shrift at all to other words printed there. These mattered not; his wife's last words did.

"There they are," he proclaimed at last.

Like a little child whose earliest drawn circles are less formed than those of an older child, Sarah's circle wandered. Yet, it was obvious what words she was determined to enclose with her blood. He stared at them and his tears fell like raindrops onto the page.

Dearly beloved, avenge not yourselves, but rather give place unto wrath: for it is written, 'Vengeance is mine; I will repay,' saith the Lord.

He grabbed the page near the spine and tore it out.

"I love you, sweetheart, but I cannot do this. I cannot let the man who did this live while I have breath in me. Please forgive me for what I am about to do."

Jesse folded the bloodied page and put it in his shirt pocket, blew out the candle and spoke under his breath. "Let my heart be black like this room until I have avenged you. Let no one stand in my way until everyone responsible for your death has a heart stilled in death." He spoke the words again. This time he swore aloud. "Let my heart be black like this room until I have avenged you. Let no one stand in my way until everyone responsible for your death has a heart stilled in death."

"Now, that frightens me," Potter said.

Jones stuffed the Bible into his saddlebag. "I've got work to do and it starts with Madame Rogers. Custus likes to hang out there so maybe he's given someone a clue where we can find him."

Jesse mounted his horse. "We'll start there and we'll start there tonight. Names. That's all I need are names. Names of the men who ride with Custus, besides Iggy and Stinson. Names of anyone who might have ridden with him when he took the lives of Sarah and our baby. Dear God give me the strength to avenge their deaths. Right now, I'd give anything for a few names."

"Alright," Potter said as he mounted. "But, I'm riding with you. This is too big a job for you to do alone."

They rode through a night with no moon, no light, yet their horses knew the way. Once in town, Jones slowed his horse to a walk. The street lights lit the way past the Lodgepole Saloon where Billie played his out-of-tune piano.

"The bars are still open and if the bars are open, so are the brothels," Jesse told Potter.

"There are three ways for a man to lose all sensibility,"

said Potter. "They are money, booze and sex. One follows directly after the other like the lethal combination of Bill Cody and his rifle named Lucretia Borgia."

Potter's comment brought a smile to Jones' lips for the first time in days. He knew Potter was right and it was only a few moments later that they saw the red light of welcome burning in the front window of Madam Roger's establishment. The place was not only open, but some of the activity reserved for inside had spilled into the streets.

"So far no one has consummated their relationship in the streets, but some are sure in the preliminary stages," Potter noted.

"Now I know why I brought you along," Jones said as he tied-off his horse in front of Madame Rogers. "You make me laugh."

Both men bypassed the siren calls of two of Madame Rogers' ladies, who had been sent outside to attract would-be visitors to step inside. Jones knew the direction he was headed, and he knew the reason. Neither was about pleasure. This was business. Strictly business.

Two henchmen sat on opposite sides of a door labeled 'Private', marking his destination, and Jones walked toward it. The bigger of the two men stood. "Are ya lost, pretty boy? The action's upstairs," the man mumbled between missing teeth.

"Not lost," Jones replied. "Lookin' fer the boss." He stood his ground. These men could not intimidate him.

"She ain't seeing anybody. She's busy."

"She'll want to see me, alright. We're old friends." Jones' words prompted the second man to stand. Empowered by the response of his friend, the big man made a play for him.

That was his first mistake. Jones' grabbed the man's beefy exposed right hand and yanked hard and down with his left hand while he smashed his fist into the man's jaw. When he slumped, Jones took him by the collar and tossed him headlong into the smaller of the two defenders in front of Potter. Helpless to stand, the man staggered to regain his feet, only to have his jaw meet Jones' fist, the same fate that befell his partner. Both men lay at Jones' feet like so much cordwood.

"What's going on out here?" said a woman's voice behind the closed door.

Jones recognized the voice behind the office door as Madame Rogers and when the doorknob turned, Jones took hold and jerked it open spilling Madame Rogers into the pile at Potter's feet. Potter reached down to help her up, but Jones grabbed hold of her wrist and pulled her in front of him. Her face was swollen and puffy and she had used makeup to hide the bruises.

"Don't look at me," Madame Rodger's protested. She tried to escape into the security of her office.

Jones followed. "Did Custus do that to you?" he asked.

"That's none of your business," she said.

"Maybe not, but it is my business if you're protecting the man who killed my wife."

He held her secure and looked her in the eyes.

"Ma'am," Potter said, "I wouldn't try Jessie's patience right now, if I was you. In fact, I'd give him what he wants."

At last she offered Jones an explanation. "I wouldn't give him the girl he wanted, so he hit me," she said and plopped down at her desk. "I hate the bas—" she interrupted her sentence with tears.

"We can stop him from ever doing this again," Jones said. "Tell me where I can find Custus. Or give me the names of the men who ride with him, and I promise that this will never happen to you again. You have my word on it."

Madame Rogers gave up the names of men who rode with Custus. Jones recognized two of them—Iggy and Stinson—but not the others.

She told him that one is called 'the old man;' and a second is called Bravo, a hired killer from south of the Mexican border. Lynch, a man so named from the rope scar around his neck, and someone called Newsome. Newsome," she said, "saw Lynch hang, cut him down and saved his life. A man called Cooper left town shortly after the gang rode in."

"Now, that wasn't so difficult was it?" Jones asked. He started for the door, but Madame Rogers yelled after him.

"You promised," she yelled. "You better not forget your promise or I'm a dead woman." She chased Jones into the street. "Do you hear me? You made me a promise!"

Jones and Potter rode east hoping to pick up Custus' trail, but the moonless night offered no help whatsoever, so they bedded down to catch some sleep before resuming their search early the next morning.

THE NEXT MORNING Potter brewed coffee. Jesse stood nearby reading again the words Sarah had circled on the page he'd torn from her Bible.

Some twenty miles to the southeast, Ned Buntline was recording these words he would send to his editor in a day or two:

Thousands of bison grazed the border between Nebraska and Kansas. The male of the species weighs every bit of two-thousand pounds or more. Majestic beasts that once supplied everything Native Americans needed to live; meat for eating, hide for tent covers, sinew for thread, and bone for needles. They were now the quarry of the greatest buffalo hunter of all time. Buffalo Bill Cody. As I stated in my earlier accounts of this man, Buffalo Bill earned his reputation supplying meat for the Kansas Pacific Railroad, but now hides took precedence and he was about to put on an exhibition that General Sheridan and his guests would not soon forget.

Cody took his time picking the bull he wanted to shoot first and methodically sighted on his kill shot at a distance of five hundred yards. In eager anticipation, a bevy of celebrities, among them General George Armstrong Custer and Duke Alexis of Russia. For show, Cody removed a glove, licked his index finger, and held it in the air as if determining wind speed and direction preparatory to the kill, something Cody had already determined. But he held them all in the palm of his hand as he played out his game. A game Cody was good at it.

His rifle? His famous Springfield Model 1866 Trapdoor to which he'd given the name Lucretia Borgia.

Cody opened the breech to place a center-fire .50-70 cartridge into the chamber and then closed it. He slid his hat back so that it hung by its straps, revealing his collar-length blond hair. Taking great care, he placed Lucretia Borgia on a stand and sighted her on a large bull buffalo.

Lucretia Borgia roared to life, sending a thumb-sized projectile into the animal's massive skull, crumpling its legs and thudding it to the ground. Two buffalo birds on the animals' back took flight, but the rest of the herd grazed as if nothing out of the ordinary had happened.

Lucretia Borgia belched forth another round. Still, they grazed. Their tiny brains never associated the sound of Cody's rifle with instant death. Cody reloaded and fired with the same results. A third bull fell to its knees, dead. A fourth. A fifth. Time after time, Buffalo Bill displayed a skill he alone possessed, but all men admired, stopping only when he had struck down twenty in a row which brought the crowd, who up to now remained silent, to life giving him a thunderous approval. With great flourish, Cody laid Lucretia Borgia on a table, and took a bow.

General Sheridan greeted him. "It's too bad folks back east can't see such a display of marksmanship," Sheridan noted. He shook Cody's hand.

I, Ned Buntline, wondered how that might happen, and shared this thought with Frank North, Head of the Pawnee Scouts.

Soon wagons arrived to take the onlookers to the site where skinners removed the hide and butchers harvested the meat for the evening meal. They scurried about the carcasses like ants. Each head was removed and carefully examined by Sheridan's guests. They marveled at Cody's accuracy, eyeing the heads and looking up-range to where a fence post marked the spot from whence Cody had fired.

Workmen erected awnings to shelter the hunting party from the sun, and it was not long before liquor flowed in abundance and the sublime smell of cigar smoke filled the air. Under these awnings, stories flowed in direct proportion to the liquor consumed.

While Cody traipsed about receiving congratulatory handshakes, North and I exchanged ideas about how a Wild West show might fulfill General Sheridan's comments.

I was the first to notice a lone rider kicking up dust behind these two men as they talked. A lone rider pulled up, dusted himself off and was escorted to General Sheridan. The young rider was so flustered by Sheridan's presence that he did not know whether to salute first or hand him the message pouch he carried.

While he fumbled about, General Sheridan smiled. "At ease, soldier," he laughed, "No need to stand on formality today. What brings you out here?"

"I have an urgent message for Bill Cody from the Commander of Fort Sidney, sir," he said. At last, he managed a proper salute.

"Colonel Cody is right here, son. You can deliver your message in person."

Cody stepped forward and the messenger, who stood erect with his right hand placed at the correct slant above his right eye and snapped it back against his right thigh. The on-lookers found entertainment in the cavalryman's attempt at military protocol in such a casual setting.

"Do you want to hand me that satchel, Private?" Cody said. He did.

Cody unfolded the message to read its contents. "General Sheridan, may I have a word with you in private, sir?" Cody said. The two walked a few paces from the others.

But I overheard him say, "General, I've been asked to return to Fort Sidney. The wife of a man I recruited was murdered. Colonel Englewood at Fort Sidney requests my return to help find the murderer. There is a second message attached that Colonel Englewood asks me to give to you."

Taking the message, General Sheridan read it. He nodded in reply to its contents. "Go, and may God speed," Sheridan said.

CHAPTER TWENTY-FOUR

Custus Leaverette was many things, conniving, malicious, evil, hateful, but the one thing he was not —he was not stupid. He had left the 'old man' in town to keep an eye out for Jones.

The 'old man' poured coffee. "I seen Jones with my own eyes. He's back in Sidney. How he got there I ain't got no idea."

Custus figured Abel would send a telegraph telling Jones of the death of his wife, and Jones would respond by returning at once to Sidney. He was proven correct with the 'old man's' words.

"Boys," Custus said, "the old man says he spotted Jones. He was at his wife's funeral, so settin' an ambush when he heads back this way is no good. He's already back."

"We could split up and ride into town separately and get Jones in an ambush," Lynch said.

"Dumb idea." Custus thought a moment. "Now that the fort has moved into town proper, Jones has lots of back-up."

"Me and Iggy could ride into town and lure him into the Lodgepole Saloon for ya," Stinson offered.

"Another dumb idea. As much as I'd like to ride in and harass Billie again, I gotta say no. I want to plan something that will go down in one of them dime novels folks is readin'."

Custus paced back and forth in front of the fire. He took out his knife and with its bladetip cleaned the dirt from under his fingernails. Without warning he let out a war whoop and heaved the knife and imbedded it half-way to the hilt in a nearby oak. "I got it," he yelled. "I want Jones to chase us right into an ambush. I want to pick the spot where I kill him. Knife or bare hands it don't matter. I want to watch as life leaves him. To see the lights go out in his eyes."

He fetched his knife.

"The best way," Custus continued, "is to create a trail for Jones to follow, making it obvious, so overtly obvious; Jones would not shy away from it. An' I know where to lead him. Its a few days' ride from here just outside Laramie. I been there a couple of times to out run the law. A place called Turtle Rock. We'll ambush Jones there. Kill those with him and then I'll kill him. The terrain at Turtle Rock gives us the high ground like they say Joshua Chamberlain had at Gettysburg."

Custus took his men and headed north, looped west and made a bee-line for Wyoming Territory. Custus glanced over his shoulder at Iggy and Stinson. *Where is a good place to put these two where they can be in the line of fire and out of my hair permanently?*

He made Iggy and Stinson bring up the rear. Their dumb ideas made them expendable. Custus was tired of carrying around dead weight.

Wyoming Territory was reached in two days on the

fifteenth of September. *Now I got two objectives,* Custus thought, *to rid myself of Iggy and Stinson. Then get rid of Jones.*

Custus found an ambush site. It was an abandoned sod house just north of the trail. There were two graves under a dead cottonwood tree nearby to remind passersby of the difficult existence of the desolate prairie. A grove of trees and underbrush gave adequate shelter for two men to set a trap for Jones. Those two men were Iggy and Stinson.

Custus stepped inside the sod house. Cobwebs told the story of a home deprived of occupants. He loved it. The interior had but one room. Tattered drapes partitioned off the room into livable spaces. Empty shelves, abandoned cookware, an unmade bed created a creepy morgue-like appearance. Perfect.

"Iggy, you and Stinson stay here. I want you to kill as many men as you can if'n Jones brings a posse with him. Don't kill Jones. I want him all for myself. Do I make myself clear?" They nodded. "Kill 'em if you can, but leave Jones to me."

Custus pointed to a copse of trees. "There's plenty of shelter over there by them trees, and for one of ya by the house. Don't much care who is where. You two work that out 'fer yerselves. My guess is that Jones will be along in a day 'er two. If he's alone or if that Potter fella is with him, let 'em right through. If a posse rides in, take out the posse. That'll give me time enough to get ready."

Jones tracked Custus east out of town and discovered where he and his men had doubled back on themselves and had headed west.

"Sakes alive," Potter said. "Looks like they deliberately

want us to follow their trail. Here's where they camped and over here is where they spun around and headed off to the west."

"Not sure where they're headed." Jones mused. "If they go back to Fort Laramie, they'll be recognized. If they head further north, they'll be in danger from Dull Knife's braves. They'll kill Custus and his men for what they've done."

He drew in his reins and stopped his horse in its tracks. "Wait one dad-gum minute," Jones said. Potter drew his horse beside him.

"What are you thinking?" Potter asked.

"I'm thinking that this is way too easy. Custus knows we're after him, yet he hasn't attempted to cover his tracks. He wants us to follow him. We're on the way to an ambush."

Potter agreed.

JONES AND POTTER rode into Wyoming Territory two days after Custus. As a precaution, they laid their rifles across their laps in anticipation of a trap. At the crest of a hill, a soddy came into view about a half mile away on their right. There was an outline of trees on the property, a second scruffy tree-line, and what appeared to be two wooden grave markers.

"My gut instincts tell me that this is the perfect place for Custus to get the drop on us," Jones said. "It would be easy to put two or three men in the tree-line and the others in the soddy and catch us in a cross-fire. Jones and Potter made their way closer to the soddy. Their horses walked at a steady, methodical pace.

"Did you see that?" Jones asked. He pointed to movement among the trees.

"Sure did," Potter answered. "The way the sun danced among those trees over there, there has to be metal. Probably a rifle barrel."

"Yep," Jones said. "Wonder how many men?"

"Darned if I know. If we get a little closer I'll bet we'll find out."

Potter's words found their answer in a heartbeat when a puff of smoke appeared near the trees and a bullet sped past his ear.

"That's close enough," he told Jones. Potter returned fire. He had no distinct target to shoot at, just the tree near where he thought the shot had come from.

Jones dismounted and used his horse as a shield. "Hold 'yer fire," Jones said. "Save 'yer ammunition for when you have somethin' to shoot at. From here, you can't tell what yer aiming at."

"I'm aiming at the tree down there where the bullet came from. It darn near took my right ear off."

"Whoever fired the shot is shooting uphill. We have the advantage if we just sit tight," Jones said. "Get behind that clump of rocks."

The men moved to their left where a couple of boulders shielded them from two more bullets that ricocheted nearby.

"There they go again. They're deliberately shooting at me. It wasn't you he's aiming at, Jones, just me."

"He missed you, didn't he?" Jones said. "He can't hit an elephant from that distance."

"General Sedgwick said those same words only to have a rebel kill him from seven hundred yards away," Potter said. "What do we do now?"

"Hold tight. Let whoever fired at us make the next move.

We've got a good view from up here. We've just got to make sure no one flanks us."

FROM THE BOTTOM of the hill, Jones heard an argument underway between the two would-be ambushers. He recognized the voices as belonging to Stinson near the trees and Iggy near the soddy.

"Stinson, what do you think you're doing? They're not close enough to get a good bead on. And be careful so you don't hit Jones. Custus wants him all to himself, you imbecile."

"They're close enough alright. I got Potter. Didn't you see how quickly he hit the dirt? Why didn't you fire?"

"I didn't want to give away my position and I was afraid I'd hit Jones. Right now they think that you're all alone down here."

Iggy thought about their situation for a moment and then offered his thoughts. "We gotta come up with some way to draw them in. Otherwise, we're just sitting ducks. You keep 'em busy and then play along with me if I walk toward ya."

Stinson fired several shots toward the position held by Jones and Potter. They returned fire and stripped bark from the tree just wide enough to hide Stinson's rotund body.

Jones nodded with satisfaction. "They have no idea that we heard every word they said. This valley is carrying their voices."

"So, that's what they're up to. Custus wants me dead so that he can have you to himself to kill you."

"That's what they said. Let's see if we can somehow use that to our advantage."

They watched as Iggy emerged with his rifle pointed right at Stinson, and ordered him to stand up. "Alright, drop your gun," he yelled.

"What the..." Stinson said.

"Do as you're told," Iggy muttered under his breath. "I told you to play along. Shut up and get to your feet, so we can lure them in."

At the top of the hill Jones and Potter heard every word.

Iggy shouted up the hill. "You on the hill, c'mon down, I've got him covered."

Back up the hill, Jones retrieved his spyglass from his saddlebag and reconnoitered the scene. "Yep, its Iggy and Stinson alright. Just as I suspected. Custus must have left them behind to do his dirty work."

"What are we gonna do?" Potter said.

Jones rose to his feet. "We're gonna play along," he said.

Jones led the way down the hill; eyes focused on the scene in front of him.

Iggy sidled closer to Stinson while at the same time keeping up the pretense of holding Stinson captive. He sidled until a gap of about twenty feet existed between him and Stinson and there he stopped.

Jones noted the fear on the faces of the two men in the clearing. He watched their eyes and with his peripheral vision noted Stinson had dropped his rifle to the ground but kept his sidearm.

Potter made the same mental note while walking. Out of the side of his mouth, he intoned sotto voce, "I wish you'd tell me what you're up to."

Jones did not answer. He kept walking, a steel-willed man seeking to avenge his wife and child. His right hand swung inches from the handle of his treasured LeMat. It wasn't the best gun to draw during a gunfight, but was all he had. What he didn't have in the speed of the draw was made up for with the volume of the pistol's firepower.

When they reached the bottom of the hill, the path flattened out to present the valley where once a family had attempted to live. Iggy halted them in their tracks.

"That's far enough," Iggy said. The two parties were within thirty feet of each other. "See, I told you I could get 'em down," Iggy said. He turned to his companion, who had widened his stance for gunplay. Iggy cast his rifle aside leaving only the six-gun strapped to his waist.

"Where's Custus?" Jones asked.

"Now, that's none of 'yer business," Iggy said.

"Yea," said Stinson. "Ain't you two the ones who came into my camp a few nights back? And ain't you the two who stepped between Custus and that gal? What was her name, Iggy?"

"Sarah," Iggy said. "Ain't she yer wife, Jones?"

"The same," Jones said.

"I didn't get a chance to tell you thanks for the hooch," Stinson said.

"You're welcome," Potter said. "Give me a moment and I'll tie up the horses and we can talk some more."

Potter led the two horses to a small tree and tied them there before standing apart from Jones and facing Stinson.

"Where's Custus?" Jones repeated. "And that's the last time I'm gonna ask ya. You see, I'm making it my business," Jones said. He looked each man in the eye. "Were you there the day Custus killed my wife?"

"Yeah, Stinson and me was there. It's a shame she had to put up such a fight. Custus wasn't gonna kill her until she slung her Bible and hit him in the back of the head. Look, we're just carrying out Custus' orders."

Stinson patted his gun. "Which means we gotta kill ya, Potter. No hard feelings, this is business."

"Did you know my wife circled words in that same Bible before she died?" There was no emotion behind Jones' words. The statement came from a man who had died the day his wife was killed.

Jones reached for his shirt pocket and removed the page he had torn from Sarah's Bible. "Now, before I kill you, let me read the words to you." He unfolded the paper. "It says, "'Vengeance is mine,' says the Lord."

He paused and then asked again, "Where's Custus?"

"If you kill us, you'll never find out," Stinson said.

"It won't matter 'cuz whether you tell us or not, you are both dead men. Somehow, someway, I'll track Custus down, and when I do he'll be just as dead as you. I want you both to know that I'm not waiting for God to take His vengeance. It's this simple. You killed my wife, now it's your turn to die."

His expression emotionless, Jones folded the paper and put it back in his shirt pocket.

"Are you sure this is how you want to play it?" Stinson said. He removed the bandage from his arm, freeing his gun hand for the work ahead.

"Yep," Jones replied.

At a signal from Iggy, he and Stinson made a play for their guns.

There were two fresh graves under the cottonwood.

CHAPTER TWENTY-FIVE

Parson Abel rose at five a.m. to rehearse his sermon. There was a routine he followed each Sunday morning. He'd rise and dress in his best trousers and a white shirt, take his coffee to the study and read over the sermon written earlier in the week. He practiced his delivery aloud to hear the spoken words. This allowed him to memorize parts of it. He said in this way the Holy Spirit could work as he delivered his message. He would allow the Spirit to walk him away from the podium for what he called 'a more personal sermon delivery.'

"My sermon this week," he'd told his wife three days ago, "is titled Forgive like Christ. I'm taking everyone to the Sea of Galilee, where Jesus forgave Peter three times, one for each of his three denials."

"Forgiveness seems to be your topic *du jour* since Sarah's death. Sadly, the only one who needs to hear it won't be here," she'd said earlier in the week.

At six when he'd finished his sermon preparation, he raised the curtains to let a new Sunday morning shine in.

Today the sun shone blood red. He called Adeline to his side to view it together.

"What do you make of this?" he asked, pointing the red sky out to her.

"It's as if God is sending a warning of impending doom and the heavens are conveying His message," she said. "Something is going to happen."

As usual, Doc joined them at six-thirty for eggs, sausage, and fried potatoes. "My wife likes sleeping in on Sunday mornings," he'd tell them. "And that means I'm on my own for breakfast. She'll make it to church alright; she just doesn't see any sense in getting up at six in the morning when she doesn't have to." Doc continued, "Did you see the sky this morning? If I were a bettin' man, I'd say the man upstairs is telling us somethin'."

"That's just what I was telling Adeline," Abel said. "It's like this whole murder thing has put things out of whack."

Doc held out his cup for a refill. "I'll take another shot of that mud, if you don't mind." Adeline poured more coffee. "Can't help but think about Jones. It's been a while since he left town with revenge painted on his face like makeup on a two-bit whore."

Doc caught himself. "I'm sorry, it just slipped out," he said. The Abels ignored his remark. "Everything's out of kilter seems to me."

"I like that," Parson Abel said. "Mind if I borrow those words to lead into my sermon on forgiveness this morning?"

"Seems you've been borrowing a lot of my words lately. I didn't know that I was such a good source for all your sermonizing."

Abel enjoyed trying his sermon ideas out on Doc before he preached them. Doc was a good sounding board.

"At least you could do me the honor of being in attendance today so you can hear where your words will lead me," said Abel.

"No thanks. I heard your sermon outline earlier in the week and we talked about it. Don't need to sit in the pews and hear it again."

Doc took his religious beliefs only so far. Hearing Abel's Sunday morning sermon idea earlier in the week was as far as Doc was willing to go. "Puttin' my butt in a pew is another matter altogether."

MILES AWAY, in Wyoming Territory, Jones and Potter sat around a campfire that sustained them with heat and promised coffee from the pot that sat above the fire.

"That sky looks horrible," Potter said. He took a cloth in hand and removed the coffee pot from the fire.

"Something's in the air and it ain't good," Jones said. "I can't remember the Lakota word for it."

He nodded at Potter's unspoken question about whether he wanted coffee. Potter poured Jones' tin cup full of coffee. With no thought at all, Jones withdrew the folded page from his pocket, unfolded it, and stared at its contents.

"Are you alright?" Potter said.

"Why shouldn't I be?" Jones fired back. He felt like he was caught in the act of doing something he shouldn't. He pushed the paper back into his pocket.

"What's eating you? I never meant nothin' by it," Potter said.

Jones stood and kicked dirt into the fire to put it out. "Let's get out of here, we've got work to do and the day ain't gettin' any younger."

Potter decided it was better to leave well enough alone.

Some people have kicked a sleeping dog only to have the dog bite them.

Packing was done in silence. Both men kept their thoughts to themselves. The day grew hotter with humidity to match. It wasn't long into their ride that the wind kicked up dust. The men found it hard to breathe. They tied their kerchiefs to cover their nose and mouth.

They rode on. Jones led. Potter followed into the teeth of the storm they knew was ahead.

IN HIS JOURNAL with the same date, Ned Buntline recorded the adventures in Buffalo Bill Cody's camp.

Buffalo Bill rose to an ominous Sunday morning. He and his party had camped for the night about eight miles southeast of Sidney. In his lifetime, he could not remember a dawn like this with such stillness to it. It was as if all the creatures on earth had taken a holiday. Even the effervescent Meadowlarks that normally chattered their 'good-mornin'-to-ya-all,' were silent.

"They were seen, but not heard," is how Buffalo Bill described it.

Today everything was silent. Redwing Blackbirds hung sideways from the cattails at the banks of Lodgepole Creek, but they too, remained uncharacteristically silent. Then the wind kicked up.

This was the scene as the famous Bill Cody surveyed the world from the opening of his tent while buttoning his tasseled shirt. One young soldier who had also risen early that morning to add wood to the campfire and bring a pot of coffee to a boil, found the wind blowing with such force that it sent sand in everyone's faces. When he finished the task of stoking the fire, the young man turned his back to the wind.

"Mornin', Colonel," he said with a salute. "The weather is unusual this morning."

"At ease," Cody said. In his wisdom he knew there was a storm brewing somewhere, and expressed his opinion to the young man who nodded in agreement. "So, how's the coffee this morning?" He sipped and then gave the trooper a wide smile. "Now, that's a lot better than yesterday's. I swear if I'd poured yesterday's coffee on the ground, it would have marched off. This isn't bad. It isn't bad at all."

"Thank you, sir. I had hand-to-hand combat with the wind to get it done."

"I'll bet you did. Never seen a day quite like this one. Refresh my memory, would you? What is it exactly that the Colonel wants me to do?" Cody said.

"The Colonel said that he wants you to track down Jones, to lend him support in whatever he does. The Colonel heard that Custus has called in reinforcements and he doesn't like the seven to two odds Custus gave him and Potter, so he wants you to take about a half-dozen men and help him out."

"Jones has a big head start. He's an excellent tracker and has the tenacity of a bulldog. Once he starts something, he's gonna finish it. I wouldn't want to be Custus right about now. Let's pack it up and make tracks, soldier."

The wind howled and the storm brewed, but it was no match whatsoever for Bill Cody.

CUSTUS RODE into Cheyenne that same morning. He took no

stock in the weather and the omens his men yakked about on their early morning ride.

Cheyenne, as he remembered it, was a hardscrabble town named for the Native American people of the area. Like Sidney, it was the railroad that made the town what it was. Grenville Dodge chose the site for the city in July 1867, with the first train arriving in November of that year. The speed with which Cheyenne grew gave cause to the nick-name it soon received, 'Magic City of the Plains.'

Custus took no stock in that either. He rode with one purpose; to fill his belly with something other than the slop the old man tried to pass off for food.

WHEN CUSTUS RODE IN, Red Hand was across the street loading supplies into his wagon. Custus saw him, but had no idea who he was. Red Hand was dressed in 'white man's clothes.' The only evidence he was an Indian were the two long sable braids that streamed from either side of his head.

Red Hand had risen that morning to the same ill-tempered sky. He considered it an omen that the spirits would grant him victory over his enemy. When Custus rode into town and hitched his horse in front of the hotel Red Hand drew the conclusion the victory would be over Custus.

"The Great Spirit," he whispered to himself, "has brought Custus to me so that I can avenge myself on him for kidnapping Two Moons."

This would be no easy task because he first had to separate Custus from his men before he could make his play. To fight Custus alone might be suicide, but to fight Custus with his men present would be just plain stupid. For now, Red Hand pulled his hat up and stuffed his braids inside it and continued to load his wagon in the wind.

Custus led his men inside.

"Why are we stoppin' here?" the old man asked.

"'Cuz I can't stand that slop you try to pass off for breakfast," Custus replied. The old man did not like the insult Custus dished out to him, nor did he like his friends to side with Custus, but they did.

"'Sides," Custus added, "we got a day or two lead on Jones."

He was certain Iggy and Stinson had met their Maker. Their deaths did not matter to him. He thought only of the added time the dead men bought him.

Inside the hotel, Custus liked what he saw. On the far side of the room, hotel guests dined. Between the door and the dining room, eight gambling tables invited all who entered to try their luck.

"Go on over and get somethin' to eat," Custus said. "I'll eat later. Gonna win me my breakfast money."

He separated himself from his men and waited until one player slammed his cards on the table in disgust and left. "Mind if I join ya?" Custus asked in a tone of voice half-asking and half-commanding.

"Suit yerself," came the reply from a man whom Custus thought was a professional gambler. The man was the best dressed in the hotel and he shuffled the desk with an ease that impressed all who watched him. That is, all but Custus.

"The game is Five-Card Stud." The gambler looked at Custus while he shuffled. "Ever played this game before?" he asked sarcastically.

"Just cut all this fancy bull-crap and deal the cards," Custus said. Custus flopped himself down in the chair opposite the gambler. He liked this spot at the table. He could keep his eyes on the professional, and he didn't have his back to the door. No one came in or out of the place without Custus noticing it. It was a little trick he'd learned from Bill Hickok.

"The ante is a silver dollar, friend," the gambler said. He tossed his dollar into the middle of the table. Three others followed, Custus included. All the while, Custus followed the gambler's hands while he shuffled and reshuffled the deck.

At the far side of the room, Custus watched the old man and others find a place to sit, and a waitress greeted them. *By the looks of her, she can't be a day younger than the old man. Her skin looks like shoe leather with wrinkles, and her smile is missing more teeth than those present.*

"What can I get ya?" Custus heard her say and watched as she leaned forward so far over the table that her ample cleavage showed like a valley between two mountains.

"The special is steak and fried potatoes, boys. What'll ya have?" she said.

"Tamales!" Bravo said with an explosive laugh.

"No, sir," she said, "just the special." The little lady rose to her full height of five feet, put both hands on her big hips and shouted toward the kitchen, "Four specials for table six!"

Custus turned back to the game. He watched as the gambler dealt the cards, keeping up his banter as he did so to focus the players' attention on his face and away from his hands.

Custus pulled his pistol and he fired. He stood. The last wisps of gunsmoke fled Custus' gun. The gambler slumped over the table, blood oozing from the hole in the middle of his chest.

"If there's one thing I can't stand, it's a dad-blamed cheater," Custus announced. He looked about the room. "The buzzard dealt off the bottom of the deck and didn't think I'd see it."

Custus scraped all the money off the table and stuffed it in his pocket. "C'mon, boys, we better get outta here," Custus yelled.

"What about our breakfast?" Lynch asked.

"Never mind breakfast," Custus replied. "This cardsharp spoiled it."

Custus sauntered to the door; his men were close behind him. With guns drawn, they covered Custus' exit.

"The first person to come after me," Custus shouted, "will get a bullet in him."

Custus stepped outside.

It was ten o'clock.

CHAPTER TWENTY-SIX

Jesse Jones and Adam Potter faced struggles of their own; a strong northwest wind and heavy drizzle. The ominous red sky that morning gave way to weather that justified it. A cold rain fell to chill both horse and rider to the bone. The wind and rain smothered every attempt at a campfire.

Both men stopped long enough to pull waterproof ponchos from their saddlebags and put them on. If there were any positives from such weather it was that a mind had ample time to think. Jesse kept replaying his last conversation with Parson Abel:

"I can tell by your voice that you're going after Custus," Abel had said. "Before you do, I want you to look at what Sarah underlined in blood in her Bible before she died." He had Sarah's Bible open and read the words, 'Vengeance is mine, says the Lord.' Sarah didn't want violence in return for what happened that day."

Parson Abel's words echoed over and over again in

Jesse's mind. They grew louder and more forceful with each repetition.

"Sarah didn't want violence."

"Sarah didn't want violence."

"Sarah didn't want violence."

He remembered his own words. "The Bible also says, 'an eye fer an eye, and a tooth for a tooth."

He'd left Parson Abel standing at Sarah's grave as he and Potter made their exit.

Now in the wind and weather, he rode oblivious to Potter's presence.

"What are you thinking about?" Potter asked him. Jones didn't answer, he was buried deep in his own thoughts.

The man who killed Sarah is out there somewhere, and he will be met with my justice. I will mete out vengeance before God has any chance of intervening. No matter what, this man's life was forfeit. Storm or no storm he is as good as dead. Custus may be alive now, but he's a dead man.

At precisely ten a.m., as Custus fled after killing the gambler in Laramie and Jones and Potter battled the bitter elements, Parson Abel stood in the pulpit, looking out over his flock.

Abel saw the regulars in their regular pews. It's as if someone had assigned them their places; everyone sitting in the same place week after week without fail.

His eyes came upon Adeline who also sat in the same place each week, right in front of the pulpit. Today, a prostitute sat beside her. Madame Rogers sat there welcomed, not shunned. Custus had beaten her and that had drawn Adeline to her.

Adeline has such a welcoming heart. She has a way with the down-casts and her winsomeness has rallied the congregation around Madame Rogers despite her vocation and reputation, Abel thought.

All of these thoughts flashed into his mind, as thoughts sometimes do, as he stood there preparing to speak. Abel smiled at Adeline and gripped the pulpit.

"I'm sure that many of you were up early enough to see the blood red sunrise this morning. Doc and I talked about that when he came for breakfast. He told me 'everything's out of kilter seems to me' and I agreed with him. Since the tragic death of Sarah Jones and the dear child she was carrying that fateful day, things have been out of kilter. I want you also to know that the one person above all others that I wanted to hear this sermon, Sarah's dear husband, Jesse, is not here among us today. So, I'll deliver my sermon to you just as if he was, and together we'll pray that somehow God would lay these words on his heart."

Quietly the door of the little church opened. In walked Doc. He never seated himself, but stood near the door. Few heard him, but his presence didn't go unnoticed by Parson Abel.

"Morning, Doc," he said. "Glad you could make it." All eyes shifted to the back of the room.

"Don't let me interrupt you. I just had to see if you used my comment this morning about things being out of kilter or if you were just sayin' you would to be kind."

The congregation chuckled.

"I used it just like I promised. You can ask anyone here."

"He used it alright," Adeline said, coming to her husband's defense.

"You gotta agree with him because he's yer husband," Doc replied.

"But, *I* don't," said another woman seated closer to the

back. "I'm your wife, and I say that he said it. Now, what do you say to that?"

Doc stammered for words for a moment then answered. "Then, I'd say that he said it."

"And I'd say I agree with Parson Abel that everything's out of kilter this morning. It's the first time in years that I've seen you in church," Doc's wife said. "Care to join me or are you just gonna stand at the back of the room?"

Doc thought for a moment and then joined his wife in the pew.

"As I was saying," Parson Abel began anew. "Everything's out of kilter this morning."

Everyone laughed and turned their attention back to Parson Abel.

"Personally, I cannot cite an example of when anything permanent was accomplished at the point of a gun," he continued. "Many of you remember with horror what happened in this great nation of ours a few short years ago. In fact, many of you know someone killed in the Civil War. We all came west, didn't we, to make a new beginning? To put behind us the violence of another time and place.

"Yet, violence has followed us here. Violence does that, you know. It follows God's people and lures them to seek revenge. But revenge is not God's desire. Our Lord Jesus Christ, when He hung on the cross, did not seek vengeance on those taking His life. No!

"Instead He looked down and said, 'Father, forgive them for they know not what they do.'

"The Greek verb in our text shows that this forgiveness seeking is ongoing. It was done continually throughout the crucifixion process. He who could call heaven's legions and free Himself from such a horrible death did not do that. He asked God to forgive those murdering Him.

"Later, after Jesus rose from the dead, He met His disciples at the Sea of Galilee. There, John's Gospel tells us, Jesus forgave the disciple who had denied Him three times before the cock crowed. This man was Peter."

He surveyed his congregation and continued.

"Recently, a man stormed into my house with a knife and carved a wound into my face. This same man beat the woman seated next to my wife." He pointed to Madame Rogers. "Are we seeking revenge? No, we are not. We are asking God to handle these situations."

"Amens," followed from the seated throng.

"Our dear sister Sarah suffered a fate no one should suffer. That same man who viciously attacked me, and later attacked Mary Rogers, also took Sarah's life and the life of her unborn child. When Sarah was slipping into the hands of her Savior Jesus Christ, she took her own precious blood and circled these words in her Bible, 'Vengeance is mine, says the Lord.' These are powerful words. These are words to be heeded."

Still more "Amens," erupted.

"It's as if Our Lord Himself was present when Sarah died —and He was! My dear brothers and sisters, a manhunt is underway. Sarah's husband is chasing her murderer with a vengeful heart even while I speak to you this morning. What we are going to do is pray that he not take Custus Leaverette's life, but leaves this matter in the hands of God.

"Perhaps you noticed the ill look in the sky this morning. I believe God is calling us to plead for the life of a murderer that he might come to repentance before God and receive His forgiveness. Pray with me now," Abel concluded.

Heads bowed.

"O Lord, You desire the salvation of all men. Turn hearts to you this day. Stop the violence. Bring an end to the killing.

Your servant Sarah calls from the grave in the hope that her husband might put down his gun and not take a life. Lord, we pray this with all our hearts. Amen."

BULLETS FLEW like angry hornets when Custus mounted and galloped away from the Cheyenne Hotel. The old man took a bullet in the back of his left shoulder and dropped his reins. Lynch rode up beside him and propped him upright in his saddle, grabbed the reins of the old man's horse, and headed west out of town.

Newsome wasn't so lucky. He took an arrow in the middle of the back and flipped backward from his horse and thudded to the ground. Riderless, his palomino continued to run.

"Let's get outta here!" Custus yelled. He led the way for his men to follow. "Where's Newsome?" he asked when Newsome's palomino raced by.

"Back in the street," Lynch answered.

Custus turned in the saddle to see Newsome face down in the street with an arrow protruding from back.

"Where did that come from? Who brought a bow to a gunfight?" he asked, not expecting an answer.

A posse of men soon galloped in hot pursuit, their rifles spitting bullets. To the benefit of Custus and his men, the posse had no success firing from horseback.

Bravo pulled his horse side-by-side with Custus while they fled through the western outskirts of Cheyenne. "Dis is a lot hotter than a jalapeño," he said with a smile that showed every tooth in his mouth.

"We've got to make it to higher ground," Custus yelled, "or we won't have any chance at all."

WHEN GUNFIRE HAD ERUPTED in the Cheyenne Hotel, Red Hand had rushed into the street unnoticed by Custus and his men in their haste to leave town. Red Hand drew an arrow on Custus, but Newsome rode between them just as he loosed it and he'd sent the wrong man to an early grave. Red Hand nocked another arrow, but the moving posse hid Custus from view.

"Red Hand," a voice called to him. He turned and found Jones staring down from his horse. Jones dismounted and Potter followed.

"What have you been up to?" Jones asked.

"Takin' a shot at a friend of yours," he replied.

"And just who might that be?" Jones asked.

"Remember our old friend Custus?" Red Hand said.

"Sure do. What about him?"

"He just killed someone in the hotel across the street. Now there's a posse hot on his tail."

"Dang," Potter said, "Sounds like we've got company. We're after him, too. He killed Jones' wife and we've been following him to make things right."

"I'm so sorry to hear that, but I think you're gonna have to wait your turn," Red Hand said. "The posse's got first dibs on him now."

"Where do you think Custus might head?" Jones asked. "Is there any way we can get ahead of him?"

"Perhaps him go to Turtle Rock. That would give him the high ground. I take you there by another way. We have to hurry if we're going to get there before Custus."

Red Hand, Potter, and Jones rode north out of Cheyenne.

Red Hand angled their route to the northwest to skim along a ridgeline, rapidly gaining elevation.

At the crest of a hill, they saw a cluster of four men kick up dust a half-mile or so to their left, with a posse of eight riding hot after them. Smoke puffed from the rifles of the men giving chase with the reports reaching Jones' ear seconds later.

"Can we get ahead of them, Red Hand?" Jones asked.

Red Hand nodded and led the way along a narrow strip of land.

"There Turtle Rock," he announced. "If we come down this hill, we should win the race."

"Good job, Red Hand," Potter said.

Red Hand led the men down the hill in single file. The hill was steep, and the men did everything they could to stay in their saddles while their horses picked their way down the forty-five degree angle of the rock ledge. Once they reached the bottom, they spurred their horses across the road Custus would have to follow.

"How much time do we have before Custus gets here?" Jones asked.

"Five minutes. Maybe ten," Red Hand answered.

"That's all the time we need," Jones said.

The three men found shelter for their horses and began the steep ascent up the side of Turtle Rock to set their ambush, finding rocks sufficient for concealment about forty feet above the valley floor. There they waited.

Jones took the page from Sarah's Bible from his pocket to read and reread the words circled in blood. 'Vengeance is mine, says the Lord.'

Parson Abel's voice came to him. "Sarah didn't want violence in return for what happened that day."

"Sarah didn't want violence."

"Sarah didn't want violence"

"Sarah didn't want violence!"

Hooves reverberated through the valley. Jones stuffed the note into his pocket.

CUSTUS LED HIS MEN. Bravo was right on his heels. Three lengths behind, Lynch raced into the canyon holding the lead of the old man's horse with the old man draped over his horse's neck. Custus looked back. The posse was gaining on them. They entered the valley. Sporadic gunfire in their rear told them stopping was not an option.

"Fire," Jones yelled. Red Hand and Potter joined him to send hellfire down on Custus. The old man was hit multiple times, so was Lynch. Both fell to the valley floor.

Custus and Bravo clamored for the boulders at the base of Turtle Rock and returned fire.

"Is that you, Jonzie?" Custus yelled.

"You know it is," Jones said. "Been lookin' for you. I'm about to send you to your Maker."

"Yer wife screamed, you know? She didn't want me to cut up yer pretty face when I caught up with ya. But, that's just what I'm gonna do while I kill ya. Do you hear me, Jonzie?" Custus yelled.

His words echoed through the rocks.

CHAPTER TWENTY-SEVEN

The posse thundering into the valley gave Custus and Bravo more to worry about than just the three men hidden among the rocks above them. If he wasn't careful, Custus would find himself trapped between hostile forces on two fronts.

"Let's concentrate on the men we can see and not the men we can't for the time being," Custus said. "When the posse comes into view, let 'em have it."

Two members of the posse came into view. Custus stood and his Winchester belched fire, dropping one of the men. Bravo dismounted the other.

"Good shooting, Señor," Bravo said.

"Don't get too cocky," Custus yelled. "There's more men coming and we're not out of the woods yet."

From the rocks overhead, Red Hand saw Custus rise to fire at the posse and he let an arrow fly. It glanced off the rocks near Custus. The flint arrowhead struck the rocks and the wooden shaft splintered. Custus turned and returned fire, nearly hitting Red Hand before he could take shelter.

"Dang!" Custus yelled. "We need better cover or we'll be dropped dead in our tracks."

Custus and Bravo crawled among the boulders in a frantic search for an unseen path to lead them upward to better cover. The trees on the far side of a rill near the road caught Custus' attention.

"If we can make it to those trees over there we'll have even more shelter," he said. There was twenty-five yards of open area between life and death and Custus would have to risk it. Posse or no posse. Jones or no Jones.

He and Bravo made an all-out sprint for the trees as the remaining members of the posse rode into view.

FROM THE CORNER of his eye, Jones saw Red Hand crouched and running through the rocks, trying to get behind Custus and Bravo.

"Let's give him some cover," Jones yelled. He and Potter fired trying to keep Custus focused on seeking shelter rather than on Red Hand. Custus zig-zagged his way to cover, leaping across the rill while bullets whistled and ricocheted off the rocks.

Red Hand waved to signal that he had crossed the rill further upstream.

"Hello, in the rocks. Identify yourselves," a member of the posse shouted.

"Jesse Jones and Adam Potter," Jones yelled back.

"I'm Sheriff Bart Masters," the man shouted. "I've got jurisdiction over this posse. State your business."

"Sheriff, we're after the same man. His name is Custus Leverette and he killed my wife and unborn child. I'm going to bring him in dead or alive."

"And I'm after him because he killed a man in Cheyenne a few hours ago."

"Sheriff, would you mind giving me the first go at this man? I want to take him back to Sidney, Nebraska to stand trial."

"You do?" Potter interrupted in a voice loud enough for only Jesse to hear. "That ain't what you have in mind at all."

"Can we discuss this later?"

"You're willing to lie to get your way?" Potter asked.

"Custus can always die attempting to escape, can't he? But, I've got to have him in custody for him to escape."

"You'd deliberately do that?"

"In a heartbeat," Jones said then cupped his hands around his mouth to shout at the posse. "What do you say Sheriff, have we got a deal?"

"You can have the first attempt at bringing him in, but if you fail, then it's my turn. Stand down, men," Masters said and the posse dismounted to wait by the side of the road for Jones to make the first move.

Red Hand had planted himself safely behind Custus. Jones elbowed Potter. "An elk can enter a thicket and disappear without a trace. Likewise, Red Hand can melt into the underbrush."

THE INTENSE EXCHANGE of fire by Jones and Potter signaled to Custus that they were providing cover for someone, putting him on high alert. Custus turned to Bravo.

"I ain't lived to my fortieth birthday without a sixth sense of danger. "Somethin's goin' on," he said. "Keep yer eyes peeled. We can expect company."

Bravo nodded in response.

Sure enough, it wasn't long before Custus spotted Red Hand weaving in and out of brush with all the stealth of his Indian heritage.

"Well, looky here," Custus said. "We got us a visitor."

"Si, Señor Custus. I think we should welcome him. What do you think?"

"I think that if you can hide behind those trees. I'll pretend I'm hit. That's what I think," Custus said.

"My pleasure, Amigo." Bravo flipped his sombrero back off his head and eased his way between two trees and out of sight. Custus rose to his feet and fired a couple of rounds in Jones' direction. He hoped they would return fire, and they did. When they did, he pretended to be hit.

"Awww," he screamed and fell headlong to the dirt and waited. The bait was set, but would Red Hand take it?

It was not long until Custus sensed someone's approach. He hoped against hope his ruse had worked and Red Hand would be sucked into the trap laid for him.

From the rocks above, Jones' gut instinct led him to believe Custus had set a trap, but he didn't fire for fear of accidentally hitting Red Hand. He couldn't yell out a warning for fear of giving Red Hand's position away. It was darned if he did and darned if he didn't.

He didn't.

"Hold yer fire," he told Potter. "Red Hand's in danger and right now I'm not sure where he is."

Moments later, Red Hand arrived at the scene to find Custus sprawled out on the ground, probably from a well-placed bullet spinning him around. Bravo was nowhere to be seen. Red Hand concluded Bravo must have escaped after Custus died.

"Come on down," Red Hand yelled toward where Jones and Potter hid.

Jones answered, "I think it's a trap. I don't think either of us hit Custus."

"Custus is dead. He's not moving."

Red Hand kicked Custus over onto his back but found no wound. He knelt down.

With the speed of a rattlesnake, Custus struck. His left hand grabbed Red Hand by the neck while his right pulled his Bowie knife and placed the tip in the flesh under Red Hand's chin. Red Hand stiffened and the warmth of his own blood trickled down his neck.

"Why if it ain't our little red friend," Custus gloated. "Stand up slowly and ya won't get hurt."

Red Hand obeyed.

Custus moved to stand and while he did, he kept the knife point at his captive's throat.

"For a while there, I thought I'd never see you again. Now, looky here. Here you are," Custus said.

Bravo squeezed into view. "Señor Custus, what have you found?"

"The little bugger who ruined my plans to keep Dull Knife at bay. How's that little squaw of yours? Two Moons, ain't it?"

Bravo tied Red Hand's hands in front of him using a strip of leather and forced him to stand erect. Custus gathered himself.

"Bravo," Custus said, "Looks like we got ourselves a ticket out of this predicament." He pushed Red Hand in front of him so all could see he was held captive. Custus kept his Bowie Knife at Red Hand's throat.

"Jonzie, are you still there?" he yelled.

"Still here," Jones said. "What do ya want?"

"Well, it seems my situation has changed a mite. I got yer Indian friend. I want ya to put down yer guns. Me and Bravo are comin' out and if I see a glint of steel, I'm cuttin' his throat. Do I make myself clear?" He paused then asked again. "Do I make myself clear?"

"We hear ya," Jones said.

"Next time don't wait so long to answer or I'll slit Red Hand's throat. Now drop yer gun belts, we're comin' out. That goes fer yer posse, too."

"Do what he says," Jones yelled down to the posse. "We don't want the blood of Dull Knife's grandson-in-law on our hands."

"I can sneak behind them," Potter whispered.

"No, ya can't," Jones replied. "We can't take that chance."

One after the other, gun belts fell to the ground. Posse, Jones, and Potter.

"Come ahead," Jones commanded Custus. "We're unarmed."

Custus and Bravo followed Red Hand and emerged from behind the trees forty yards away. "My, my, how the tide has turned," Custus bragged. "You had the drop on me and ya cut down two of my men. Now, I got the drop on you."

"Why don't ya turn Red Hand loose? It's me ya want," said Jones.

"Yeah, it is," Custus said. "But this ain't the time nor the place fer it."

"You can kill unarmed women, but ya can't fight like a man," Jones yelled down at him.

"Tell me, if you make me mad and I kill Red Hand here, how ya gonna explain things to Dull Knife?" Custus laughed a laugh that came straight from the depths of Hades. "When the time is right, Jonzie, you and I will have our little time together. In the meantime, Bravo, me, and Red Hand are riding outta here." Custus motioned for Bravo to untie all the horses, including releasing all but three of the horses held by the posse.

"Sorry, Amigos, but you're gonna be on foot now," Bravo said. Bravo gathered the leads of three horses and led them back to Custus, who forced Red Hand to mount. He held Red Hand's leads until Bravo climbed into the saddle. Custus tied Red Hand's bindings over the saddle horn, took the leads of Red Hand's horse and climbed into his saddle.

Custus' revolver came to life with a pair of shots that scattered all the other horses.

"Keep yer eye on Red Hand from the back," Custus instructed Bravo. Custus spurred his horse onto the road and away from the unarmed men.

"Get," Bravo yelled.

There followed a mad scramble while each man fastened his gun-belt and took off in hot pursuit of his mount. It was a half-hour before horses and riders were reunited. A half-hour head start for Custus.

Custus pulled his horse to a stop. His arm was tired from holding the leads on the pony carrying Red Hand.

"Gotta rest my arm a little," Custus said.

That was cue Red Hand had waited for. He applied both heels to the sides of his horse and it jerked free, dismounting Custus. Red Hand white knuckled his hold on the saddle horn while his horse bolted to freedom. The only chance Red Hand had was to steer his horse with his legs which he did with a lean in the direction he wanted the steed to go. Not an easy thing to do, but not unprecedented among those of his people who often rode bareback, leaving their hands free to fire arrows into stampeding buffalo. The process was made difficult with the saddle between his legs and the animal's flank, but Red Hand managed. He freed his hands tied around the saddle.

"After him! Don't just sit there," Custus shouted.

Bravo gave chase and Custus swung back into his saddle and galloped after the others. A quarter-mile gap developed between Red Hand and Bravo, with Custus an additional quarter-mile behind. A hard right turn near a rocky outcropping shielded Red Hands' jumping dismount. He rolled twice, but regained his footing. He dove behind the rocks while his horse raced on.

Bravo raced by, then Custus. Red Hand's horse led the two men onward, dodging in and out of the rocks. Custus could see the horse's rump and nothing more.

Red Hand freed his hands from the leather strap and sprinted away.

Custus did not give up easily after Red Hand's escape. He and Bravo prowled the area, but all traces of Red Hand's whereabouts had vanished. Bravo warned against too much time spent in one place because a pursuit by the posse was inevitable, but Custus persisted. He bristled at talk they should cut their losses and move on. At last, he agreed with Bravo and rode cross-country toward the Oregon Trail and safety.

Jones did not wait for the posse to retrieve their horses. He found his mount, and the pursuit was on. He knew Custus had a huge lead so he raced onward. He left Potter behind to melt away the miles. He knew that if Custus had taken off at a gallop, he would have to slow down some time to rest his horse. He surmised that at its peak, Custus' horse could run two and a half miles. After that, the horse would need time to catch his breath. If Custus slowed the horse's pace to a trot, the animal could cover eight miles but even after that a rest would be necessary. Jones alternated his horse's pace between a walk and a trot to maximize the distance covered between periods of rest. He easily found the trail Custus left behind.

To a veteran tracker, the trail was obvious. Three sets of hoof prints pointed to Custus' direction and rate of travel. Jones was on the right trail and rode alone for several miles before he rested.

When he did, he removed the paper from his pocket and unfolded it. All he noticed this time was the blood. His wife's blood. He didn't know why, but the words she'd circled melted into the page. He saw only Sarah's blood.

Because of one man, she was no longer alive. Because of one man, the baby she had carried was also dead. His plans, his hopes, his dreams all died in their cabin's bedroom.

He could see Sarah's smile and hear her laughter. Memories washed over him of the day when he saw her for the first time and had stepped in between her and Custus. He wished now he had shot Custus between the eyes then, but he hadn't. He'd give anything to have that moment back. He wished he'd aimed at Custus' heart the night when he rescued Two Moons. He wished he had gone after Custus after learning he had cut up Parson Abel's face.

Jones had let his love for Sarah temper him. With her death, he was no longer in control of his emotions. He saw only red. He looked once more at the page. He saw the words not there earlier:

'Vengeance is mine; I will repay, saith the Lord.'

Jones did not want those words to be there, he was convicted by them.

God forgive me. But this is the way it's got to be. An eye for an eye.

CHAPTER TWENTY-EIGHT

Days on the move put Custus and Bravo at a point west of Fort Laramie, where the Oregon Trail met a place called Register Cliff. Here they approached a wagon train that had halted to rest a few days before pressing westward.

"Been here a couple of times before," Custus said.

"What is this strange place?" Bravo asked.

"Register Cliff is a stopping place for weary travelers. The rock cliff is so soft that you can cut your name in it. Look up there." Custus pointed. "Put my name there six years ago."

Custus and Bravo stopped to rest. Because of the sheer number of those traveling on the wagon train, they blended in and shared in their anonymity.

A young mother in her early twenties offered Custus a plate of beans cooked over an open flame. Custus took the plate but kept his eyes on her. His lustful eyes watched her every move; his mind undressed her.

"Thank ya, ma'am," he said. Bravo helped himself to

some biscuits. The young woman continued her cooking while her husband and children crowded near her by the fire.

"Where are you headed?" Custus asked.

"Oregon," came the husband's swift reply. "They say there's a lot of land there. I hear the coast is beautiful and the weather is more predictable than anything around here."

"Never been that far west," Custus said. "My friend here has."

"What's it like?" the young woman asked of Bravo. She sat the youngest of her three children in her lap.

"It's a nice place with lots of ground for farming," Bravo said. "I think you will like it, señora. But the road between here and there, she is not so good."

"Mountains?" her husband asked.

"Sí, señor. Mountains. Lots of mountains. Freezing cold," Bravo said.

"So, where are you two headed?" the man asked.

"Back to Nebraska. We've been hunting in Wyoming." Custus pushed himself away from the fire to cut short more questions. "Thanks again fer yer hospitality, but my friend and I are gonna call it a day."

Custus laid his head on his saddle and pulled up his blanket. He pretended to sleep, but watched the young mother clean up the pots and pans.

TEN MILES FURTHER WEST, the same starlit night found Jones and Potter around a fire of their own. Potter had trailed after Jones and had only recently arrived in camp. Jones was a terrible cook and Potter was no better. Jones burned the beans. No matter how hard he had tried to disguise the scorched taste by adding a bit of ground coffee, the beans still tasted scorched.

"When did you learn to cook?" Potter asked.

"During the war," Jones said.

"Guess I got spoiled during the war. We had cooks that actually knew how to cook."

"Well, that wasn't the case with my regiment. I insulted our cook once and our commanding officer overheard me and gave me a month's detail in the mess. In my regiment, mess was just that. A mess."

"Ya mean if we shot a deer tomorrow, the results would be the same at supper tomorrow night?"

"You got it," Jones said.

After supper, the two men sat around the campfire and talked. Before long, Jones took the paper from his pocket, unfolded it, and read it.

"Why do you keep doing that?" Potter asked.

"I don't know," Jones replied. He folded the paper and put it away. "Guess it's the only tangible thing I have left that belonged to Sarah. Does that make any sense?"

Potter nodded.

Jones took out the page and read it again. "When I read this paper, I hear her voice telling me not to avenge her death. Think of what she went through, all the reasons she had for hating men, and yet she loved me. I don't get it."

"I wouldn't either. I mean, I've never been married and chances are good I'll stay that way. I like not havin' to answer to anybody when I wanna do somethin'."

"That was me 'til I met Sarah. Do ya remember the day at the lumberyard when Custus was chasin' after her like an elk in rut?"

"How could I forget? You knocked him flat on his butt."

"I wanna do somethin' more permanent than that now. But Sarah's words call me from the grave. With her own blood she circled the words in the Bible Parson Abel gave her." He read the words aloud, "'Vengeance is mine, says the Lord.'"

He looked up. Time passed before he asked, "When?"

"How would I know?" Potter said.

"God promised vengeance and I wanna know when?" Jones' voice gave away his agitation. "When will God do as He says? When will He take vengeance on Custus for what he did? It ain't fair what he did." He looked heavenward. "Ya hear me? It ain't fair what he did? If you ain't gonna do somethin' about it, I will. Do you hear me? I will."

A KNOCK DREW Parson Abel's attention away from the newspaper he was reading.

"Would you please see who that is, Mary?" Abel said then listened to the exchange at the door.

"Who is it?" she asked.

"You tell Parson Abel that it's Doc and I got a couple of questions for him."

"Let him in, will you, Mary," Abel said. "Tell him I'm in the parlor and he's interrupting my newspaper reading."

"The Parson said—"

"I heard him, Mary." Doc barged through the door and into the parlor.

"Evening, Doc." Abel said. "What brings you by on such a crisp fall evening? I thought you'd be hitting the hay early to get in some end of the season fishing in the morning."

"Had my mind all made up to do it, too. But, I've had

somethin' gnaw on me ever since Jones rode out. Then, there was yer sermon."

"Pull up a chair, will you? You're making me nervous hovering over me like a hawk."

Doc sat.

"There, that's better. What about my sermon?" Abel asked. "You're not getting all sentimental on me, are you?"

"Don't think I'd call it sentimental." Doc learned forward. "I just need an explanation. That's all."

"An explanation about what?"

"Well, I'd like you to explain how someone like Sarah would do somethin' like she did. I mean, I'd like to know why she used her own blood in an attempt to stop Jones. It's as if she knew Jones would go after Custus with vengeance as the first order of business. I don't understand that at all. It makes little sense to me."

"I want to tell you something, but I know it will come across all preachy."

Doc shrugged and waited for an answer.

"All I can tell you is exactly what Jesus did. On the cross, he asked His Father to forgive those who crucified Him. Don't understand it to this day, but there it is, and I have to deal with it. During all the hate and death, Jesus spoke of forgiveness."

"What kinda man would do that?" Doc asked.

"The true Son of God. God knew hatred and violence gives birth to more hatred and violence. Until someone stands in the gap and says, 'No more!' everything continues like it is. God calls us to love our enemies, not hate them."

"That's the complete opposite of normal, ain't it? In fact, that's kinda what you did after Custus cut yer face. You didn't strike back or nothin'. You just took it. You returned good for evil. How did you do that? I don't understand that one either."

"Jesus changed everything. He changed me, I know that for sure. There is no way I could have done that before I met Jesus. I *am* getting a little preachy, aren't I?"

"Naw." Doc paused a moment to think. "So, this Jesus changed you and helped you change Sarah's life and now Mary's life?"

"Yes, something like that. I haven't changed anybody, not even myself. When God leads us to faith, *He* changes everything. That takes me to baptism. When we're baptized, Jesus comes in and cleans house."

"Like yer wife cleans this place every Saturday night?" Doc asked with a wry smile.

"Kinda of like that," Abel replied with a laugh. "Jesus comes in and does housekeeping. He takes our old self with our hatred and such and changes us to be more like Him, more loving, forgiving, and accepting of others. Even when they hurt us."

Silence fell in the room, an emptiness no one rushed in to fill, at least not right away.

Then Doc broke that silence. "Do you remember the day I thought I might slide into the creek while you baptized everybody?"

Abel nodded at the pleasant memory.

"I think I'm ready now," Doc said.

"Ready for what?" Abel asked.

"Ah, come on, you know very well what I'm talking about. I'm ready to be baptized. Am I right, you said that God changes us in Baptism?"

"Yes, God does that."

"Can I have a new name, too? I've never liked Aloysius."

Jones tossed his blanket off and stretched. It had been a short night and his sleep had been fitful. Custus was out there somewhere. He was ahead of them, but how far ahead?

"Wake up, Potter. I can't sleep so we might as well be in the saddle."

"What time is it anyway?"

"I'd guess somewhere around three."

Potter curled under his blanket. "A perfect time to sleep."

"Custus is out there. I know it."

"He's probably sleeping right now, so what's the rush?" Potter said.

"If he's sleeping, we can gain on him. C'mon get up. Let's get started."

Using the light of the moon, the men saddled their horses and rode to the northeast, aiming for the spot known as Register Cliff. After a couple of hours riding Jones reigned in his horse.

"Give 'em a rest," he said and dismounted. He hung onto the reins, but loosed them enough the horse could nibble on the scrub grass along the side of the road.

Potter did likewise.

Borrowing Potter's spyglass, Jones peered into the eastern horizon where the sun was just high enough that it didn't send sunrays into the lens, blinding him. He looked once, and then looked again. "There's Register Cliff and it looks like a wagon train stopped along the base of it."

He handed the spyglass back to Potter. "What do you see?" Potter looked.

"It's the cliff alright. And, yes there is a wagon train up ahead. Looks like they are packing and getting ready to move out."

"That would be a perfect place for Custus to be. There'd be food and water and the safety of blending in with other travelers. It's gonna be hard, but let's see if we can pick up Custus' trail once we get closer to that wagon train."

"Prepare to move out!"

The wagon master's voice carried the length of the train. In response, packing began and the trappings that provided breakfast on the plains were stowed and tied down.

Soon the wagon master would sound, "Wagons, Ho!" The armada of covered wagons would jerk forward with oxen tugging and wheels turning, unwinding from their circle of wagons formation into one continuous stream of white-canvassed Conestogas. In numbers too vast to count, they moved westward.

Custus used this opportunity to ogle the young woman one last time. He had noticed the young man's uneasiness. *The kid won't try anything, will he?* Custus wondered. *It's a foolish thing if he does. He'd be no match.*

Yep, Custus was up. But, Bravo wasn't.

"C'mon," Custus yelled while kicking at Bravo's boot. "Time's a wastin'. Either get up or get left behind. And it don't make a bit of difference to me."

"Okay, okay, Amigo," Bravo said, rising to his feet and rolling up his blanket.

"Andale, te enternedi la primera vez," muttered Bravo under his breath.

"And don't be giving me any of that Spanish crap. You know I don't understand it."

"Sorry, Amigo. I only said, 'Okay, I heard you the first time.'"

"You bet, you did," Custus said. It wasn't long before the two men were mounted and with the long westward wagon train on their left, they headed in the opposite direction.

"I've thought it through," Custus said. "I think that when we get to Sidney, we should have us some fun."

Custus and Bravo rode in silence. Custus had a plan and usually nothing on God's green earth could disturb that plan. Jones was out of town, in fact, probably back there on his rear somewhere. It was Custus' race to win. *Ride into Sidney. Burn down Swede's. Why not set the store on fire and wait for Jones to get there and kill him with his store burning in the background? Sounds like a dime novel to me.*

FROM A MILE away Jones and Potter watched the wagon train inch along the trail and then as the last part of the train passed in front of Register Cliff, they spotted two horsemen riding in the opposite direction.

"Look there!" Jones shouted. "That's Custus and Bravo right there."

They spurred their horses and began the chase.

"HEY, AMIGO," Bravo said, drawing his horse parallel to Custus'. "I've been watching two men on horseback behind us. Isn't that Senor Jones?"

Custus stopped. He drew out his field glasses and looked

back in the direction Bravo pointed. "Well, I'll be," he said. "Looks like we got company. We've walked our horses most of the day, so they ought to have plenty left to out run Jones. What do ya say we try it? I'd still like to burn his place down. Maybe we still can."

Custus spurred his horse and Bravo followed.

"The race to Sidney is on," Custus shouted.

CHAPTER TWENTY-NINE

Bravo bolted through the door of Swede's Mercantile, raced through the crowd of customers, shoving them out of his way.

"Hey, what do you think you're doing?" Abel stood his ground between Bravo and the stairs.

"Out of the way, old man," Bravo shouted. He delivered a right fist to Abel's chin, dropping him in his tracks. Abel watched from the floor as Bravo took the stairs two at a time and disappeared.

Custus stood in front of the hotel, watching Bravo crawl out a second story window onto the balcony and lay prone with his rifle pointed eastward up the street. Custus anticipated Jones would ride in from that direction. With Bravo in place across the street, Custus was in the choicest spot to get Jones in a cross-fire.

There was a fight coming and Custus was ready. He casually counted the rounds in his revolver like a man might count livestock. He felt for his knife. It was there waiting to slice into Jones.

A wry smile crossed his lips when he sat down in the Moore Hotel's front porch rocking chair, which felt very comfortable after days in the saddle. After noting how well Bravo followed directions and was ready to back him up when the gunplay started, Custus gave Bravo a thumbs up.

Town folks sensed that gunplay was near, so their personal safety trumped their curiosity and they ran and hid seeking shelter wherever they could find it.

Word spread like wildfire Custus was back and trouble rode with him. Parents hustled their children off the street. Someone ran for Sheriff Blanton. He strapped on his sidearm, made a pretense of preparation, but never left his office. He was not about to step between Custus and Jones. Like the other observers, Blanton elected to part the curtains of his office window and peer into the street.

Jones and Potter passed by the cemetery at the north edge of town in mid-afternoon. Jones spotted Sarah's fresh grave among the others.

"Let's do this," Jones said. "I'll go around and come in from the east and you from the west. It'll be a very crude pincer movement, but a movement none-the-less."

Jones wheeled his horse onto Illinois Street, at the east end of town. Potter did likewise to the west. What awaited them mid-town they did not know; only that it was not good because Custus was involved.

Jones removed a piece of paper from the safety of his shirt pocket and unfolded it. The words remained unchanged, no matter how many times he read them. 'Vengeance is mine, says the Lord.' *Not today it isn't*, he thought.

He folded the paper and stuck it back in his pocket. He pulled his LeMat and counted the chambered rounds. Nine rounds in nine chambers. He broke the pistol open. The shotgun shell was in place.

"Good." He holstered his weapon and nudged his horse forward down Illinois Street, the main artery through town. To his left he watched soldiers drill on the parade grounds of Fort Sidney, unaware of what the town knew. Death rode into town today.

Standing on Jones' left as he rode by, Bill Cody caught his attention.

"Got the Black Arrow matter settled."

"When did you do that?" Jones asked.

"Couple of days ago. Found his camp and razed it. I killed Black Arrow in hand to hand combat. Buntline's writing it all down."

"Good. I'll read it when I get back. Gotta face Custus alone."

"Sure you don't want any help."

"Nope. I'm good," Jones said.

As he traveled further down the street, Jones watched Potter backing his horse down an alley.

"Must see something I don't." He saw Custus two blocks down the street in front of the hotel. "Oh, that's it. Where is the man who rode with Custus?"

After a moment of studying the street, he nodded. "That's a rifle barrel on the second-floor balcony above Swede's right across the street from Custus. I hope Potter sees him."

His military instincts taught Jones to trust. He'd have to trust Potter to react and cover him. It all came down to trust. Jones reined up in front of the hotel with his back to Bravo. He did not climb down from his horse.

"Well, I'll be. If it ain't my old friend, Jonzie," Custus chortled. "Where ya been, Jonzie?"

"Lookin' fer you," Jones said. "I wanna talk to ya."

"Now, that's right neighborly of ya. What do ya want to talk about?" Custus rocked back in his chair, keeping his right hand near the butt of his pistol.

Jones brought his hidden right hand to his LeMat.

Custus stopped rocking. He was all attention. "Easy does it, Jonzie. I don't want nothin' to happen to ya. Not yet, anyway."

Behind Jones, Bravo moved to get a bead on Jones and with his move, he gave his position away to Potter, who eased from his horse and used the corner of a building to stabilize himself while he took aim at Bravo. "That's gonna be one tough shot," he said under his breath.

"I need to show you something," Jones said.

"Alright," Custus responded. "But nice and easy like. Don't make no sudden moves or you'll be dead before you hit the ground."

Jones fetched the paper from his left shirt pocket and flipped it onto Custus' lap.

"What is this?" he asked.

"It's the reason I'm here. Pick it up. Read it."

Custus unfolded the paper. He recognized the torn page from a Bible. On the page, he saw blood circled words, 'Vengeance is mine, saith the Lord.' Custus looked up into Jones' vengeful eyes.

Jones' saw fear and anger in Custus' eyes. *That's to his undoing.*

"I'm here to kill ya or die tryin'," Jones said. "My wife circled those words before she died. Now, vengeance might belong to the Lord, but I'm tellin' ya that I'm here as yer judge, jury, and executioner. I ain't waitin' 'til God takes His vengeance. It's an eye for an eye. Sarah's life for yours." The words came out with steely confidence, icy enough to rile Custus to the bone.

"Prove it," he answered, going for his revolver and firing off a shot that narrowly missed its mark.

Jones tumbled from his horse, rolled and fired a return shot, striking the rocking chair where Custus had sat only moments before.

Bravo stood up to get a better angle on Jones and that was all Potter needed to squeeze off a shot that sent him over the balcony railing to the dusty street below.

Custus ran down the alley between two stores, Jones in hot pursuit.

Custus fired a shot that struck a rain barrel.

Jones returned fire but missed his mark. He ran down the alley to find Custus nowhere in sight. An open door caught his attention about midway up the alley. He raced toward it. Potter ran up the alley from the other end and met Jones at the door.

"Good shootin', back there," Jones said. "I trusted, and you delivered. I've got it from here."

"You sure?" Potter asked.

"Yep. I wouldn't want it any other way. Vengeance is mine."

Jones followed Custus into the building under construction. Three workmen fled in haste when Custus entered with his gun drawn.

Jones crept into the main room.

Custus fired. Jones ducked, and the bullet struck the doorframe.

Custus smashed through the front window and into the street. He fired twice more to cover his exit.

Jones opened the front door.

Wood splintered over Jones' head. Again, Custus' anger had caused him to fire wildly.

Jones stepped into the street to meet him. "You shouldn't have wasted your ammo like that. Now, yer out," Jones said.

Custus threw away his gun. He unbuckled his gun belt and dropped it in the street. With a crooked smile, he unsheathed his Bowie knife.

Jones drew and fired.

The knife flew out of Custus' hand.

"Now, it's fair. I don't carry a knife." Jones unbuckled his gun belt, and let it thud to the ground.

Custus charged Jones, ramming his shoulder into Jones' midsection so hard that it sent him reeling backward. Custus followed with a fist to Jones' jaw.

Jones shook off the punch and plowed his left fist into the right side of Custus' face.

A crowd gathered to watch, Doc and Parson Abel among them.

Custus landed a blow that drove Jones backward and off balance. Doc and another man in the crowd caught him and kept him upright.

"Keep yer hands up," Doc said.

"Thanks, Doc, I'll remember that next time," he replied.

Custus rushed in again and ran straight into Jones' right hand. Custus' knees buckled, and he dropped to the ground. In an instant, Jones was atop him, pummeling his face to a bloody pulp. He grabbed Custus by the neck and squeezed. This was a hot rage like Jones had experienced once before when he killed the rebel colonel and stole his LeMat.

Custus' eyes bulged and he stared blankly up at him. Jones squeezed tighter.

"Jones."

Jones tried to ignore the voice breaking through his rage. "Jones."

There it was again. Whose voice was that?

"Remember what Sarah wanted. Do you hear me? Sarah didn't want you to kill him. Remember?"

That's Parson Abel's voice. He eased his grip, aware of a hand on his shoulder.

Custus sputtered and coughed, desperately trying to breathe again.

"Let him go. Let the *Lord* handle this. Sarah would have wanted it this way."

Abel was there alright.

Jones' rage subsided, and he could see again through the red haze of his own anger. He stood and Parson Abel welcomed him back to reality. They hugged. Doc joined in to the surprise of both men.

Custus revived. His knife was only a foot away and he reached his hand out to retrieve it. Advantage Custus. Jones had his back to Custus.

"Look out, he's got a knife," someone in the crowd screamed. Custus drew back his arm to throw his Bowie knife.

An arrow slammed into Custus with an ominous thud. His eyes widened in disbelief. He looked down in amazement at the shaft with a bloody arrowhead protruding from his chest. His knife fell from his hand and his lifeless body pitched forward and fell, face down in the dust.

Red Hand walked over to Jones, bow in hand. "Followed Custus here," he said. "No more bad medicine."

Parson Abel's congregation gathered around the banks of Lodgepole Creek. It was a special day. A joyous day. A fall day. The day of Doc's Baptism. There was a name on the certificate, Doc's given name. Only Parson Abel and his wife Adeline saw that name written in hand calligraphy.

Aloysius Edward Hardesty

CHAPTER 30

Parson Abel and Adeline had sworn to secrecy never to disclose this name. They agreed to always call him 'Doc' and not Aloysius. Parson Abel stood knee deep in the water.

"Doc, come down," he beckoned. Doc was dressed in dark pants and a white linen shirt. He refused to wear a white robe. Two men already in the water presented him with a pathway to Parson Abel. They assisted Doc so he wouldn't slide down the bank like he feared he might. He approached Parson Abel, saying sotto voce, "And so help me if you say my first name while baptizing me, I'll strangle you right here. There's not a jury in the world that would convict me. Now, what are we standing here for? Get on with it."

Parson Abel dipped Doc under the water. "Doc Hardesty, I baptize you in the name of the Father, and of the Son, and of the Holy Ghost. Amen."

Water dripped down Doc's face. Someone handed him a towel.

"Well, that wasn't so bad," Doc said.

"What's say we get out of the water and get something to eat?" Parson Abel said.

Doc nodded his approval.

It was quite a celebration. Not only had Doc come to the waters of baptism, but Jones was feted for the way he handled the Custus affair. If there is one thing to say about how a small town handles a celebration, it would be found in the amount of food they served. One generous member provided the meat, a whole hog roasted over coals. The ladies outdid themselves with casseroles of all kinds made from fresh potatoes and beans from their own vegetable gardens. And desserts galore.

Parson Able clasped Jones' hands. "You did the right thing. Sarah would have been so very proud of you."

"Parson, can I ask you somethin'? When does the hurt go away?"

"It doesn't. There will be times when you hurt less. Think of it like a scab over a wound. There will be times when you'll do fine, but then someone or something will come along and rip the scab off and you'll have to grieve again. There's an old saying that time heals all wounds. Not so. In your case, you have a wound only God can heal. My best advice is to go on living and let God handle the rest. What do you think of that advice, Doc?"

After Doc nodded, Potter added, "Dang right."

"Parson, just one more question." Jones said. "What about baptizing me?"

EPILOGUE

What I've put on paper is one part of my great-grandfather's journal and some extraneous clippings of accounts written by Ned Buntline stuffed in that journal. I don't know if I'll find time to thumb through any more of it. This whole process was just that time-consuming.

My wife will tell you of one instance when this journal became so all-consuming it nearly cost me my marriage. After working all day, I'd come home and have an evening meal with my young family. After eating, it became my habit to go downstairs to my office and work on this project until ten-thirty. I'd sleep, go to work, eat dinner with my family and then go downstairs to write. One evening, after spending several weeks in a row in the aforementioned routine, I heard my wife creeping down the stairs. She came about half-way.

"You do know that you have a family upstairs, right?" she said.

Ouch.

I've kept my family intact, but what that has meant is that it took me a lot longer to translate my great-grandfather's diary from his lingo into readable English. I smoothed out the rough edges of the language. The way he swore throughout, you would have thought him a sailor instead of a soldier. One thing I've discovered is that some of my great-grandfather's legend is true while some of it is exaggeration.

But, I've spent a lot of time reading, writing and rewriting what he wrote. It was life changing for me now that I look back on the two most memorable incidents of his life and times.

I've also discovered that no man really lives his life alone, although some may want to. Life is really built on relationships that impact and change us into whom God wants us to be. Had it not been for other people—like his first wife, Sarah, Parson Abel and his wife Adeline, Doc, and a friend named Potter, and, as Ned Buntline would put it, the legendary Buffalo Bill Cody, my great-grandfather would not have become the man he was.

Oh, and by the way, I have since discovered the title of the John Wayne movie that provided the line *When legend becomes fact, print the legend.*

It's *The Man Who Shot Liberty Valance.* If you haven't watched it, I'd encourage you to.

Jesse Jones IV

P.S. You'd be interested to know that tucked into the old Bible my great-grandfather put between the laths in his house along Lodgepole Creek I found a folded piece of paper with the words 'Vengeance is mine, saith the Lord' circled in blood.

DEAR READER

Thank you for reading **Death Rode to Lodgepole Creek,** the first book in the Man With The LeMat series. Jesse Jones' story continues in book 2, **At The Point of A Gun** and concludes with **Gunfight at Camp Clarke Bridge.**

Reviews are lifeblood to authors. Please consider leaving a review of this book at your retailer's website or at places like Goodreads and BookBub.

At The Point Of A Gun

Man With The LeMat book 2

It's been a year since Custus and Jesse fought over Sarah, and Sidney, Nebraska, the wickedest town in the west, is returning to normal. Except for Cincinnati Culver, owner of the Last Chance Saloon. Using his gang of thugs and misfits, the small man with a big ego is hell-bent on controlling every business in town. Including Swede's Mercantile.

Jesse Jones now owns the mercantile and isn't about to sell out. No matter the price. No matter the threats. A young woman searching for her brother, and a shootist following his sister's trail arrive in town, complicating Cincinnati's plans and Jesse's life.

Gunfire occasionally lights Sidney's dark streets. Far too often the horseplay turns to gunplay where blood is spilled and men die.

Gunfight at Camp Clarke Bridge

Man With The LeMat book 3

The promise of Black Hills gold is drawing prospectors and greedy men to Sidney. Plans are made for a bridge to span the Platte River, cutting days off travel time to the Dakota Territory. Jesse Jones and Swede's Mercantile are chosen to supply the materials needed to build the Camp Clarke Bridge.

Jesse leases a warehouse from banker Swan Holmes, a cheerful man who often claims, "God helps those that help themselves." When the phrase is repeated by the one armed man, Bill DuFreeze, and the town is overrun with shady men all wearing black bandanas, Jesse takes on the job of acting sheriff. In his search for answers he faces rustlers, accusations, destruction, and fear. What price will he have to pay to finally bring peace to Sidney, Nebraska?

ABOUT THE AUTHOR

Zachary Lane is a native Nebraskan; a small town kid who has always had a big imagination. A family vacation to a battlefield sparked his interest in the Civil War. The 'old shed' in his back yard soon became an officer's quarters or a fort. Lane fueled his imagination by reading books about this epic war that pitted brother against brother. His personal library is filled with books. Lots and lots of books. So many books that an ultimatum has been issued in the Lane household—if a new book comes in, an older one must be boxed up and put on a shelf in the garage.

Zachary began writing seriously after visiting a rest stop near Sidney, Nebraska. Observing and reading a historical marker overlooking the railroad and town in valley below set his imagination free to tell the story of life there in the 1860's and 1870's.

He still lives in Nebraska where he enjoys walks with his wife, playing with grandchildren, grilling on summer's evenings, smoking ribs and pork butts and stretching his imagination by writing new stories about early Nebraska.